Rafael

Stone Society Book 1

Faith Gibson

missy
keep Atm &
Gargoyl ou!

Faith G

Copyright © 2014 by Faith Gibson

Published by Faith Gibson

First e-book edition: November 2014

First print edition: November 2014

Cover design by KPG

ISBN 10: 0692311955

ISBN 13: 978-0692311950

This book is intended for mature audiences only.

Dedication

To Jennifer – from a telephone conversation, this series was born. Your ideas and your comments have helped shape it into something stellar. You are forever my girl.

To the man – thank you for putting up with the out-of-the blue epiphanies and random plot ideas as we're walking the dogs or driving down the road, and just basically dealing with my absence mentally as I get engrossed in all things Gargoyle. I love you.

Acknowledgements

As always, I have to thank my writing posse: Kendall, Jen, and Nikki - you encourage me to color outside the lines.

Thank you to Alex B, Sharon B and Tanya R for reading Rafael and loving him as much as I do. And for telling me you're ready for more Gargoyles.

KPG – You took an idea and a few pictures and turned them into an amazing cover. That right there is priceless.

Kendall FG, the best f'n PA a girl could want. You keep me from coloring too far outside the lines, my little comma queen.

To the ladies at Tasty Wordgasms, thank you for blogging and pimping me. It is mucho appreciated.

Jen, this book is all you, baby. Thank you for all your stellar ideas and for being there with me non-stop. You keep me sane.

Prologue

2014

As the beautiful redhead paced back and forth, cooing her equally beautiful baby girl, Dr. Jonas Montague examined a baby boy. The woman would stop and peer over the doctor's shoulder to check out the notations he was making about her other child. The doctor didn't utter a sound until he had written the last note. As carefully as his mother would, Dr. Montague redressed the boy then picked him up gently and held him close to his chest.

The doctor's hair and clothes were disheveled as if he hadn't slept in days. Still, there was an air of excitement about him that couldn't be suppressed by lack of sleep. Grinning, he said, "We did it my dear. He is as healthy as his sister."

The examination room door burst open. Dr. Montague's assistant, Julia, was frantic. "Jonas, there's a man here demanding to see you. He said his name's Flanagan. He's ranting about *his* wife and *his* child."

"No, Uncle, NO." The redhead was in full blown panic mode.

Calmly, Jonas handed the baby to Julia and instructed them both, "We are prepared for this. Remember the plan. Julia, you take the boy, and both of you get to the tunnel, now."

The loud commotion that was Gordon Flanagan became even louder as he closed in on them. Jonas waited until the two women disappeared through a secret panel in the wall behind a bookcase and then stepped through the door to the lobby. A mammoth of

1

a man rushed him, catching him by the throat. "Where is she? What have you done with my wife?"

Montague couldn't breathe much less respond. "Answer me!" Gordon yelled as he threw the doctor up against the nearest wall. He hit so hard the sheetrock dented. Jonas had to give the women time to get away. Far away.

Holding his hands up defensively, knowing it would do no good, he tried to catch his breath. Flanagan loomed above him, face red from the obvious rise in his blood pressure. "I will kill you with my bare hands if you don't tell me what you have done with my wife."

The front door to the building flew open, and a man dressed in black military style fatigues strode to Flanagan. "Sir, we need to leave. We just received a tip that the rioters are making their move today, now."

Flanagan glanced down at the doctor who appeared to have lost consciousness. He kicked him in the ribs, "Wake up and tell me where she is!" His voice thundered throughout the building. The doctor slumped even farther toward the floor.

"Sir, we have to move out now." The man made his way to the door, holding it for Gordon.

Realizing he was going to get nothing out of the doctor, Flanagan followed his guard outside. They'd barely cleared the building when the first explosion hit.

The Mayans got it right. Almost. The bombing of Dr. Jonas Montague's clinic in Atlanta, Georgia by a group of religious heretics set off a chain of events that left the world in a state of de-evolution. The country was divided, literally. Bombings across America caused the underground fault lines to fissure. The result was a canyon as large as the one named Grand, splitting the US of A almost exactly in half. Civil wars broke out. Governments crumbled.

Worldwide travel was halted for many years as humanity fell to a level dating back to biblical times. Dr. Montague's notes on human cloning were scattered causing mass chaos. His body was never recovered, and after several years he was finally declared dead. The cloning research he perfected was eventually achieved once again, and cloning became routine.

When Gordon Flanagan's wife disappeared with their daughter, he lost his mind. His twin brother, Magnus, also disappeared. It was assumed that Magnus took the baby that was cloned from his niece, but it couldn't be proven. Thirty-three years passed and none of them surfaced. Gordon blamed both his brother and Montague for ripping his family in two, and he vowed to find them all, no matter what it took.

Being one of the richest men in America, he used his money and abused his power to put his hat into the cloning ring. Since most of the military unraveled in the wars, Gordon Flanagan began building his own army. The experimentation by his team of scientists skirted the fringes of ethical. Eventually, those fringes unraveled, and the humans that volunteered to serve Flanagan slowly lost their humanity.

The cloning that produced healthy, intelligent babies met little opposition. The religious zealots that marched against and eventually leveled Montague's clinic claimed all clones were unholy and damned by God. Over the years, the media adopted the name Unholy for those less than human clones that were being created by Gordon Flanagan. His clones were a mixture of super soldier and monster.

The leaders of the nation began rebuilding but found they couldn't contain the Unholy. Without the necessary military intact, the people needed a miracle. What they got was The Stone Society.

Chapter 1

Present Day, 2047

The streets of New Atlanta were in utter chaos. Rafael Stone, King of the Gargouille, rarely flew on scouting missions. However, with the Unholy wreaking havoc at every turn, he wasn't about to sit on the sidelines and allow his brothers to have all the fun. He may be the leader of the Stone Society, but he wasn't afraid to get his claws dirty. He streamlined his wings and flew right into the middle of a group of the monsters who were battling each other.

Something about this felt wrong. Rafe quickly took out four of the Unholy only to find five more ready to take their place. "What the fuck is going on, Rafe?" Frey, one of his Clan, was guarding his back. "Why are they fighting each other?"

"That is a good question. It's like they were sent on a suicide mission to draw us out. I'm going to have a look around." Rafe launched himself back into the sky and flew around the city, taking in the fighting down below. The Unholy were rarely seen in public but when they were, they weren't known to fight amongst themselves. Their job was to target humans. Rafael didn't care if they took each other out. That was less scum he had to put in the Basement at the prison. The fighting was mass confusion, and it reeked of a distraction. From what, he didn't know.

As he passed over each of his brothers below, he let out a loud whistle, calling them back. When Rafael had gathered everyone, they flew to his office to regroup. Stone, Incorporated was situated on the top floor of the Walnut Street Towers so that he and the Clan could land on the back side of the building without being seen by others.

Once they were assembled in his office he said, "Whatever is going on out there doesn't sit well with me. It felt like a diversion. Frey, you and your men take the north quadrant. Jules, head south. Nikolas, take your team and head west. I will contact Gregor and tell him to check around the Pen, and then I will go east. Let them kill each other and then whoever's left we will load up for the Basement. Keep an eye out to see where they are not fighting. That will be where the real danger lies."

Rafael's younger brother, Gregor, was the Warden at the penitentiary. Once he had given him a heads up, Rafe headed back to the skies. There was something amiss this night, and he needed to find out what.

Police Chief Kaya Kane walked the length of the loading dock where the bodies of eleven delegates from the World Council were stretched along the edge: bound, gagged, dead. Twelve delegates had disappeared, so there was still a body missing. Make that a person missing. Kaya was going to assume the twelfth was still alive until she saw a body.

Fucking hell. Kaya had tried several times to convince Governor Jackson Wallace that New Atlanta was no place to hold the World Council Delegation, especially with the Vice President of the United States

6

in attendance. Wallace had argued that the near apocalyptical mess that ruined Atlanta happened a long time ago and this conference was just the thing that was needed to bring some positive light back to their once fair city.

"Find out who owns this building. I want a name and number," Kaya told her lead detective, Dane Abbott. She already knew the building would belong to Stone, Incorporated. Rafael Stone and his family owned most of the real estate in New Atlanta, whether it was gorgeous downtown architecture or an abandoned warehouse.

Kaya stood back out of the way, allowing the Crime Scene Unit to do their job while she thought about the mysterious man. She had never met the elusive Mr. Stone, at least not that one. The Stone name popped up all over New Atlanta from the prison to the hospital to the airport. The family's fingerprints were on just about every pot in the city.

She had met a couple of his relatives: his brother Gregor, and his cousin Geoffrey. Both men were intense. Gregor, the Warden at the penitentiary, represented the name Stone well. He was hard, cold, and unmoving. Geoffrey Hartley, owner of the gym where she had trained in martial arts for several years, was just as stern as his cousin.

Dane returned with the information she asked for. "Stone, Incorporated. I put in a call to Stone's office, but he wasn't available so I left a message with his assistant. Here's his number."

Kaya took the piece of paper from Dane and put it in her jacket pocket. She wouldn't hold her breath for a phone call from the man himself. No, someone as powerful as Rafael Stone would employ minions to take calls, make appearances, see to the little people.

"Has CSU come up with COD?" Cause of Death was not clearly detectable. Other than the ligature marks from the ropes binding their hands, there were no visible signs of trauma to the bodies.

Dane shook his head. "They will have to take the bodies back to the lab and run some tests. Some type of injection is Dante's first guess. He's already called for the buses to come retrieve the victims. Speak of the devil."

Dante Di Pietro, medical examiner, approached with a scowl on his face. It was a look Kaya never got used to. Standing well over six foot tall, the ME was handsome in a rugged sort of way. He spoke with a slight accent that might be Italian. It wasn't prominent and came and went depending on his mood. The moodier he was, the thicker the accent. "Chief Kane, with your permission I will take the bodies and begin testing. Upon initial observation, I believe the victims to have been poisoned but until I get them to my lab, I am only speculating."

"Of course, Dante. Please keep me posted." He didn't bother to respond, just nodded to both Kaya and Dane and stalked off. "Friendly sort." Dane muttered.

"I don't give a rat's ass if he's friendly or not as long as he discovers the COD. Come on, we have a missing person to find." Kaya's cell phone vibrated on her hip. She pulled it out of its holder and without looking at the caller ID she answered, "Kane."

"Chief Kane, this is Willow Bridges, assistant to Mr. Rafael Stone. He asked that I call and provide any information you might need."

"I will need to speak to Mr. Stone personally since he is the owner of a building involved in a crime scene. No offense, sweetheart, but this is a police matter. If he cannot oblige me by returning my call, I will have a police officer escort him to the precinct. Please tell him it's his choice." Kaya hung up her cell phone. She was used to dealing with men such as Rafael Stone. She would not be bullied.

Dane was smirking at her. He flirted with her constantly, but she did not fraternize with her employees even if they were gorgeous blonds with eyes the color of the clearest sea in the Caribbean. Dane was former military and a damn good cop. If they were ever in a desperate situation, she knew he would have her back. Besides, she knew the type of women he went after, and it wasn't older women who were tall and on the thick side. He chased those young, petite girls.

"What?" She didn't bother waiting for an answer. There was a delegate missing and the longer they stood around, the less chance that person had of living. "Do we know who the twelfth person is?"

"Yeah, Magnus Flanagan."

She stopped walking. "You have got to be kidding me. Magnus Flanagan as in Gordon Flanagan's brother?"

"One in the same."

"This just went from a bad dream to a fucking nightmare. And speaking of nightmares, how in the hell did *she* get wind of this?"

Dane turned from his scowling boss to see Katherine Fox and the Channel 5 news crew van pulling into the lot. Once parked, the petite reporter slid out of the passenger seat, landing on five inch stiletto heels with the grace of a ballerina. Flipping open her notepad, she stopped Dante before he could get into his SUV.

"No worries, Boss, I got this." Dane headed toward the auburn-haired beauty before Kaya could stop him.

"Yeah, I just bet you do," Kaya mumbled. "Get rid of her then meet me at the hotel. We need to interview the other delegates." Dane gave her a two-fingered salute over his head letting her know he heard.

An albino looking brute leaned against an older model van; long legs crossed at the ankle while smoking a cigarette. Pulling off a kidnapping of this scale would secure his place in Mr. Flanagan's organization. The cigarette was down to the filter as he sucked in one last lungful of nicotine then flicked the butt to the ground. A black sedan with dark windows pulled up, stopping just short of his boots. The driver's door opened, and a man dressed in black camouflage angled out. He stalked around to the passenger side and opened the back door. Mr. Flanagan himself slid out of the car.

Without a thank you or a job well done, he rounded the car and demanded, "Where is he?"

The kidnapper thumbed over his shoulder at the building. Flanagan headed that direction, telling him, "I'll be in touch."

Chapter 2

The previous night had been a long one with the Clan fighting and capturing Unholy until three in the morning. Rafael was still uneasy and the ringing phone didn't help. His brother Dante, the city's medical examiner, rarely called just to chat.

"Rafe."

"I wish I had good news, Brother, but I do not. Twelve delegates were abducted from the World Council, and one is still missing. The bodies were dumped at one of our warehouses, the one out on Oakley. All eleven were poisoned. There are no visible puncture wounds, but I can smell the offensive odor seeping through their skin. I am on my way back to the morgue to conduct the examination. I overheard the Chief's conversation with one of her detectives. You know she's a tenacious one. Miss Kane is not going to stop until you call her back."

Rafael sighed. "She's already threatened me through Willow, so yes; I will give her a call. Do they have any clues to who is behind the killings?"

"Magnus Flanagan is the missing twelfth delegate, so speculation is his brother at this point."

"Fucking Gordon Flanagan. It's been a while since he surfaced. I guess Magnus would bring him out of hiding though. Okay, go do your job little brother, and I will see you tonight at the family meeting."

"Later."

Rafe picked up his office phone and asked Willow for the phone number to the police chief. Over a hundred years had passed since Rafe allowed himself to become openly involved with a police investigation.

11

It was risky to the family, but Gordon Flanagan was not going to stop killing until he found what he was looking for: his child. If he indeed kidnapped his brother, he could be one step closer to finding his daughter.

Rafe dialed Kaya Kane's number. Miss Kane might be a woman, but she was more than capable of doing the job of chief of police. Rafe kept tabs on whoever was in office, assuring his city was kept as safe as possible where humans were concerned. He and his brothers stepped in when the non-humans were involved. The prison they built was filling up with the dregs of society, mostly those cloned experiments gone wrong.

"Kane." That one word coming through the airwaves sent a wake-up message straight to his cock. *What the hell?*

"Miss Kane, this is Rafael Stone." No niceties, no pleasantness.

"Ah, Mr. Stone, thank you for returning my call. We have a situation at one of your properties, and I'd like to ask you a few questions."

Another twitch in the groin area. "Proceed."

"I would rather do this in person, if you don't mind."

A full blown hard-on. "I do mind, Miss Kane. I am a very busy man. If you have questions, ask. If a face to face is necessary, one of my associates should suffice." What in the name of the gods was happening? His dick was straining against the zipper in his jeans as if he were in the presence of his mate. Since this woman was a human, that wasn't possible.

"Mr. Stone, do you have something to hide?"

At the moment, he did: a throbbing erection. "Miss Kane, I assure you I am an open book. If you insist on speaking directly to me, come to my office within the hour. I will postpone my other meetings until I have satisfied you."

"I look forward to it. I will see you soon." The phone disconnected.

His body was willing to satisfy her any way she pleased. "Are you out of your fucking head? The woman causes this type of reaction over the phone, and you invite her to your office?" Rafe didn't understand how only a voice could cause his body to betray him. Goyles were not easily affected. It took the nearness of their mate to produce that type of sexual arousal, and she could not be his mate. Could she?

The Stone Society was a family of Gargoyle shifters dating back hundreds of thousands of years. Rafael's family, the Di Pietros, migrated from Europe over two hundred years ago, right before the civil war broke out. When his father was slain in a coup to take over the throne, Rafael became King since he was the oldest son. Once King, he took on the less formal name of Stone. Their Clan was the largest in the Americas with Rafe having several brothers and cousins living in New Atlanta with him. He regarded those closest to him as his inner circle and called them all *Brother.*

The females of his kind were almost extinct. It had been years since a new shifter was born; fifteen to be exact. Mason, a distant cousin, was a teenager in human years, but Gargoyles aged at an accelerated rate causing Mason to appear to be in his twenties. Once the shifters reached maturity, the aging process all but stopped. This was the main reason Rafael remained hidden. You could only explain your youthful good looks with plastic surgery for so long.

Julian and Nikolas were the faces of Stone, Incorporated. They could pull off being thirty something for several more years, then they would have to change cities and take on new identities. Rafael, being King, stayed out of the public eye so he could remain in New Atlanta indefinitely.

There were no appointments to cancel since he did not actually attend meetings. What he did have was time on his hands until Miss Kane arrived. If he couldn't handle talking to her on the phone, how did he think he could manage being in her presence? However, he needed to know if that had been a fluke. Rafe hadn't been with a woman in a very long time. The near apocalypse thirty years earlier caused so much destruction that he spent those years helping to rebuild their city.

Modern high-rises were replaced with ornate stone structures. Sure, it might take the city back to a time of long ago as far as architecture was concerned, but it was the style of his people, and the buildings were easier to secure. To keep up the façade of having canceled meetings, Rafe changed from casual jeans and an untucked button-down to a pair of slacks and a dress shirt. Just as he exited his private apartment, the desk phone rang. He didn't have to answer it to know Willow was calling to announce Kaya Kane. He could feel her heart beating in his own chest.

Chapter 3

Kaya called Dane to tell him she would be meeting Rafael Stone before she came to the hotel. She didn't waste any time heading to the tall, gothic building. Stone, Incorporated was the largest architecture firm in the South. Ironically, the brothers specialized in stone structures. Kaya was always amazed whenever she saw one of their buildings. She hadn't traveled much in her thirty-six years, but she had visited Europe just after college. Knowing she wouldn't be able to take time off once she began her career, Kaya spent a couple of weeks abroad. The buildings in New Atlanta would rival any of those she saw on her trip.

Rafael Stone was a genius when it came to design, assuming he actually was the designer in the family. He could just be the face behind the name. One of his brothers could be the true talent. The directory in the lobby showed the office to be on the top floor.

The elevator doors silently opened, and she stepped into a plush outer office. The furnishings were as opulent as she expected. A very pretty younger lady was sitting behind the desk. She stood as Kaya approached, offering a warm smile along with her hand. "You must be the chief; we spoke earlier. I'm Willow."

"It's a pleasure to meet you, Willow." She shook the younger woman's hand noticing a genuine face. Kaya met all kinds in her line of work and was pleasantly surprised that Mr. Stone employed a nice looking young lady, not a bleached blonde bimbo. *Why do you care who he hires?*

15

"I will let Mr. Stone know you're here, if you would like to have a seat." Willow gestured to the plush chairs in the waiting area. Kaya chose to stand. Hopefully, he wouldn't make her wait long. She strolled along the office, taking in the paintings and photos on the walls. She recognized some of the local buildings in the photos as those constructed by the brothers. Some appeared to be really old but just as spectacular.

Willow spoke directly behind her, "Mr. Stone will see you now. If you will, please follow me."

Kaya walked behind the assistant until they reached the first office on the right. Willow waited for her to step through and then silently closed the door, leaving her alone with the man of the hour.

Kaya often imagined Rafael Stone would look similar to his brother Gregor. Her imagination was nowhere close to the man standing before her. Where Gregor was closer to her height of five nine, Rafael was well over six feet. Longish black hair was styled away from his face. Dark eyes stared at her. From this distance, she couldn't tell if they were brown or blue. A short beard covered his jaw.

The sleeves of his dress shirt were rolled up to his elbows, showing off well-defined forearms. His shoulders were broad. This man was thick. Dress slacks were straining across the muscles in his thighs. He stood unmoving, hands in his pockets, head slightly cocked to one side. As she was taking in his features, he was doing the same to her.

Why hadn't she changed out of her uniform? *Wait, why would you? You're here on official business. Get your head out of your ass, Kane.* "Mr. Stone, I appreciate

16

you taking the time to speak with me." She walked forward holding her hand out. At first she didn't think he was going to take it. He lowered his gaze from her eyes to her hand then took it in his own, shaking firmly. The current she felt radiating through his skin into hers took her by surprise, reminding her of the time she was stunned by a taser.

"Can I offer you something to drink, Miss Kane?" Kaya preferred to be addressed by her title of Chief. After all, it was a title she had earned, but she was not going to press the matter with this man. "No thank you. If you don't mind, I'll get right to the questions so I don't waste either of our time."

"Spending leisurely time with a beautiful woman is never a waste, Miss Kane." He motioned to an empty chair then proceeded to his own behind the desk.

"Flattery is not necessary, Mr. Stone, but I do appreciate the sentiment all the same. Now, can you please tell me your whereabouts the last twenty-four hours?" Instead of taking notes in her notepad, she took advantage of the closeness to study his face. She would probably never have the opportunity again. He was not Hollywood good-looking. His face, while handsome in a rugged way, appeared weathered like he spent a lot of time outdoors. An olive complexion hinted at an Italian or Greek heritage. He had thick eyebrows, the left having a deep scar traveling down to the corner of his eye. Nostrils were flaring in a slightly wide nose as she waited for an answer.

"I drove straight here from my home. I remained here until five-thirty at which time I returned home, not stopping until I arrived. It's a rare occasion I go anywhere else, Miss Kane, unless my presence is required on a jobsite. I have witnesses that can attest to my whereabouts, if you need to verify what I'm saying is the truth." His nostrils flared again. Was he smelling her? She'd used a spritz of vanilla lavender body spray after her shower, but surely it had worn off by now. His intense scrutiny was causing her to become uncomfortable. She uncrossed her legs then crossed them to the other side.

Kaya was pretty good at reading people. It was a requirement in her line of work. The vibe coming from Rafael Stone was that he was not someone to be messed with. No, this Mr. Stone was as intense as his brother. Powerful. Why would an architect be built like a Mack truck?

"I will need to verify that. While I am certain you wouldn't lie to me, I hope you won't take offense that I prefer to do my job properly. I need to ask you about the abandoned property on Oakley Industrial Boulevard. When was the last time you were there?" He didn't blink, didn't flinch. That was a good sign.

"I've never been there, Miss Kane. Do you mind telling me what this is about?"

"You own the property yet you've never been there? Do you buy a lot of property sight unseen, Mr. Stone?" There was a slight twitch to the right side of his mouth. He was not enjoying this.

"As a matter of fact, I do. Unseen by me anyway. My cousin Julian handles all property purchases in our family, Miss Kane. As I previously stated, I rarely go anywhere other than my office or home. I am a very private person."

Private people usually have something to hide. What was he hiding?

"Do you have any type of security on your properties? We didn't find cameras when we searched the premises."

"Under what circumstances did you find yourself searching my property? Did you have a search warrant?" She was losing ground instead of getting any useful answers.

"Are you familiar with the World Council Delegation?" How could he sit so still? Other than an occasional blink of the eye, Kaya could detect absolutely no movement at all.

"Of course I am. The Delegation is being held at one of my properties. What does my warehouse have to do with the Delegation?" He was cool. No, cold. Stone cold. Just like his brother.

"Twelve delegates were kidnapped. Eleven of them were found on the dock of your warehouse, Mr. Stone. Dead."

Chapter 4

Rafael had perfected his stony facade over the years. He could pass any polygraph test given. Gargoyles were capable of slowing their heart rate at will, allowing them to maintain a level head in any situation. "Dead? Miss Kane, I assure you I know nothing of these deaths nor did I have anything to do with them. I'm not sure how you think I can help you. There are no security cameras at any of the abandoned warehouses we have purchased. Our intent with these properties is to raze them and put beautiful buildings or parks in their place."

Rafe rose from his seat and walked around the desk to settle directly in front of Kaya. So far, he was able to keep his dick in check. Now that he was closer, he may have made a mistake. Her delicious scent was enticing him like a raw steak would a ravenous lion. He was a starving man, and this delicious meal sitting in front of him was going to cause him to totally blow his celibacy diet.

Her face flushed as his legs brushed hers. He could smell her arousal mixed with her shampoo, her soap, and her perfume. Miss Kaya Kane was no more immune to him than he was her. Most women were easily turned on by a strong male, but he should not be having these stirrings. She was a human. A feisty, beautiful, strong human, but a human none the less. Rafe may just have to break his own rule and bed this creature.

"Who knows you own these properties, Mr. Stone? Is it possible someone is trying to set you up?" Kaya shifted in her seat causing her leg to brush his.

20

Once again, his cock stirred to life. Crossing his hands in front of his groin, he told her, "Property purchases are public record, Miss Kane. I am an architect. I have no enemies. I strive to provide New Atlanta with beautiful buildings to replace those that have been lost over the years. The economy has not recovered such that the warehouses will be used for their former purposes. Also, I am a philanthropist. The only reason someone would want to pin this on me is to direct attention away from themselves. Now tell me, Chief, who would do that?"

Rafe pushed away from the desk and braced his hands on either side of her chair. Leaning in to her, close enough that he could smell her minty breath, he whispered against her ear, "Tell me, Kaya. Do you think I am a killer?"

Her heartbeat was speeding, her breathing getting shallower. His proximity to her was causing chaos. "I, no... I don't know you well enough to make that assumption, Mr. Stone."

Calming his own racing heart, Rafe leaned away from her. Of course, she wouldn't know whether he was a killer or not. He hid from society, a mystery man. "Then, Miss Kane, if you have no more questions, I have business to attend."

Kaya stood from her seat. With him still standing in front of her chair, she was close to him. Too close. If he didn't get her out of his office, he would be doing more than answering questions. Looking up at him, she replied, "Yes, Mr. Stone, I do have more questions, though they are for your alibis. If you would be so kind as to provide the names of the people who can verify your whereabouts for the last twenty-four hours, I would greatly appreciate it."

Rafe was getting light-headed at the nearness of this woman. He had to get away from her and get to the archives. Surely there was something written about human bonding. There was no other explanation for the effect she was having on him, unless she herself was a shifter. There was no way a female could have slipped into New Atlanta undetected. Both Gregor and Dante spent time with Kaya and neither suspected that she was anything other than human. Female Goyles put off a pheromone of sorts that was detectable only by males of their species.

Speaking of his brothers, they should have already arrived, and he needed her gone, for more reasons than one. Even though she was standing, she was not making her way to the door. Oh yes, she wanted a list of alibis. "If you stop by Miss Bridges' desk, she can provide a list of names for you."

There was a look in Kaya's eyes that hinted of jealousy. Her scent morphed from one of arousal to annoyance. The good chief definitely felt something for him, but then the few human women he encountered reacted the same way. Why did it puff up his pride that this particular human felt it?

"Thank you, Mr. Stone. I will do that. You have my phone number should you think of anything that could help us find Magnus Flanagan."

"Wait, did you say *Magnus* Flanagan?"

"Yes, why?"

"It just seems odd that a man who has stayed hidden for over thirty years should surface now. I would think his brother Gordon would be your number one suspect, not me."

"He is a suspect but then again, so are you, Mr. Stone. Now, if you have nothing further for me?"

Oh, I have something for you all right. "No, but I do have your number, Miss Kane, and I won't hesitate to use it."

Kaya once again held out her hand for him. Instead of shaking, he turned her smaller hand over and kissed her knuckles, inhaling her scent as he did so. Her gasp was audible as his lips touched her skin. He lingered a moment longer than was appropriate, but he wanted her scent tattooed on his brain.

He released her and stepped away from the desk, dismissing her. She folded her unused notepad and slid it into her jacket pocket. Getting in the last word as she reached the door, she looked back over her shoulder, "It was a pleasure."

When she was down the hall, Rafe muttered, "That was not pleasure. That was pain, pure and simple." He was in trouble. Her scent was imbedded in his nostrils and would remain in his subconscious for a long time to come. Noticing the lateness of the day, he made his way to the conference room where his brothers should already be waiting.

Chapter 5

Gordon Flanagan disappeared into the building. With barely any light filtering through the dingy windows, it took him a few seconds to adjust to the dark. Not seeing the man, he stepped further into the dimly lit warehouse. Hanging from a rafter was the twelfth missing delegate; his mouth covered with duct tape, hands bound with thick rope. Both his body and head were hanging limp.

Looking around, Gordon found the ladder the albino must have used when securing the man to the beams. Carefully, he climbed far enough up to cut the rope. The lifeless body dropped ten feet, landing hard on the concrete floor. A few broken bones wouldn't make a difference in the end.

For a few moments, Flanagan just stared at the face that had haunted him for years. A face he saw in the mirror every day. Nudging the body with his foot, he rolled him over until he was flat on his back, hands that were still bound by the rope lying askew.

Gordon bent down and grabbed his cheeks with one hand and shook. "Wake up, Magnus." Getting no response, he slapped him across the face, leaving a huge hand print on his left cheek.

"I said wake up Goddammit!" After another slap to the face, the man's eyelids fluttered, focusing enough to tell who was yelling at him.

Gordon ripped the tape off his mouth, knowing the man wouldn't scream, but even if he could, nobody would hear him. "Hello, Magnus. It's been a long time, *Brother.*"

"Now, tell me where she is…"

Rafe's brothers Dante and Gregor, along with their cousins Julian, Geoffrey, Nikolas, and Mason, were standing around the conference room. Dante was the only one using the family surname of Di Pietro. The others adopted more common, modernized names when they left Europe. There were many more of their kind scattered throughout the city and surrounding states. Rafael was their King, and he and his circle ruled all of the Society in the Americas. His brother Sinclair ruled over the west coast. Each led a team that took turns patrolling the city for Unholy.

"Sorry I'm late. I'm sure by now you've all heard about the killings at the warehouse. Dante, what did you find out?" The men took their seats, and Dante confirmed what he suspected earlier.

"I was right about them being poisoned. It was a super strain of wolfsbane. It was injected through the scalp making a puncture wound virtually undetectable."

"Wolfsbane? Isn't that harvested in the Alps?" Julian was practically a walking encyclopedia.

"Yes, Jules. Someone would need resources overseas." Dante confirmed his cousin's question. "I put in a call to the chief to relay this information, but I have yet to hear from her."

Still standing, Rafe crossed his arms over his chest. "That's because she was here." There was a rumble throughout the room that included a medley of *What?* Excuse me? *Here?* And, you're fucking kidding me. Rafe waited for the surprised men to quiet down. "Yes, I allowed an outsider in, but there's a reason. A very good reason and we'll get to that in a minute. First, back to the murders. If Magnus Flanagan is alive, we need to help find him. Gordon is going to cause chaos until he finds his wife and daughter. If he has his twin, the turmoil will be unlike anything we've seen in a long time. I just don't understand why Magnus would choose to surface now after hiding for so long.

"Julian, I want your team to install security systems on all the warehouses. Have them monitor the feed around the clock. If someone used our property as a dumping ground once, there's a chance they'll do it again. Then I want you to personally inspect the hotel. I want DNA samples from Magnus Flanagan's room. Something about him showing up in public after all this time doesn't make sense. Even if he were trying to draw his brother out, he could have done it in a more subtle way.

"I will take your patrol tonight. Mason, you're with me. Dante, you and your crew take the south, west, and east. Mason and I will take north. Gregor, any rumors from inside the Pen?"

"Some, but not any we can verify as of yet. We should probably put someone undercover on the inside. If Flanagan does have Magnus, we need to find his base camp and quickly."

"I think that's a good idea. We have been too lax in looking for him over the years. I will leave the details of that up to you and Geoffrey. Does anyone have anything else?"

Nikolas spoke up, "Yeah, why was the sexy chief of police visiting you?"

Rafe arched an eyebrow at his cousin, "Sexy?"

Nik just shrugged while grinning at him.

"Since you asked, I require your help with the archives. I want you to look up anything and everything that has to do with bonding to a human." That brought on more rumblings through the room, everyone asking questions at the same time.

He held up his hands. When the men calmed down he continued, "Gregor and Dante, you two have been around Chief Kane. Have you ever felt anything out of the ordinary from being in her presence?"

Both men shook their heads no.

"Frey, what about when you trained her at the gym, anything?"

Geoffrey also confirmed that he did not.

"Earlier when I returned her phone call, her voice alone caused the same type of stirrings that are brought on by the nearness of one's mate."

Julian clarified, "You mean you got wood?" This was not meant as a joke, and the other circle members were equally as intrigued. Finding a mate as a Goyle was a rare occurrence, and if there were any possibility of mating with a human, it would be a blessing. It just wasn't heard of.

"Yes, Jules. If she could cause that type of reaction over the phone, I wanted to find out what would happen in her presence. So I invited her to come to my office for her interrogation. I just left my meeting with her before I walked in here."

Gregor asked, "How did that go? Were you able to control yourself?"

"It was very difficult. Her scent alone is intoxicating, and when I brushed against her, I thought

27

I would pass out. Nik, please go to the family library immediately and search every book, every journal. I prefer to keep this between us for now. I do not want to get hopes up where there are none."

"You have my word, my King; I will find an answer for you." Nik bowed his head in respect. Rafe did not rule with an iron fist nor did he expect to be put on a pedestal. He treated his Clan as brothers, family. When one of them did bow to him, he felt it in his heart. They loved him and would do anything for him. He was a good and just ruler.

"Thank you my brother. If there is nothing further, I am ready to hit the air."

On their way out the door, Rafael stopped Julian. "I want you to get me everything you can find on Chief Kane."

Julian nodded, "Will do."

Chapter 6

Kaya could not concentrate on anything other than Rafael Stone. Driving to the hotel, she missed more than one turn. She finally pulled into the circular drive at the Westwood Plaza, formerly the Westin. It was one of the few larger hotels that had not been leveled in 2014. The area was slowly seeing a renewed growth, but New Atlanta was not the international hub it had once been. She pulled her cruiser to the front door and flashed her badge at the valet.

Walking through the sliding-glass doors into the lobby, she surveyed the surroundings. She had sent another detective, Kyle Jorgenson, on ahead to lock down the hotel and begin the initial investigation. Either he had all the news people tied up in a room or the hotel staff had done an excellent job in concealing the kidnapping. She was certainly surprised to not see Katherine Fox nosing around.

Dane and Jorgenson stepped out of the elevator together. As she approached them she asked, "Kyle, what do we have?"

"The delegates were to begin the day together with breakfast at 8:00. The Vice President, his aide, and four others were the only ones in attendance. After waiting on the other delegates for thirty minutes, Vice President Reed sent several of his security detail to look for them. When there was no answer at any of the doors, they alerted the hotel manager who gave them access to the rooms. All of them were found empty. Nothing appeared out of the ordinary; all beds looked like they had been slept in. The Vice President has gone back to his own hotel."

Kyle had gone over the security footage. Somewhere around one a.m. the video feed had been set on a loop and then was reset around four a.m. That meant they needed to find out what had transpired in the three missing hours. Whoever pulled this off must have had inside help.

Kaya held a printout listing the delegates in attendance. "I have already sent the list of names of the deceased to the Governor's office. I'm going to let him notify the families. You two interview the staff and go back over the rooms when CSU is finished."

Dane took the list and asked, "How did the meeting with Rafael Stone go?"

She pulled another list out of her pocket and handed it to him. "He has several alibis for the time of the murders. Call them tomorrow and set up interviews to get their statements. Also, we need to find Elizabeth Flanagan and figure out why her brother-in-law decided to surface now."

"I will call the people on the list but finding Elizabeth Flanagan is going to take time. I have a lead to check out too, but I'll wait to see if it pans out before I give you the details."

"Okay, call me when you two are finished here." She left them to their work and headed out.

Driving home, her thoughts once again drifted to Rafael. Sitting in close proximity to the man caused her pussy to throb with a need like she had never felt before. Being a police officer was not a good occupation for a healthy relationship, and she wasn't the one night stand type. Many years had passed since she'd been with a man. Being the chief of police was like a dating death sentence. She didn't have time to date, but even if she took time her choices were almost nil as she refused to go out with anyone she worked with. The list of available bachelors in New Atlanta was a short one.

Rafael was on that list, as were his brothers, but dating a suspect went against all protocol. Until he was cleared, he was off-limits. Besides, a man like Rafael Stone probably preferred petite, frilly women over athletic tomboys. Her closet was lacking in the fancy dress section. The policeman's ball was the only time she ever dressed up.

Kaya counted herself lucky to have seen the man in person. He was an enigma, and rumors ran amok from him being disfigured to hideously ugly to gay. Rafael was definitely no monster. It was possible he was agoraphobic, but she didn't think so. The family built beautiful buildings including the state penitentiary that his brother Gregor oversaw. One wouldn't normally describe a prison as beautiful, but the same ornate stonework was used on it as with the downtown office buildings. If the newspaper reports were correct, Rafael and the Stone family donated millions to local charities.

Kaya, having arrived home, parked at the side of her two-bedroom house and shut the engine off. She leaned her forearms against the steering wheel and clasped her hands together. *Why him?* She was around men all the time, but never had one affected her the way he did. She couldn't wait to get inside, grab a glass of wine, and strip down to her lace thong. She might not date, but she didn't deprive herself of artificial gratification.

31

Her modest home was situated on the north side of town and sat back off the road. Tall oak trees lined both side yards offering privacy from the prying eyes of neighbors. If her neighbors could actually see, they might be nosy, but she lived in the house she grew up in. The neighbors on either side were both getting on in age, and the only things they worried about watching were The Golden Girls reruns or the six o'clock news. Fifty years later and the four ladies of Old Florida were still making people laugh.

Now inside, she pulled off her boots and socks, scrunching her toes in the plush carpet of her living room. She enjoyed the feeling of being barefoot because it meant she was home. No boots meant she wasn't in the office doing paperwork or at a crime scene staring at the loss of humanity. Her father had been chief when she was a little girl. He was outside Jonas Montague's clinic trying to calm the rioters when the first blast went off. Kaya was three at the time. She grew up knowing she would follow in his footsteps. She had vowed at an early age to put away every derelict in her city.

Opening the refrigerator, she pulled out a bottle of Riesling and poured a tall glass. The wine was sweet and tart at the same time. The cold hit her tongue and felt good sliding down her throat. It quenched her thirst but did nothing to slake the fire that was still smoldering between her legs. She double-checked the doors and set the alarm.

Thinking of the rugged architect and drinking wine was a dangerous mixture. Both caused her body to heat from the inside out. Kaya sat her wine on the nightstand then opened the window in her bedroom.

The weather in October was a crap shoot. One year it was cool with the next being humid. Luckily this year was pleasant. The moon was almost full and was high in the sky, casting a soft glow through the window into her room. The thin lace curtain was fluttering from the breeze.

Humming a tune, she began removing her clothes, slowly, seductively, as if Rafael were watching. Starting at the top of her blouse, she slid each button through its hole. With a small shimmy of her shoulders, the top slid down her arms, falling to the floor. Next she unbuttoned her pants and slid the zipper down. Slowly. Hooking her thumbs under the waist band, she pushed them down her legs, letting her hips sway. She stepped out of each pant leg and kicked them out of the way. The clasp of her bra was between her breasts. Breasts that were now heavy with need. Her nipples hardened as the silk material scraped across the sensitive nubs. The bra landed on the floor with her shirt.

Kaya took a sip of wine and touched the glass to one nipple, then the next. She watched as they puckered even more. She downed the last of the fruit of the vine and let it intoxicate her just a little more. Tossing the now empty goblet to her bed, she allowed her body to sway in time to the sounds coming from her throat. She released her long blonde locks from the band that held them captive. Shaking it loose, her hair fell in silky waves down her back. Closing her eyes, she continued to seduce her invisible lover, circling her hips just above his ghostly lap.

She ran her hands up her smooth stomach until she reached her aching breasts. Kneading, rubbing,

33

twisting, pulling, she could feel the wet between her legs at the thought of Rafael's mouth teasing each nipple while his hand found her core. Her silky thong was soaked through with her juices. Kaya slipped her hand under the material and cupped herself. Dipping two fingers between her folds, she continued her slow lap dance for her absent tormentor. Thoughts of Rafael being the one to pleasure her body stoked the fire in her belly, flames that were ready to descend to where she was rubbing her clit. With a couple flicks of her fingers, she moaned as she came.

Chapter 7

Rafe had flown with Mason several times. The younger Goyle was mastering his changes like a pro. Gargoyle shifters were quite different than the gothic stone figures depicted on buildings. They were primordial beings. Even though they had human traits, they were full-blooded Gargoyle. There were various phases of changing, those being extending claws, elongating fangs, and unfurling wings. The skin of the male Gargoyle was virtually indestructible. It was thicker than human skin but didn't feel any different to the touch. One of the few things that could penetrate it was the fangs of another shifter. The older the Goyle, the faster and more innate the phasing became.

Rafe led Mason through the sky to the north of the city at a safe level. Humans rarely looked up. Should they happen to, they would think they were seeing a large bird.

Kaya Kane lived north of the city. It was no coincidence he chose this quadrant to patrol. The pull he felt when around her was too strong to ignore. As he and his young protégé closed in on her home, he told Mason to separate for a twenty block radius. Rafe continued to Kaya's house until he hovered just outside. The only light on in the house was on the back side. The glow from a lamp along with the moon's beams made it just bright enough that he could see Kaya through the thin curtain covering the window. Having excellent hearing, the tune she was humming sounded like a lullaby in his ear. The melody ramped up to a sexy number as she began to undress. Rafael found a tree limb to perch on so he could give the show inside all of his attention.

Her blouse fell from her arms as did her pants, then her bra. The wine glass caressing her nipples caused a jealous stir in his chest. His tongue should be the cause of moisture on her beautiful breasts, not a piece of glass. This slow dance felt as though it were choreographed just for him. His cock was straining against the fatigues he was wearing. His fangs ached to burst forth from his gums and claws scratched at the inside of his skin, begging for release. Kaya's hand slid beneath the thin layer covering her mound, and he could smell her arousal as if his nose were buried where her hand was.

Her breathing hitched, and her hand sped with the need for release. When Kaya yelled his name, Rafe had to grab his cock and squeeze. *Fucking hell. Motherfucking hell. She was thinking of him!* Mate or not, Rafael was going to bed this beauty and soon. The flap of wings brought Rafe out of his private viewing. With one last lustful gaze, he launched from the tree into the sky.

"All was quiet except for a human bar brawl that spilled into the back alley," Mason reported as they met in the air.

"Very good. Let's head toward the warehouse where the murders happened. I want to take a look around."

Mason flanked Rafael as they flew in silence, keen eyes watching the streets below. As they approached the warehouse, Rafe listened, scanning for humans. Finding none in the area, they made their descent. They landed soundlessly on the ground beside the loading dock, both tucking in their leathery wings. The King took in their surroundings, first by closing his eyes and smelling. Gargoyle senses were always heightened no matter what form they were in. Next he scanned the area, looking for anything the CSU team may have missed.

He and Mason split up to cover more ground. After several minutes he called for his young cousin, "Mason, come check this out." Rafe was squatting by a set of tire tracks hidden behind a row of saplings. "What do you see?"

Mason pointed at the tracks. "Tread, large vehicle probably a van or an SUV. Makes sense the killer would have used a van so he could haul more people. An SUV is large but the seats would have to be removed. Tread appears to be from a late model Ford panel truck with the wheels out of alignment on the right side."

Grinning, Rafe pulled out his cell phone and snapped several pictures, sending them to Julian. The Society owned a sophisticated lab that allowed them to do their own investigative work. Hopefully Jules could get the make of the tread and thus a clue to who the killer was.

When Rafe was satisfied there was nothing else to see, they once again unfurled their wings and took to the skies.

Nikolas had looked through over half of the books in the family library; a massive room that just happened to be in his home. So far there was nothing written about human bonding. One of his specialties was speed reading. He would much rather be sitting with an old book in front of a fireplace than outside patrolling. This assignment was just what he relished.

If it were true, if the Goyles could bond and mate with a human, their heritage could be preserved, and another generation of protectors could be produced. This possibility excited him, so after a quick bathroom break he dove back into the rest of the journals. He had just pulled a book down from the shelf when he heard the door open. Geoffrey, his older brother by about fifty years, walked in.

"I thought you were helping Gregor find someone to go undercover." He placed the book on the table and opened it.

"I did. One of my students, Tamian St. Claire. His skill in Muay Thai is the best I've ever seen. I'm just waiting for the day he kicks my ass," Frey said with a laugh. "He's still a little bit of a wild card. There is just something about him I can't quite shake, but he's been studying with me on and off for three years now, and I really like the guy. He has no family in the area and mostly sticks to himself. He is always talking about making a change and stepping up to better the world, that kind of thing."

Frey walked over to the bookcase pointing to the book beside the space vacated by the journal Nik was studying. "This one next?"

Nik looked at his brother and frowned. "You hate reading. And sitting still. And reading."

Frey grabbed the book and sat down in an overstuffed chair and got comfortable. "Yes, but I hate

38

being alone more. If there is something to bonding with humans, I want to know." He settled in and began reading.

Nik just shrugged his shoulders and returned his attention to the book in front of him. Being alone was just a way of life for most of their species. Nik often drove out of town to find one night stands. While he hated the lack of connection that came with that type of interaction, he craved the feel of a woman beneath him, beside him, surrounding him. Seems he wasn't the only one.

Chapter 8

Rafe woke to his personal phone ringing. He glanced at the clock: 4:17 in the fucking morning. "This better be important."

"Hello to you too, Brother. Catch you at a bad time?"

"Sin, you do realize there is a time difference?" Rafe sat up, swiping a hand through his hair. If Sin was calling so early, there was a good reason.

"Of course I do, but I wanted to give you a heads up. Since you didn't bother answering your phone *before* going to sleep or returning the message I left, I thought I better check on you. What's up?"

Rafe's thoughts were so filled with one lady cop that he hadn't looked at his phone before he lay down. "Long night, sorry. What did you need?" He wasn't ready to tell Sin about Kaya and his reaction to her. None of the brothers wanted a mate more than Sinclair. Being younger than Rafe by only a few years meant he had been lonely almost as long. Sin was like Nikolas; he wanted a woman in his life, even if it were just for a night. He had even married a couple of times over the years. As painful as it was to watch your partner age and die, Sin endured that pain just so he could enjoy a companion while the human was alive.

"I wanted to let you know that Lorenzo Campanelli and Jasper Jenkins are heading your way this afternoon. I will have Ashley forward the itinerary to Willow." The Clan moved around quite a bit, usually on the same coast. When they felt they were jeopardizing the family, they would travel cross country to start over. Some even changed countries.

"Be mindful of Jasper though. He has been showing signs of aggression lately, and he wasn't keen on the move. He more or less told me he wasn't moving and when I told him it wasn't a request, he phased. Fully. I believe if some of the others hadn't been present he might have challenged me."

"So you're sending me your problem child?" Rafe just laughed. "I'll hand him over to Frey, see how long the attitude adjustment takes."

"Not long knowing our little cousin."

"I'd really like to witness you calling Geoffrey little. He'd be offering *you* an attitude adjustment." Frey was the largest member of their Clan and being a master of several types of martial arts, he was not only the fiercest but also the scariest.

"Yeah, well I want to keep all my limbs intact as well as my head attached to my shoulders, so I think I'll pass."

Rafe laughed again. He missed Sin. Not only were they closest in age but they were close period. He and his brother were so much alike they could pass for twins and often did in their younger days. He couldn't hold back the sigh that escaped. "Miss you, Brother."

"And I you." The line went dead as it always did before he could say goodbye. Sin didn't believe in the word.

Rafe placed his phone on the night stand and then settled back into bed. Jasper. He didn't know much about the man since he was sent directly to the west coast from Scotland when he could no longer pull off his young age there.

Nikolas kept a detailed record of every Society member: their age, occupations, all former identities, as well as their mates and offspring for the few who were lucky enough to have bonded. Most chose to remain in the same occupation as before, but every once in a while a few opted for something new. When you did the same thing for hundreds of years, it could become monotonous. Whatever job they chose, Rafael would help them both adjust to their new surroundings.

Nik had found nothing to report from the archives. He was surprised that Frey helped him search. Rafe, however, was not. Theirs was a family of protectors first, and they took their role in society seriously. They also wanted to be mates and fathers like most men did. Just because they were shifters didn't mean the longing for that soul mate wasn't there. If anything, it was a deeper want, a greater longing since they couldn't choose just any woman.

If they never found their mate, they lived alone until they were no longer of this world. They could have sex, but it wasn't a lasting fulfillment. It quenched the thirst for a moment, but the parched feeling came back quickly.

Would Kaya Kane even desire him? Right now, probably not. Until he was no longer a suspect for the recent murders, she no doubt wanted nothing to do with him. He hoped the man Gregor and Frey were putting inside the pen would come up with some answers and quickly.

Wanting a few more hours rest, Rafe closed his eyes. As with the night before when trying to go to sleep, his thoughts turned to Kaya and the way she affected him. He loved the fact that she was tall and toned. All of his past lovers had fit the same description. No petite women for Rafe. He was a big man and wanted a woman who wouldn't break when he bedded her. His sexual tendencies leaned to the rough side. If by some miracle Kaya was his mate, he would thank the gods every day and night, and worship and cherish her until her dying days.

Kaya stood at the kitchen table scooping seeds out of the pumpkin she was going to carve. A dark haired little boy with eyes the color of pitch stood in the chair watching intently. The back door opened, and the little boy declared, "Papa look! Momma's making us a punkin." Laughing, the father of her child picked his son up throwing him in the air, causing them both to laugh. With the boy safe in his arms again, the man leaned over and kissed *Momma* on the cheek. She smiled at her son then looked up at the man holding him: Rafael.

Kaya awoke from her dream with teeth chattering. The temperature had dropped overnight. She pulled the covers up tight under her chin. She wasn't completely certain it was the frosty morning causing her teeth to stutter together. The little boy in the dream had seemed so real.

The morning light hadn't broken so there was still a little while before her alarm would go off. She loved this time of year with the cooler weather, the harvest moons, and the wind whispering through the trees. Autumn had been her favorite season since she was a little girl.

The change in the topography of the land after the bombings seemed to affect the weather for several years. Back then, the air was almost always filled with a hazy film. The temperatures rarely fluctuated from one season to the next. The religious zealots were calling for the end of days on every street corner, quoting the book of Revelation. They obviously were wrong since the seasons leveled out as did the smog in the air.

Kaya's house was full of Halloween knickknacks, and there was even a pumpkin sitting on her front steps. Each year she planned on carving a jack-o-lantern and each year she ran out of time. She loved watching the kids come to the door in their costumes. Her neighborhood was one of the safest even with the houses sitting back from the road. She observed which parents came with their children and those that sent them out on their own. Her dreams of having her own goblin or vampire to dress up were quickly dwindling with her age. Not only was she getting too old, but her job was hard enough with nobody waiting on her at home. If she had a child to take care of, she might think twice about running the city's police department.

The scene from the dream played on a continuous loop in her mind: the beautiful boy, the handsome father. Closing her eyes made the vision even clearer. She opened her eyes, but those tiny black orbs would not vanish. Her chest ached with the longing to see his face in reality. Something about those eyes was haunting her soul, but at the same time, that little face lightened her heart in an otherwise bleak world.

Kaya turned to her side and slid one hand under her pillow, cradling her head. Her teeth no longer shivered, but she still felt the chill. After a while, she gave up on going back to sleep so she rolled over, shut off her alarm, and made her way to the shower. She might as well go on in to the office and try to get some work done.

Chapter 9

Kaya arrived at the precinct, having driven there on auto-pilot. After eighteen years of navigating the same route every day, she could do it with her eyes closed. The only change over the years was where she parked. Being chief meant the premier spot in the whole parking lot now belonged to her.

Sighing, she thought back to the days when she was just a beat cop. She didn't have to make any decisions; she just did her job and wrote a report. Now it was up to her to ensure everyone else was doing their job and to double-check all reports. She didn't trust anyone else to that task, not after the governor had questioned one that was less than perfect. Never again would her department look incompetent. If it took her all night, she looked over every report that came in before they were sent on up the judicial chain of command.

As she walked through the lobby past the bullpen, she greeted the few overnight employees by name. One thing she made sure of was that the office was stocked with decent coffee. She needed her caffeine fix as much as the next person, and she refused to drink sludge. Her team didn't make a lot of money, so she didn't want them spending what they did make on expensive, barista drinks. She poured herself a cup of hot, steamy, wake-me-up and settled in for the day.

Several cups of coffee and a couple of hours later, her day team began coming in, grumbling and complaining as they did most mornings. Being a cop was a rewarding job when the bad guys were caught, but when they had a case like they did now, it wore on

46

your soul. Kaya waited until all bodies were feeling the caffeine running through their system before she wrangled them into the conference room. She had learned a lot about dealing with a large group of mostly testosterone laden men over the years; let them know right away your balls are bigger but mother them at the same time. From the moment she was promoted to chief, she laid down the law, and her team listened. She proved herself time and again in the field, garnering the respect of those who didn't think a woman should be a cop, much less chief.

With their early morning brief over, she stopped Dane and Jorgenson. After she had left the hotel, the two of them spent the next several hours interviewing all of the hotel staff before going through the guest rooms. There was no sign of struggle, no sign of a break-in. Whoever pulled off an abduction of that magnitude could not have managed it alone. There were a few of employees they wanted to talk to again as well as all of the managers.

Jorgenson walked off to get busy, but Dane held back. "You okay, Boss? You seem tense." He usually offered up his dimpled grin that she was positive melted the panties off certain young women. Hell, if she was honest, that grin made her stop and take notice in the beginning. Today he was holding back, almost sounding concerned.

"No, Abbott, I'm really not. We have eleven dead, one missing and very few leads. We need something and soon because Magnus Flanagan's chances are sliding down the percentage scale quickly." She was shocked when he gripped her shoulder with a small squeeze. "Hang in there. I'm going to check on the lead I got. I'll let you know how that goes."

He walked away leaving Kaya speechless. Well hell.

Kaya was going over the previous night's reports when her desk phone rang. "Chief Kane."

"I have information on your murders. I saw Rafael Stone leaving the scene just after daybreak yesterday." The line went dead. The voice on the other end had been distorted by an electronic device.

She stared at the receiver a beat before hanging up. First, only those in law enforcement or higher up knew the number to her office phone. Second, time of death still had not been released. Dante had called Kaya yesterday while she had been meeting with Rafael. She later returned his call when he informed her of the cause as well as time of death. The bodies were found at approximately ten a.m., and the ME estimated the murders happened at approximately eight that same morning.

Since the sun came up right at eight, the time frame fit. Unless Dante shared TOD with someone outside of his department, he and Kaya were the only ones with that information. Well, them and the killer. She picked up her phone and dialed his department.

"Morgue. They dice 'em, we ice 'em."

Kaya would never get used to the young assistant. "Trevor, this is Chief Kane. Please put Dante on the phone."

"Hold whatcha got."

Shaking her head, she waited less than a minute for the ME to pick up.

"Chief Kane, what can I do for you?" His deep baritone voice was sexy over the phone. If the man ever chose to smile, she might consider him handsome.

"Dante, have you spoken to anyone other than me about the murders?"

"No, I ran the tests and made the notations in the computer myself."

"Does Trevor have access to the information?" Kaya could see the young man chatting up the murders over a nice game of Halo with his geek buddies.

"Yes, he does, but I can assure you, he takes his job seriously and knows not to speak about ongoing cases, the same as you and I. Is there a problem?"

"I hope not. I just received an anonymous phone call with a tip. The caller knew the approximate time of death. Let's hope it was a guess." She pressed the button that disconnected the call. When the dial tone buzzed, she punched in the number for her IT department.

"Wilkes, this is Chief Kane. A call came in to my private line, and I need it traced. Yes, about three minutes ago. This is priority." She hung up. What the hell was going on? If someone actually placed Rafael at the scene when they said they did, all of his alibis had lied to Dane. She called his cell, but it went to voicemail. "Dane, Kaya. Call me."

Needing another cup of coffee, she passed by the dispatcher's desk on her way to the kitchen. "Hey Kim, did you put a call through to my phone a few minutes ago?" The younger woman had worked at the precinct for years, and Kaya knew her well. "No, Ma'am. Is something wrong?"

"No, everything's fine. I just missed the call, and they didn't leave a message."

Her office phone was ringing as she walked back through the door. "Kane."

"Chief, Wilkes here. We couldn't get a trace on the call that came in. It was from a burner phone."

"Okay, thanks." Kaya was at a loss. She needed answers. She didn't want to be wrong about Rafael. *Mr. Stone.* Sipping her coffee, she thought back to the dream of him and the little boy. Wishful thinking was all that could be. There was no connection between them, never would be, especially as long as he was a suspect.

The anonymous tip bothered her. She received them frequently and more often than not they were bogus. Was this one real? Was someone trying to set him up? His alibi was airtight *if* his housekeeper and gardener were telling the truth. There was also the security footage at the office with timestamps. She needed to see them.

Chapter 10

Rafael's home was a large manor situated on a sprawling piece of land located on the northeast side of New Atlanta. The house boasted eight bedrooms, ten bathrooms, billiards room, dojo slash gym, state of the art kitchen, swimming pool, and his favorite area: a flower garden. The garden covered approximately three out of the fifty acres. Paths led through the various types of greenery, blooms, trees, and fountains. It was one of the most serene places he had ever enjoyed. When Rafe wanted to think, this is where he went. Benches were scattered throughout the paths, and on one of these benches is where he found himself this morning. The brisk October air kicked his senses into sixth gear.

Ever since waking, Kaya filled his thoughts. He couldn't shake the memory of their brief contact, the electricity that zinged through his arm when they shook hands. The way she trembled beneath his touch and the scent of her arousal as they stood close were tattooed on his brain. However hard it was to control his thoughts, he had to get a lock on them. There was a killer to find so that he was no longer a suspect.

He had learned the art of meditation from Geoffrey. Rafael calmed his heart rate, stilled his body, opened his mind. Breathing in through his nose slowly, all tension eased from his body. Rafael imagined he was standing on a rocky cliff looking out over a wild sea; waves rolling in, crashing over the jagged rocks that protruded from the depths like a barbed wire fence protecting a prison. The beauty of the water mixed with the turmoil of the waves somehow brought a sense of balance to Rafe. As he breathed in the scent of the saltwater, he felt a tug on his arm. Looking down, there was a small, black-haired boy reaching for his hand.

Clasping onto the child's hand, he looked back out to the sea. The tide calmed; the waves no longer crashed. The water was as smooth as glass. Glancing back down, the child was smiling up at him. "It's pretty, Papa." The boy was pointing to the horizon. The sun was peaking its head over the faraway horizontal barrier that appeared close enough to touch. "It is beautiful, my son."

Rafe came out of his trance with a start. *What the fuck?* Rarely did his meditation take him that far into his subconscious. But a child? He was not a father, of that he was certain. The fates guaranteed they could not procreate unless it was with one who could handle carrying a Goyle fetus: their mate. Would the fates have changed their minds or had they made it so the humans could carry a shifter child as well?

Meeting Kaya and the possibility of human bonding must have affected him deeper than he knew. Previously, Rafe bore little hope of finding a mate and having a family. Now, it was all he could think about. To have his home filled with children, given to him by the woman he was fated to be with, would be worth every second of loneliness he had endured for the last five hundred years. He rose from the bench and made his way through the garden, stopping to admire the last few blooms that were hanging on in spite of the cooling weather.

Grabbing his phone on the way to the shower, he rang Geoffrey. Frey was one of the more disciplined of the Clan. He didn't stay out late and he rose early. "Yo." His answer was in no way disrespectful to his King. He was answering as family.

"Yo yourself. I got a call earlier from Sin. He's sending Lorenzo Campanelli and Jasper Jenkins our way. I need you to pick them up from the airport and bring them to the manor. Sin said that Jasper is showing signs of aggression. I think I have the perfect test to see if that's true."

"Ah, let me guess. A little friendly scrimmage?"

"Right you are my brother. It's been a while since we have gathered all the family together, and I do believe today is perfect for a *meeting*."

"If Jasper isn't exactly a team player, how are you going to handle him?" Frey was the enforcer of the family. He relished bringing less than submissive members back in line.

"I won't be handling him; you will. The way you brought Michael around all those years ago was brilliant. If you can tame *his* beast, surely you can handle Jasper."

"We shall see. Are you going into the office this morning?"

"Yes, for a while. I am going to schedule a video chat with the others so we're all on the same page. I will be home by the time you bring our guests. Sin didn't give me much of a heads up, so they can stay with me until they find their own homes. I'll have Willow set up the video feed, and I will talk to you then."

Rafe stopped off in the kitchen for a cup of coffee before he made it to the shower. His housekeeper was putting something sweet smelling in the oven. "Good morning, Priscilla. We will be having new family arriving this afternoon. If you would please, make sure two of the guest rooms are ready."

The older lady walked up to Rafe and pulled his face down so she could kiss his cheek as she did every morning. She was the closest thing he'd had to a mother in almost two hundred years. Priscilla's family had been serving the Di Pietros for centuries. She and her brother, Jonathan, lived with and served Rafe and whoever stayed with him. Very few humans knew of the shifters, and those that did were as loyal as if they were shifters themselves. "Of course, my boy. You go shower. Sweets will be ready when you are finished."

"You spoil me too much." Rafe kissed her cheek and did as she said. An hour later he was pulling into the parking garage at Stone, Inc. At the back of the garage, a wrought iron gate slid open, and his car passed through. Only he and his inner circle knew the code that led to the underground lot. Everyone else parked outside the barrier.

The top floor of the building housed Rafe's office and his private apartment. His second home was spacious and included all of the amenities one could want. It, as well as all Society homes, was equipped with roof access. All were custom built and situated strategically throughout the city and surrounding states. They each contained Julian-designed security systems that were more advanced than any available to the government.

Julian was not only an expert forensics scientist but also an electronics whiz. His I.Q. was off the charts. If anyone outside their family found out what he was capable of, his life would be in jeopardy from not only the government but also the likes of Gordon Flanagan. Julian had confided in Rafe many years ago that he, too, had perfected the cloning formula, but only in theory.

It was quarter 'til eight, and Willow was sitting at her desk when Rafe arrived. "Good morning, Willow. How was your evening?"

His young assistant blushed. Even though Rafe had hired her a couple of years ago, she was still shy when he spoke to her. "It was very nice, thank you. I received an email from Ashley and forwarded it to you."

"Excellent. I would like to have a video chat with the team. Please set that up for nine, and I will let them know to be on the call. Anything else for me?" Willow was young, but she was the most efficient assistant he had ever employed. She was a very pleasant, if somewhat timid, young lady. He enjoyed her immensely.

"No, Sir, nothing else."

Rafe let her get busy with setting up the video and walked the short distance to his office. Sending out a group text, he let the others know to be on the call in an hour. He sat down at his desk and turned on his computer. As soon as it booted up he opened his email program. The first one he looked at was the itinerary. The flight was coming in at two that afternoon giving Frey plenty of time to get to the airport.

The email program was fitted with the very best spyware possible. When messages came in from anonymous accounts, they were sent to his spam folder. He noticed there was an email from an unknown source with the subject "I want to hire your firm". Knowing he should delete the message immediately, something about it nagged at Rafe, and he opened it anyway.

Mr. Stone,
Our company is looking to relocate to New Atlanta. While there are many available spaces, we prefer to have our facilities built to our own specifications, from the ground up. We are contacting several firms for bids. Attached to this email is a rough sketch of what we are looking for. If you wish to bid on the project, please reply to this email and we will contact you for a meeting.
Regards,
Bartholomew Cromwell
CEO, Cromwell, Inc.

Rafe was unfamiliar with the name Cromwell. He would have Nikolas or Julian check out the validity of the company as well as search for information on Bartholomew. Against his better judgment, he opened the attachment and found a drawing of what looked like a modern office building with a warehouse attached. This type of structure wasn't his specialty. If it turned out to be a legitimate request, he would have to think long and hard about bidding on it.

Chapter 11

Nikolas closed the last book. Not one journal noted anything on mating with humans. In fact, there wasn't much mentioned about bonding at all. That seemed odd to him. If he hurried, there would be enough time to shower before the video call. He wanted to visit the downtown library and search their archives, even though it was a long shot. Sometimes reality got buried in fiction, starting as truth that became too outlandish to believe and ended up a fairy tale.

Before he left the library, he glanced at the files on the two shifters who were moving to New Atlanta. Once they settled into their new jobs and homes, he would update the information. All of the Clan leaders had access to these files; Nikolas was the one who kept them current. Knowing where their experiences lie helped Rafe and the others in assigning them duties within the Clans.

Nik reopened the files on his computer as he was towel drying his hair. Sin was just as diligent about keeping accurate records as he was. Reading more thoroughly, he noticed there were some blanks in Jasper's file. *What the hell?* There were a few minutes before the video call started, so he dialed his cousin.

"Sinclair," he answered groggily. It was rather early on the west coast.

"Sin, Nik. Sorry to wake you so early but there's a problem with one of the archives. Jasper's employment history has gaps during three separate time periods. Was there a problem?"

"Wait, what? That's not right. You know I update the records myself. Hang on a second, I'm going to log in and have a look on this end."

Nik waited while Sin booted up. "Here it is. What in the fuck? Nik, I swear these were up to date yesterday. I looked at them before I called Rafe."

"Well, they aren't up to date now. Can you tell me what he did during those missing dates? I'll fill them in myself. We have a video call in about two minutes."

"Yeah, let's see. The time in the nineties, he was a fireman. The time in the twenties, he was a fireman. Fuck and his last job was as a fireman. That doesn't make sense though. First, there is no way someone could have hacked into the system. Second, if they did find a way in, why would they want to erase those particular dates? Nik, you get to your call. I'm going to do some digging. I'll call you later."

Nik hung up then dialed in for the video chat. Rafe was already addressing the group. "Frey will go meet them at the airport and take them to the manor. Until we find their permanent homes, they can stay with me. Nik, did you have a chance to look at their docs?"

"Yeah, sorry I'm late, but there was a problem with one of the files. Lorenzo's is complete. He has spent the last fifty years working in various stone quarries. If he wishes to continue in that capacity, that will come in handy because Finley needs to move out of the area. Jasper's file was missing jobs for three time frames. I called Sin and he let me know that during these three missing periods, Jasper was a fireman. Julian, please check the archive retrieval system. You designed the firewalls and will be able to detect if they have been hacked more readily than I can."

Rafe addressed his brother, "Jules, that's your first order of business today."

"I assure you the system is not hackable, but I'm on it."

"Keep me posted. Were you able to run analysis on the tread photos I sent over?"

Julian nodded, "Yes, Mason was spot on. The tires belong to a late model, Ford panel van that needs an alignment. That's the good news. The bad news is those vans are a dime a dozen. I have already been scanning traffic camera feed around the area of the warehouse. Also, I was able to get into the hotel rooms and take a look around. I pulled DNA from Flanagan's room. I want Dante to come by the lab and double check what I'm seeing. If what I have found is confirmed, either the missing delegate is not Magnus Flanagan or the man has shifter blood."

"Things just keep getting more interesting. One more thing. I received an email today from an anonymous account. I am going to forward it to you. If either you or Nik could run a background check on the sender and his company, I would appreciate it. Jules, please monitor our system and find out how an anonymous email got through."

"Yes, Sir." Julian's tone let everyone know he was frustrated with both breaches of security.

"Nik, did you find anything in the family library after your update last night?" Rafe's gaze was steady, matching his voice. Nikolas had called during a break in reading to let him know he hadn't found anything so far.

"Nothing. There was barely any mention of bonding at all and nothing with humans. I thought I'd go to the public library and look through some of their older stuff."

"I don't think it could hurt. Just give yourself time to get back and help Julian. Gregor, Frey told me he found a man to go inside the Pen. Are you prepared for that?"

"Yes, Frey and I are meeting Tamian this morning and briefing him on how he will get arrested and what to expect once inside. Even though his "crime" will not warrant it, I will have him in maximum security."

"Very well. If there's no other business, I would like you all to be at the manor tonight around seven. Sin reported that Jasper is showing signs of aggression. I think a little game of football will allow us to see just how aggressive our cousin can be. If he maintains his calm, then it's possible his problem was with Sin. Priscilla will have supper on the table at six, should any of you wish to arrive early. Have a good day my brothers."

"And you, our King." Sinclair was the one who started the sign off many years ago, and the other men eventually joined in. Now it was an automatic chorus of deep voices.

Nik signed off the call and put his clothes on. Opting for comfort, he dressed in his usual jeans and Henley, throwing on a hoodie, in case he needed to be a little incognito. As one of the "faces" of the family business, he was often recognized. Having been up for over twenty-four hours, Nik was tired and preferred not to be hounded by someone wanting to have their picture made with one of the illustrious Stone family. He picked out clothes appropriate for football and stuffed them in a gym bag for later.

The downtown library was busy for a Thursday morning. Nikolas found an open spot and parallel parked his two-seater perfectly. Thinking he would begin in the archives, he found the directory then made his way to the third floor. As soon as he stepped off the elevator, a wave of nausea flowed through him. Nik paused, making sure he wasn't going to throw up. When the feeling passed, he continued to the help desk.

Nik expected to find an older woman with her hair in a bun and skinny glasses perched atop the bridge of her long nose. Instead, sitting behind the desk was a younger woman with her brown hair in a messy knot and funky glasses perched atop the bridge of her very cute, button nose. "May I help you find something?" The smile she bestowed on him caused another surge of unease inside his belly. He leaned both hands on her desk and dropped his head down, taking deep breaths.

"Sir, are you okay?" she asked placing her hand on one of his. Nik felt like he was flying too close to a power line. The electricity sizzled where their skin met. "Holy shit." He glanced up to find her expression was one of worry. "Sir, can I get you something? Some water maybe?"

"Uh, no. No thank you. I have to go." Retreating the way he came in, he all but ran out of the public building.

Nikolas arrived at the lab early. Three hours early to be exact. He planned on spending that long

61

doing research, but after the librarian-induced panic attack, he found himself at the lab with his younger brother whose fingers were flying over a keyboard.

"This is bullshit, Nik." Julian rarely raised his voice being the calmest one of the Clan.

"Hey, there was an issue at the library. At least I'm early, not late."

Julian looked up. "What? No, not you. This." He waved his hands at the monitor as if Nik knew what *this* was.

"I take it you found the problem then?" If Julian couldn't find why their computers were being hacked, no one could.

"Yes but first, what happened to you? You look like you're going to hurl. If you are, you better not do it in here. I'm not cleaning up after you." He was typing as he talked.

"Yeah, well I'm not so sure I'm *not* gonna throw up. Jules, it was the weirdest thing. I got off the elevator at the library and immediately felt sick. I leaned over the desk to catch my breath, and this woman put her hand on mine. I thought for certain I was going to pass out right there."

"Nik, you're five hundred and twenty years old for fuck sake. You can't handle being around a woman?" Julian's blondish brows were dipping between his green eyes.

"Hold up. First off, I'm five hundred and twenty three. Second, you were interested when Rafe was affected by a female. Don't be giving me shit about it. If the King can't help it, why should I be able to?" At this point, Nik really wanted to leave all the security research to Julian, but he had already failed one assignment today. He wouldn't fuck up another.

"Sorry bro, I'm just pissed. Come look at this." Julian was pointing to the computer screen. It took a few seconds, but he saw the discrepancies Jules was pointing to. "What the hell?"

"My sentiments exactly. Nik, this had to have been done from the inside."

"Fuck. Did you tell Rafe?"

"No, I just found it. Hang on, let's look at the email server." A few clicks of the keys and they both saw it at the same time. "Son of a fucking bitch." Julian ran his hands through his hair and then his fingers began flying again. Nik watched in silent awe as his brother rewrote the security program. Once he felt it was secure he stood and stretched.

"I'm hungry. Did you have lunch?"

Nik shook his head, "No, I was afraid it would come back up, but I could eat now. Do you want to start the search on Rafe's mysterious e-mailer or do you want to go get lunch?"

Julian twisted his torso to both sides. "I need to get out of here for a few minutes. I'll go. Giovani's?"

"Yep, the usual." Nik sat down at his desk and began searching for information on Bartholomew Cromwell.

Chapter 12

Sitting at the corner table with his back to the wall, Dane glanced at the door every time it opened. His waitress, Marley, refilled his coffee more than was necessary, but since she was a pretty distraction, he didn't mind. One cute little red-headed reporter had told him she had a lead on Gordon Flanagan. Whether or not she was baiting him was yet to be seen, but he was supposed to be meeting her for a quick cup of coffee before heading to the doctor's office.

Thirty minutes later than scheduled, the petite spitfire came through the door, waltzing across the room in those damned stiletto heels. How any woman could walk in those needles, much less glide in them, was a mystery.

He rose from his seat, waited until she sat across from him, then sat back down. "Miss Fox, thank you for meeting with me. Can I get you something to drink?"

"No, thank you. I don't have much time. I really don't have a lot to go on. What I do have is an address where someone who matched the description of Gordon Flanagan was seen." She slid a folded sheet of paper across to Dane.

"Why are you giving this to me? Why not check this out yourself? If you could find Flanagan that would be a huge boost to such a young career, would it not?"

Katherine scowled at him. "Don't patronize me, Mr. Abbott. I'm not stupid enough to go after someone as irrational as Flanagan. That's *your* job. You chase the crazies. If you happen to find him, I will consider that boost enough." She stood but leaned over and whispered. "I don't want to be associated with anything that has the Flanagan name on it. Are we clear?"

"As freshly cleaned glass." Dane watched with a smile as she strolled out the door. He opened the paper, glanced at the address, and shoved it in his pocket. He downed the rest of his coffee then dropped an extra few dollars on the table for Marley. He headed across town for an appointment that, hopefully, wouldn't have to be rescheduled.

Even though he arrived late, the doctor didn't turn him away. The paper barrier on the examination table crinkled as Dane stood. Having sat there for the last half hour was causing his back to ache more than it had been when he came in the exam room. He retrieved his cell phone out of the pocket of his jeans. Shit. Several missed messages from Kaya. "She's gonna kill me."

"What's that?"

Dane jumped at the doctor's voice. He was so intent on his messages that he didn't hear her come in. "Just my boss. It's nothing." He returned to the table, holding the cotton gown closed behind him. When he was situated, he noticed the doctor was staring at him. "That bad?"

Dr. Isabelle Sarantos' blue eyes were hidden behind square black glasses. "Not bad, Mr. Abbott, just inconclusive. I know this isn't what you want to hear, but we are going to have to run more tests. The blood panels so far have either been compromised somehow, or there are anomalies in your white blood cells that we have never seen before. I'm going to have the tech pull more samples and then I will let you go. We will send these samples off to an independent lab for verification. I'll call you when I know something, one way or another."

She was right; that wasn't what he wanted to hear. Dane wanted to know what the fuck was wrong with him. Between his skin itching and his joints aching, he wasn't getting any sleep. He was unable to focus on his job, and it was beginning to show. He could only avoid Kaya for so long. Dane never called in sick, but he had to get some rest.

The young lab technician knocked then came in the room, setting a plastic container on the stainless steel table. She pulled several vials of blood earlier, so she didn't bother reintroducing herself. She just got busy with the tourniquet and needle. After she was finished, she removed her gloves and disposed of them before she slipped out of the room.

Dr. Sarantos was scribbling notes on Dane's chart. Without looking up, she asked, "Do you want me to write you a prescription for a sleep aid or pain pill?"

"No, I'm good."

She continued writing a few more lines. "Okay, I will let you get dressed then." She held out a business card. "Here's my number in case you change your mind."

Without another look back, she left him to put his clothes back on. He really should go check out the address Katherine had given him earlier, but Dane was feeling worse by the minute. He just wanted to go home and go to bed.

Isabelle stopped the lab technician in the hallway just before she stepped into the elevator. "Paige, I am going to run these samples myself. I have another case I'm working on, and I believe they are similar. You go ahead home and tell Dustin hello for me." The tech handed the tray of samples to her and smiled.

"Thanks, Doc!"

Isabelle laughed at her young friend. "Have a good night."

"Will do. And don't you work too late." The elevator doors closed on her last words.

"Right, me work late?" Isabelle laughed at herself. There was already a cot in her office so she could get a little sleep. This latest case was bothersome to say the least. Her background in infectious disease should be coming in handy, but this was like nothing she had ever seen before. Actually there was something like it a long time ago in her father's lab, but she was certain this could not be related.

The notes and findings her father wrote about were obscure at least and unbelievable at most. She was going to have to call in someone to help her with the research, and she knew just the person. If this was anything close to what her father worked on, her cousin Tessa would know more about it than anyone.

Now, if she could just find her world-traveling cousin. Tessa was a couple of years older than Isabelle. Where Isabelle was settled and responsible, Tessa was a wild child; moving from one location to the next when the fever struck, using the title of Archaeologist as a reason for such nomadism. As far as she knew, her cousin had never discovered anything.

Once back in her office, she placed the blood samples in the private refrigerator and found her cell phone. She skimmed the list of contacts until she found the last phone number she had for her cousin and pressed "call". After several rings, voicemail picked up. "You know the drill."

Isabelle would never get used to her cousin's disregard for those she felt she didn't have time for. "Tessa, it's Isabelle. Listen, I have a project I'm working on, and I could really use your help. I don't want to go into detail over the telephone, but let's just say it is similar to the findings in my father's journals you and I spoke of long ago. Please call me when you get this message."

Now all she could do was wait.

Chapter 13

Coffee was doing more harm than good on Kaya's empty stomach. She needed food. Dane hadn't called yet to update her on the lead he was checking out. She wanted to run the anonymous tip by him and have him question Rafael, but Kaya was tired of waiting on him to call her back. She packed her laptop in its case and grabbed her keys. After she had lunch she would have another talk with the prime suspect. Kaya passed the dispatcher on her way out. "I'm going to check on a lead. It'll take a while, so if you need me call my cell."

Kaya wanted more information on Rafael before she approached him again. She drove to Giovani's, a nearby Italian restaurant. The lunch crowd was thinning out. The lack of clientele along with a table in the back allowed her a modicum of privacy. After taking her seat, she pulled her laptop out of its case and began searching. Kaya didn't want Rafael to be guilty, but that didn't mean she shouldn't research him anyway. First she was going to look into Elizabeth Flanagan.

Even though there was no proof, the consensus at the office was that Gordon Flanagan had abducted his twin. When her uncle's clinic was bombed and Elizabeth disappeared, the media spent all their time researching the Flanagan brothers and their relationship with Elizabeth, as well as each other. When Gordon and Magnus were teenagers, they both fell in love with Elizabeth Carson. Magnus went off to medical school, and Gordon joined the military. Gordon would come home on leave as often as possible to see Beth. With Magnus out of the picture, Gordon eventually convinced her he was the brother she wanted.

Soon after they were married, Gordon began showing his true demeanor: dark. Magnus graduated and returned home to join their father's private practice. By then, Elizabeth was already married to the wrong man. She confided in her brother-in-law that she was pregnant, and soon after, she disappeared. Somehow, Gordon found out Elizabeth was hiding out in Atlanta with her uncle.

Kaya wondered if Elizabeth was still alive. Whoever helped her disappear had succeeded in erasing all trace of the woman and her daughter. If Gordon had managed to track down his brother after thirty-three years, it was possible he could find his wife as well. Not likely, but possible. Kaya had encountered quite a few rich and powerful men over the years, but none as hell bent on revenge. If Flanagan was indeed behind these murders, she was going to need an army of her own.

The waitress cleared away the dishes and asked Kaya if she was ready for her check. She noticed the time in the corner of her computer. *Shit.* She had been sitting there for over three hours with no more information on Rafael than she already knew. She would just have to go talk to the man. She packed her laptop and left enough money on the table to cover the tab.

Twenty minutes later Kaya was pulling into the parking lot at Stone, Inc. for the second time in two days. She shut the engine off and was opening her door when she saw a sleek black Jaguar convertible pulling through the security gate that led from the underground parking garage. Rafael Stone was behind the wheel. Kaya ducked down in her seat quickly, hoping he didn't see her. Her vehicle, being a standard issue cop car, was pretty conspicuous. She rose up slowly to see the tail lights disappearing down the street, heading out of town. She started her engine and backed out of the spot, hoping to follow him wherever he was going.

He surprised her by taking New Buford Highway instead of getting on the interstate. She kept several cars between them so he wouldn't notice her tailing him. A few miles down he turned off toward the abandoned Country Club. When they were the only cars on the deserted country road, Kaya backed off. More than likely she would miss where he turned, but she didn't want him to know she was back there.

Tall trees lined the road on both sides. If it were summer, the road would be canopied by green branches reaching toward each other. With it being late October, the leaves were now vibrant oranges and reds. If she had been any closer to Rafael, she would have blown her tail for certain. He turned into a driveway, stopping at the gated entrance to enter his code. Kaya pulled over on the shoulder, waiting until he drove on, out of sight. Was this where the elusive Rafael Stone called home? She glanced in her rearview mirror and noticed another car coming up behind her. She couldn't just sit there, so she pulled back onto the road and drove off. The car, a dark SUV with tinted windows, turned into the same driveway as Rafael.

Kaya reached a dead-end. She waited, hoping she wouldn't be joined in the turn-around. When she thought enough time had elapsed, she drove back the way she came. *Shit.* Kaya passed several more cars and a few motorcycles headed toward Rafael's. Since there were no other driveways past his house, it only made sense they were all headed to the same place. What was going on? Was he having a party? She was pretty sure her cover was blown.

She could always gate crash. Not literally, but she was within her rights to question him. He was under investigation, and she was saving him the trouble of coming downtown. *Right.* She just wanted to see how the other half lived. Her little two-bedroom would probably fit in his living room. Not that she could see his house from the road. What if it wasn't a house? She needed more information. Her search earlier didn't allude to his home address. It was almost six so calling Wilkes was out of the question. Shit, she needed Dane.

Rafael had called Priscilla earlier to tell her that most of the men were coming for dinner. He requested the back patio and deck area be set up so they could enjoy the cool air. The brothers never passed up the opportunity to eat one of Priscilla's home-cooked meals. While most of them employed their own housekeepers, none had a Priscilla. Rafe was climbing out of his Jag when he heard the rumble of the bikes.

The men parked in the drive just outside the garage. Geoffrey, along with Lor and Jasper were exiting the Suburban. Rafe smiled at his cousins. He had met Lorenzo about fifty years prior but Jasper was new to him even though he was probably four hundred years old. Lorenzo approached and bowed his head, "My King." Rafe pulled him in for a friendly hug. "My brother."

Jasper looked less than thrilled as he approached Rafe. Bowing his head, "My King." Rafe didn't pull him in for a hug, instead held his hand out to shake. "Jasper, welcome to New Atlanta." They shook hands, and Rafe headed toward the house, his Clan in tow.

A bar was set up off to one side of the enormous deck. Jonathan was handing out drinks as Priscilla was placing the steaming pans of food into the warmers that were situated on a couple of side tables. The men all grabbed their drink of choice then started filling their plates with food. There was no formality when they gathered like this. They were just a family sitting down to a meal together.

Rafe grabbed his plate and sat at the head of the table. Once everyone was seated he began eating. Small talk was made while they ate. Nothing serious was spoken about in front of the newcomers, not until Rafe felt them out, got a sense for where their heads were. He stood to refill his drink and felt someone behind him.

Frey, who was grabbing a beer, held an expression of amusement as he clapped Rafe on the shoulder. "Did you happen to notice one police issue vehicle earlier?"

Rafe nodded, grinning. "Yeah, for her to be chief she sure can't tail someone for shit. I clocked her as I

73

was leaving the office." They both enjoyed a chuckle then Rafe grew serious. "We really can't have her seeing us all together. We'd have some serious explaining to do."

"Truth, Brother, truth, unless..."

Rafe cut him off. "I need to speak to Jonathan, then on to the fun and games." Rafe found his old friend inside the house eating with his sister. "Priscilla, dinner was excellent as always. Jonathan, when you are finished eating I need a favor. The chief of police followed me home. I'm not worried that she knows where I live, but I do not want her nosing around when all of the Clan are gathered together. If you would, please monitor the perimeter cameras to be sure she is not trying to find another way in."

"I will be glad to, my Lord." Jonathan inclined his head.

Rafe returned to the gathered men. He could tell Gregor was anxious to get the game started. He loved the full contact. Rafe and Gregor were almost always captains when they played. Today he decided to switch it up. He raised his hand, and everyone got quiet. "Now that you all have your bellies full, I think we should play a little football. We have new family among us, therefore I have decided we'll let them be captains. Lor, Jasper, I'll flip a coin and you two can choose your teams. Jasper, you call it."

Rafe flipped the coin and Jasper called tails. Tails it was. Pointing to opposite sides of the deck, he separated the captains. Jasper eyed all of the men and chose Gregor. Lorenzo chose Rafe. They went back and forth until everyone was on a team. Rafe picked up the football he'd stashed earlier and led the way down to the back field. "You chose first, so we get the ball first," he told Jasper and his crew.

"Any rules?" the newcomer asked a little warily.

"Just one: no phasing." Rafe grinned at him and trotted off to his team.

Chapter 14

All the men were shirtless. No reason to tear apart perfectly good clothing and as rough as they could get, that is exactly what would happen. Gregor and Rafe lined up facing each other. Gregor loved the chance at rushing his brother and knocking him on his ass. This was one time when Rafe was not King but just another player on the field. Nikolas, in the quarterback position, called the play and Rafe snapped the football between his legs. Players scrambled all over the field trying to get away from the defense. Being shifters, they were equally matched in speed and strength.

Lorenzo zigzagged and used his muscular legs to jump a little higher than his opponent, snagging the pass out of the air. Strong arms wrapped around his waist taking him down. If he were human, the breath would have left his chest as he hit the ground with a thud. "Good catch, cousin." Frey offered his hand to help Lor up.

After the snap, Nik handed the ball off just before he was knocked to the ground by Jasper, their bare chests pressed together. "If I didn't really like women, I might think this was hot." Nik laughed as the newcomer scrambled away from him. The plays continued with Jasper's team holding Lorenzo's to no score.

Now on offense, Gregor snapped the ball to Julian. He handed it off to Jasper who ran up the middle for about ten yards until he was tackled by Sixx. Next play, Julian pumped the ball a couple of times, muscles rippling in his toned arms. He wasn't as bulky as some of the others who spent a lot of time in the gym. He was more streamlined and sleek, like a panther. He passed a perfect spiral to Dante who ran the ball in for a touchdown.

Play continued for about an hour until Rafe called the game a tie. Jasper didn't show any signs of aggression other than tackling really well. At some point during the game, Jonathan brought water bottles down to the field. They all clapped each other on the back recalling catches and tackles while they rehydrated.

"Great job men. Nothing like a friendly game to welcome family. Jasper, you and Lorenzo will be staying here at the manor with me until we find your permanent homes. Tonight we will let you settle in. Tomorrow night you can begin scouting rotation. Before any of you leave, I'd like to speak with Jonathan. He's been monitoring the perimeter for any sign of Miss Kane. I want to make sure she isn't hanging out by the road. It's bad enough she saw all your vehicles coming in at once. Should she single any of you out and ask what you were doing here, tell her we were playing poker."

Once Jonathan gave the all-clear, the men headed to their respective transportation. They all said goodbye and left for home. Frey helped the two new members grab their luggage, and Priscilla directed them to their rooms.

Rafe walked him to his SUV. "Well, what do you think?" Rafe respected Frey's opinion as much as anyone's.

"I have a feeling I know what the problem is, but until I know for sure, I'd rather not speculate. If I'm correct, we need to speak to Sin. Have Jasper and Lor come see me tomorrow at the dojo."

Rafe clasped his hand, shaking it then pulled him in for a hug. "Thank you, Brother. I will talk to you tomorrow." He waited until Frey was out of sight then went in search of his new houseguests. Voices coming from the kitchen told him Priscilla was entertaining them.

Rafe leaned against the door jamb while Lorenzo was telling Priscilla all about Sinclair's housekeeper, Ingrid. Jasper was watching Lorenzo intently. Rafe's laughter startled them all but none more than Jasper. If a Gargoyle could blush, his face would be scarlet. The fact that he wouldn't meet Rafe's gaze was a clear sign he was embarrassed. Rafe walked up behind his cousin and placed his hands on his shoulders, offering a comforting gesture.

"Priscilla, how long has it been since you spoke to Ingrid?" Most of the servants came from the same family lines, and he should have realized they were related.

"I talked to her just yesterday. She called to warn me about these two." She pointed at them with the spoon she was using to stir some sort of sweet batter. Priscilla was always baking something sinful and fattening since Rafe loved his sweets. "She told me that Lorenzo is a health nut and that Jasper really likes his meat."

Rafe could feel the younger man tense beneath his hands. Instead of playing off the double meaning, he patted his cousin on the shoulder and let it go. "Then Jas and I will get along famously since I love a good steak as well." He used the shortened name hoping to ease the tension he felt pouring off his new brother. Is this what Frey was going to find out for certain, that Jasper preferred men? Rafe didn't care who he liked as long as he was loyal to the family and did his job. He wouldn't be the first gay Clan member. Rafe realized a long time ago that love was love, no matter the gender.

Jasper relaxed, glancing back at his King. Rafe squeezed his shoulder for extra reassurance. "If you two are okay with your accommodations, I will leave you in good hands and say good night."

Both men stood, shaking Rafe's hand. He excused himself to his suite. He wanted to call Sin, but he would allow Frey time to come to the same conclusion he had about Jasper. Rafael felt an unrest in his body, the yearning to let go, unfurl his wings, and fly high above the city. He wouldn't kid himself. He was headed to Kaya's again.

It wasn't often one of the Clan broke the law willingly. Nik felt that sneaking into the public library after hours technically wasn't wrong. He wanted to research the public information, and he could not do that with a certain librarian in attendance. Therefore, Julian hacked into the security system and allowed Nikolas entrance when no one else was there.

Instead of taking the elevator, he took the steps to the third floor. That familiar scent filled his senses, causing a slight flutter in his stomach. Pushing the memory to the back of his mind, he strolled past the desk where the cute brunette was sitting earlier. He made his way to the computer bank and typed *gargoyle* into the search field. Thousands of references came up, most having to do with the stone structures that paid homage to his bloodline. It took several hours, but Nik scrolled through every mention of gargoyle on the system. He began writing down reference books that mentioned origins.

He walked through the rows of books until he found the ones that weren't solely based on folklore. His excellent night vision squelched the need for lighting. When he was about to give up, he happened upon one passage that mentioned the shifters and their origins. The footnote mentioned the source of the passage that led to another book. He returned to the computer and researched the book and its author. Locating the mentioned book, he pulled it off the shelf and was just about to sit down to look through it when his cell phone buzzed.

He looked at the text message from Julian: "Get out of there now."

Nik placed all the books back where they came from with the exception of the last one he picked out. He would borrow it and return it tomorrow night. He paused and listened. Footsteps were coming up the stairwell on the first floor. If he hurried, he could make it to the roof before the security guard found an intruder. As quietly as a mouse hiding from a tomcat, he opened the door to the stairs and ran two steps at a time to the top floor. He exited onto the roof, thankful Julian was manning the alarm. He tucked the book into the waistband of his jeans and removed his shirt, tying it around his waist. He phased as he was running to the edge of the roof and launched into the night sky.

Chapter 15

Kaya dragged herself into the precinct, tired from lack of sleep. It had been a long time since she felt as aggravated in her job as she did at this moment. She knew the routine: discover, research, follow, investigate, solve. This case left her feeling like a rookie. A certain suspect kept her distracted to the point of frustration. What was it about him that demanded her attention? He was just a man after all. On top of that, the last few nights had been restless. She felt as if she were being watched.

If she could connect with Dane, Kaya would feel better about taking the weekend off to relax. Rarely did she take time off from work. Her last vacation, about five years ago, had been mandatory after being shot during a drug bust. The scar on her right shoulder still ached when it was going to rain. Not that she was able to get out of town, but even if she could, she had nowhere she wanted to go.

If Kaya were a girly girl, she would go to the spa for a relaxing massage and pedicure. Manicures were out of the question. She long ago gave up painting her nails. They would chip within an hour and just piss her off for wasting the money. Maybe a shopping trip was in order. Right. What did she need? New uniforms? Maybe she would buy a new dress for the ball. Just because she went alone didn't mean she couldn't look her best.

Sighing, she opened her laptop. Before she could worry about the weekend, she had to get through today. The first email was from the Governor's office reminding her to RSVP for the ball. She looked closer at the message. It contained a copy of the invitation. This year's ball was themed: Masquerade. That might be interesting. She hit reply just as the dispatch band announced an assault in progress at Lion Hart Dojo and Gym. It was said to be the elite training facility in the south. Geoffrey Hartley, owner, was a cousin of the Stone brothers.

Rodgers and Smithson were in the vicinity and took the call. Kaya had trained at the dojo. Geoffrey Hartley ran a tight ship and took no shit from anyone. He was a mixed martial arts trainer, former Marine, and all around badass. If there was a dispute, Kaya hated to see what the other guy looked like. Soon enough she would read the report when it came across her desk.

Her desk phone rang. "Kane."

"Hey boss, it's Dane. I need to take a couple of days off. I've come down with a virus, and it's contagious."

"No problem. Did you check out that lead yesterday? Do you have anything to report?"

"I did check it out but nothing came from it so far. Look, Chief, I'm sorry to bail on you. I'll be back in as soon as my fever breaks, yeah?"

"Yeah. Feel better, Abbott." She hung up the phone. Something was up with him. He never missed work. She often made him go home when she was afraid he was going to get the rest of her team sick.

Sitting back in her chair, she flicked her ink pin back and forth between her forefinger and thumb. She stared at the ceiling as though it would give her the answers she sought.

Screw it. She was going to talk to Rafael Stone. He said he could provide video verification of his whereabouts. She opened her cell phone and called his number.

"Stone, Incorporated. How may I direct your call?" She recognized Willow's voice.

"Willow, this is Chief Kane. I need to speak to Mr. Stone, please."

"I'm sorry, he isn't in yet. May I have him call you?"

"Yes, tell him it's important."

"Yes Chief, I'll let him know right away."

"Thank you, Willow." She thumbed off her phone.

One of her other detectives walked in and placed a file on her desk. "Here you go, Chief. The report on the armed robbery from last night."

"Thanks." At least she had a file to look over, anything to keep her mind busy.

All of the lights in Dane's apartment were off, the curtains drawn. Never having had a migraine, he wasn't one hundred percent sure he knew what one felt like, but he imagined it felt like this. Every sound was amplified so much that he thought his head was going to explode.

His skin itched like he was infected with the worst case of chicken pox known to mankind. His joints ached, his gums hurt. He truly felt like he was dying. Why didn't he get that pain prescription when

Dr. Sarantos offered it? He could call her now, but there was no way he could go get it. He could ask Kaya to bring it to him, but he didn't want her to see him this way: fucking curled up in the fetal position on the floor. The tile was cooler on his skin than the cotton of his comforter. He heard the door slam down the hall and knew it was the kid who worked at the morgue. Trevor was weird, but he was friendly enough and often kept Dane entertained on boring Friday nights.

He dragged himself off the floor and made it to the front door before his neighbor had time to disappear down the steps. "Trevor. Hey Trevor." It took him a couple of tries before his voice caught.

The kid turned around and looked surprised. "Dude, what the fuck is wrong with you? Are you fucking contagious? Whatever the fuck *that* is, I don't want it." He was pointing his finger at Dane and circling it to emphasize *that*.

"I don't know what this is, but I need meds. Will you stop at the pharmacy on your way home for me?"

"Sure, but do you think you'll live that long? I mean fuck bro, you look like shit on a stick."

"Yeah, *bro* and I feel a million times worse. If I happen to kick it before you get back, you can have my gaming system." Trevor was an all-around great guy. He loved his job and talked about it non-stop when they spent time together. His didn't take life too serious and lack of maturity made him that much more enjoyable to be around.

"Fuck man, don't talk the morbid talk. I was kidding. Shouldn't you maybe, I don't know, go see a doctor?"

"I did, yesterday. Until she gets the test results back, the jury's still out."

"Okay, which pharmacy? And for the record, I think you should call her back and tell her the fucking jury better hurry the hell up."

"I'll have her use the one at the hospital so you don't have to go out of your way. Now, I'm going back in here and pass out. Thanks, Trevor."

"Yeah man, I'll see you later."

Dane shut the door and went to the thermostat on the wall. Even though it was October and the weather was cooling off outside, it felt like a furnace in his apartment. He cranked the AC down to fifty.

Chapter 16

Breakfast dishes were cleared away, and the men were enjoying their coffee on the patio. "I've read your files. Lor, if you want to continue working at the quarries we could use you. Finley, like yourself, is ready for a change of scenery. He's been with us quite a while, and the workers are getting a little suspicious that their boss of almost twenty years still looks to be in his thirties. Good genes can only be explained for so long."

"Yeah, I'd be honored Rafe. It's almost a passion of mine and where I feel most useful."

"Jasper, what about you? Your employment hasn't been consistent like Lorenzo's, but you have been a fireman several times. Is that something you're interested in?"

His cousin was nodding his head. "Yes, it is. I really enjoy serving the community and being a fireman is one of the more exciting jobs. That or being a police officer. Where am I most needed? Do we have anyone on the inside?"

Rafe was glad to see Jasper truly was a team player. "As a matter of fact, we do not have anyone on the force at the moment. There's nothing in your file about you being a cop before now. Are you sure that is something you want to commit to?"

"Definitely. There were already several men on the inside on the west coast, so I opted for the next best thing. If it pleases you, I would love the opportunity. It's something I've always wanted to do."

"Well then, I will get Jules on your paperwork and we'll get you transferred immediately. Thank you, Jasper. Lorenzo, you can start at the quarry tomorrow. I will let Fin know he can make plans to head west. He can show you the ropes for a few days then head out. Today, I would like for you both to spend some time at the gym with Frey. Being shifters, we don't need to work out, but we do it to keep up appearances. He also teaches martial arts, if that is something you are into. It does come in handy, being able to explain our hand-to-hand abilities.

"Now, I have business to see to so I will leave you to your coffee. Jonathan will drive you downtown around ten. Just meet him out front. Good day my brothers."

"And to you our King." Both men stood as Rafe did, but he waved them off.

Priscilla was holding the coffee pot when he met her in the kitchen. Holding his cup out, he watched his faithful servant as she poured the hot liquid. "Sir, I put your mail on your desk. I noticed the invitation to the Police and Fireman's Ball is not in the trash. Are you considering going this year?"

"As a matter of fact I am. It's a masquerade ball. Since the invitation does not indicate the name of the invitee, I could go and still keep my anonymity." Rafe had thrown the invitation in the garbage can. As soon as he met Kaya Kane in his office, he came home and pulled it back out. "I have plenty of suits. What I do not have is a mask. Can you see to that for me?"

"It would be my pleasure."

Rafe kissed her on the cheek and headed to his office to make a few phone calls. The first one was to Sin. His brother should be up by now.

"Yo. How are my two transfers doing?" The cheeriness in Sin's voice was a pleasant surprise. The last few times Rafe had spoken to him he sounded stressed.

"Actually they are doing remarkably well. That's why I'm calling. Well, that and I need to send Finley your way. Have you already replaced Lor at the quarry?"

"No, I was going to look into that today. If Fin wants the job, it's his."

"Good, I will speak to him this morning. Lorenzo is assuming Fin's role here. Jasper has agreed to join the police force since we have no one on the inside at the moment."

"Really? And he's showing no signs of aggression?" Sinclair sounded completely amazed.

"No, he's not. He's the picture of the perfect brother, Sin. I want to ask you what the problem was on your end. Was there something about him that caused you to treat him differently than the others?"

"He was shy and I couldn't really get him to talk to me. I guess I may have pushed him too hard to come out of his shell. Why, do you know something I should know?"

"I believe I do. Until I know for certain, I am keeping it to myself though. I do not want to speak out of turn if what I think is not true. When I find out for sure, I will let you know. I believe his aggression was a defense mechanism."

"As long as he is working out for you that is all that matters. Has Julian been able to determine how the files were hacked? That is still troubling to me."

"As it is to me, Brother. He informed me last night the he has the system updated and it should now be impenetrable. He is afraid the hack came from inside the family. He is supposed to call this morning with an update."

"Who on the inside would fuck with the system?"

"That is a very good question. One I hope he finds the answer to."

"Any other business before I go?"

No, my brother. Have a good day."

"Same to you." Rafe disconnected the phone then waited for a dial tone, calling Willow.

"Good morning, Willow, how are you today? Excellent. Yes, thank you. Please RSVP to the Governor's office that I will be attending the Ball this year. Yes, you heard correctly. Yes, I have that covered. No, I will not be taking a date. She did? Thank you, I will return her call. Yes, I will see you later."

Before he could think about Chief Kane calling him, his phone rang. Julian. "Good morning, Brother. Do you have good news for me?"

"Maybe. I am still digging into the firewall breach. As for the email from Bartholomew Cromwell, it seems to have gotten through because it was sent at the same time the firewall was down. Even though it appears to be a coincidence, I am not taking any chances.

"I have researched Cromwell and his company. He tried to bury the true company behind several false

90

fronts, but I was able to get several layers deep. The odd thing about it all is the parent company, WSD, Inc. is owned by a Richard Adams."

"That name sounds familiar... Richard Adams..."

"If you were Nik, you would have picked up on it immediately. Since you do not read as often as our dear brother, I will tell you. Richard Adams wrote *Watership Down*, the dystopian novel about rabbits. Thus the initials for his company, WSD. Now, I do not believe this to be the true Richard Adams since he is no longer of this world."

"So what you're saying is, we still have no idea who sent the email?"

"That's what I'm saying. I will keep digging. Also, Nik wanted me to tell you he may have come across something. A book he found at the library seems interesting, with the interesting part being the author: J.V. Montague."

"Montague, as in Jonas Montague?"

"One in the same. This was written as fiction many years before the clone wars. In this novel, the heroine is human, and her mate is a shifter. His shifter isn't named by species, but it does have similar characteristics with Gargoyles. This seems too much of a coincidence to let it go. I am researching his whereabouts as well as his next of kin. If we can find him or his other writings, we might find out if he knew the truth of us."

"I thought he was dead."

"From what I can tell, there was never a burial, just a memorial service. No body could mean no death."

"Tell Nikolas that is his primary focus. I will reschedule his place in the rotation. He is to continue digging until he finds this man or at least someone related to him."

"Yes my King. Any more from your lady?"

"She's not my lady. However, I have decided to go to the Ball this year. It's a masquerade affair so I will be able to observe her more closely."

"This oughta be good." Julian rarely allowed his vocabulary to lax into slang the way Nik's did. Rafe laughed at his cousin.

"Yes, it oughta." With that, he disconnected.

Rafe dialed the number he had memorized after the first time she called. "Kane." Sweet gods, that voice.

"Chief Kane, this is Rafael Stone returning your call. What may I do for you?" Besides throw you down, strip you naked, and ravish your body?

"Mr. Stone, there are a few more questions I have for you. I also need to get that security footage you assured me would put you at the office at the time of the murders."

"Ah, back to that. I was hoping this was a social call. I will have the security feed sent to your office, unless you would like to look at it here?" What the fuck was he doing? Inviting her to his office last time had been a test of willpower like nothing he'd ever endured and now, he was willingly going to go through it again?

"As a matter of fact, I would like to see it at your office, not that I think you would tamper with the evidence."

"Of course. I have a few errands to run, but I can meet you at my office around noon. Will that be sufficient?"

"Yes, I will see you then." The phone disconnected in his ear.

Obviously his charm was losing its luster. Hers, however, was not. He adjusted the erection that was pushing against his zipper. He could either wait for it to subside, or he could take care of it in the shower. He opted for the latter.

Chapter 17

Rafe's nose picked up the delicious aroma of lavender and vanilla. Today it was mixed with something else: metal? Willow escorted Kaya into his office, and he noted she was wearing her pistol. For some reason, he found her even sexier when she was armed.

"Please, come in Chief Kane. Willow, we will require the security footage from the day of the murders. We will view it in the conference room. Thank you."

"Won't you have a seat?" Rafe gestured to the same chair she sat in last time she was here. Again she wore the obligatory uniform that did nothing to showcase her figure. Rafe wanted to see her in something more casual, more flattering.

"No, thank you, Mr. Stone. I have things to do, so I'd prefer to get on with viewing the footage." Her demeanor was all business. This was very disappointing.

"Very well, follow me then." He led her to the room just down the hall where he had earlier set up an elaborate meal. "I was hoping you would join me for lunch. I am starving and cannot eat all of this by myself." He gestured to the spread of pastas, salad and French bread.

"Mr. Stone, this isn't a social visit. I am a busy woman." A busy woman who was taking inventory of the food in front of her.

"A busy woman who needs to eat. Miss Kane, when is the last time you enjoyed a home cooked meal?"

"Are you insinuating I can't cook?" She had her hands on her hips and a scowl on her face.

Ah hell. "Not at all, but if you are as busy as I believe you to be, you probably do not take the time to cook for yourself. You either eat out or grab something quick on the way out the door. Am I correct?" Her eyes flashed with annoyance. Yes, he was correct.

"I would hate for you to throw this out after you went to the trouble of cooking it." Was she goading him or just being curious?

"Oh, Miss Kane, I assure you I didn't cook this. My housekeeper did. My cooking skills are lacking at best. Grilled cheese sandwich is about the extent of my expertise in the kitchen." Her smile at his honesty lit up the room as well as his libido. Before she could see the evidence rising behind his zipper, he rounded the table and stood behind a tall chair. "Please, have a seat."

Kaya took the chair directly across from his, and they dished food onto their plates in silence. Willow came into the room, pushed a button on the wall causing the projector screen to descend from the ceiling. She laid the remote beside Rafe. A few minutes later she returned carrying a tray of drinks. She set them down and left the room without a word.

"Now, Miss Kane, would you like to watch the footage while we eat or would you rather wait?" Of course, he asked her just as she put a bite of food in her mouth. He watched as she chewed, her tongue sneaking out to lick red sauce off her lips. It was a good thing there was a table between them. Rafe wasn't sure he had the strength to resist kissing those lips.

"Now is good. I'm sure it's going to show exactly what you said. Otherwise we wouldn't be sitting here." Of course, she was correct.

Rafe pressed play on the remote and observed Kaya's face as she watched the screen. He didn't have to watch to know what it showed. Were he guilty, Julian could have doctored the feed so well that not even the best forensic lab would be able to tell. As it were, he had nothing to hide. Except the ever present erection in his pants.

Her face showed nothing other than the acceptance that he told her the truth. He didn't bother turning the feed off. It continued on throughout the day showing her coming into the office. He knew this part by heart. He had played and rewound this scene until he could see it in his mind without error. He found it most interesting when she stopped and studied the various pictures. "Have you traveled much, Miss Kane?"

Startled, she jerked her head to look at him. "What?"

"Travel, have you done much of it? I noticed you looking at the photographs on the wall as if you were reminiscing." He hoped she said no. He wanted to be the one who showed her the world.

"Oh, yes. I mean no. I traveled to Europe right after college, but it was a short trip. I wanted to see the world before I got pinned down in a job."

Kaya's mouth held him mesmerized. Her bottom lip was slightly fuller than the top; the kind women paid money to get. Her teeth were white, but the bottom front were slightly crooked. Her eyes lit up when she mentioned Europe, but just as quickly dulled when she spoke of her career. Rafe had inquired into her background and already knew she had followed in her father's footsteps as one often did when a parent's life was cut down too early.

"How do you feel about your career now, Chief? Still living to fight the good fight or are you ready to pass the white hat to someone else?"

Her face shifted back to that look she got when she was thinking how best to answer as she pushed the empty plate away from her. Rafe wanted to see more looks on her beautiful face, namely those when she was lying underneath him in the throes of passion. He wanted to be closer to her, damn his body's reaction. He stood and circled the table. He leaned his backside against it, leaving his legs spread to give his twitching cock room to expand. He looked down at her, waiting on a response.

"Most days, I still feel like I'm making a difference, doing what I am meant to do. Others, I feel like I'm losing traction and the bad guys are winning. What about you, Mr. Stone?"

"What about me?"

"You've been an architect your whole adult life, correct? Is it still as satisfying as it was the first time you designed a building?"

Rafe rewarded her with a rare smile. If she only knew the first building he designed was one of those in a painting she gazed upon in the lobby, she would probably run screaming. "Yes, it is. Designing a building that stands hundreds of years is almost indescribable. When you stop to think of all the people who come and go, whose lives leave a footprint in that building and then multiply it by hundreds of

97

buildings; it is really astounding. I feel like I design more than just the building, Miss Kane. I create the backdrop to the plays that are life."

"Wow, that was…beautiful. Can I ask you something personal?"

"You can ask, doesn't mean I'll answer."

"Why the anonymity? Why hide out instead of showing the world who you are?"

"Is it that important that the people see my face? I am not a Hollywood star who wishes to have his personal life exploited in the tabloids for the world to pick apart. I'm a private person, Miss Kane; I do not crave the limelight. What's mine is for me to enjoy. Should I ever find someone to share my life with, that will also be done in private."

Kaya leaned forward in her chair as if to better hear him. Maybe she just wanted to be closer to him, he wasn't sure. He took a chance and softly stroked his forefinger along the top of her hand. Instinctively, her hand turned over and clasped his fingers with hers. The look in her eyes was a mixture of lust and uncertainty. Keeping their hands locked, he pulled her to her feet and angled her between his open legs.

She didn't hesitate; Kaya moved her body closer to his. In this position, they were almost eye to eye. She reached up with her fingers and touched the scar running through his eyebrow. She would probably wonder what happened there. Hopefully one day he could tell her. Then she traced her fingers down his cheek to run her hand along his jaw. She seemed mesmerized by his whiskers.

Rafael placed one hand behind her neck, under her ponytail. Wanting to see her blonde hair down, he removed the rubber band, allowing her locks to fall along her back. She seemed to be holding her breath. He threaded his fingers through her hair and pulled her face to his. He rested his forehead against hers, not wanting to move too fast.

Kaya exhaled and touched her lips to his. Rafe stood from the table and pulled her head back so that she was looking up at him. He grazed his lips over hers, barely on a whisper. When she closed her eyes, he pressed their mouths together. The hum flowing through their bodies was heady. He pulled her hips to his knowing she would feel his erection against her stomach. He wanted her to know how she affected him. When he felt the gasp escape her throat, he lost his control.

He licked the seam of her lips, asking to be let in. Once she granted permission, he let his lust for her flow through his mouth, rolling off his tongue onto hers. Kaya's hands moved from his shoulders up into his hair. With every twirl of their tongues, her grip became more frantic; pulling him closer, but at the same time pushing him away. She was as conflicted as he. His hand on her hip moved down to her ass, squeezing. She moaned into his mouth and moved her hips so that she rubbed against his cock.

The blood was coursing through Rafael's body, pounding loudly in his ears. If he were smart, he would use his shifter instincts to calm himself, but this out-of-control feeling was new to him. If this was what being mated felt like, he wanted to lock Kaya in his bedroom and never leave.

When the kiss broke, she pulled away, placing her fingers on her swollen lips. The look she gave him was tormented. "I have to go. I'm...." She didn't finish her thought. She just rushed out the conference room.

Fuck. It was probably a good thing she left. Rafe was about 2.5 seconds away from coming in his pants like a teenage boy watching porn for the first time. He raised the rubber band to his nose and inhaled the scent of her shampoo. If he wasn't sure she was his mate before, he was now.

Chapter 18

"This is Katherine Fox reporting live from Lion Hart Gym where New Atlanta resident, Timothy St. Claire, has just been arrested for the assault on several members of the facility. Owner, Geoffrey Hartley, would not give us an interview but eyewitnesses have confirmed that Mr. St. Claire apparently went berserk and attacked not only Mr. Hartley but two of his gym members. We will have a follow-up story tonight at six. Reporting live, this is Katherine Fox."

The camera panned out showing the front of the gym. *Timothy* St. Claire was in handcuffs being put into a patrol car. Bystanders were gaping at the scene, and police were speaking with Mr. Hartley.

Tessa Blackmore muted the sound on the television when her burner phone rang. "Hello."

"Are you watching the news?"

"Yes, that's bullshit and we both know it. Tamian is the calmest person alive, well next to you. I didn't realize he was going by Timothy now. Don't worry, I'll get to the bottom of it. Anyway, I'm glad you called. Isabelle left me a voice message. She wants my help with some blood samples. I think she's stumbled on another one."

"You know what to do."

"Yep, I'm on it." She thumbed her phone off and turned the volume back up on the TV. Katherine Fox was a hot little redhead. "Reminds me of myself," she mused aloud. Once the news report switched back to regularly scheduled programming, Tessa turned the television off and dialed Isabelle's number.

"Tessa, I am so glad you returned my call. Please tell me you are in the states and can help me." Isabelle was always serious and most of the time a little dramatic. She was the polar opposite to her cousin. Even though they were close in age, they didn't socialize together. Tessa just couldn't see Belle hanging out at a biker bar.

Laughing, Tessa replied, "Slow down, Belle. You sound like you're about to find the cure for cancer."

"If I didn't need your help so bad I would hang up on you. You know I hate Belle."

"No, you hate the cartoon. Just remember, Belle's beast ended up being a handsome prince. Besides, coming from me it's cute."

"You think everything coming from you is cute. Anyway, where are you?"

"Well, Cuz, you're in luck. I'm in New Atlanta."

"Wait, how long have you been here, and why haven't you called before now? You know I always want to see you." Since when? Isabelle never once asked her to visit unless she needed her help. Obviously she needed her now or she wouldn't be calling.

"Jesus H, I just got here. Now, give me a few hours to throw my shit together, and I'll come to you. Are you still at the clinic?"

"How do you know I'm at the clinic?" Isabelle sounded irritated.

"Where else would you be? You're like a dog with a bone when you get your nose to something new or obscure." Tessa didn't bother to tell her she had eyes on her cousin. Being the daughter of one of the most

102

infamous doctors in history could lead to danger. Now that Belle had discovered another anomaly in a blood sample, Tessa was afraid shit was fixing to get real.

"Whatever. And yes, meet me at the clinic."

Tessa looked at the phone when she heard the dial tone. Isabelle must be stressing for her just to hang up, but like her cousin said, whatever. She looked at the monitor that was feeding from Isabelle's office. Her cousin was sitting at her desk, head in her hands. Yep, definitely stressing.

Isabelle needed a break. She'd been at it all night with no answers. Combing through her father's journals proved more frustrating than helpful. Her cell phone rang, and she looked at the caller I.D. Not recognizing the number, she almost let it go to voicemail, but she was a doctor. If someone needed her, she should answer.

"Dr. Sarantos speaking."

"Doctor Sarantos, it's Dane. Dane Abbott. Listen, I know I said I didn't want any pain pills, but it's getting worse. Doc, I think I'm dying."

"Dane, let me send an ambulance to get you, bring you back in."

"No, I don't want to be a burden. Just please call in the pain medicine to the pharmacy at the hospital. My neighbor's gonna pick up the scrip for me."

"Mr. Abbott, are you sure? I don't like this. If you won't come to me, at least let me bring the medicine to you now so you don't have to wait."

"Yeah, okay. You have my address right?"

"Yes, it's in your file. I'm leaving now."

Isabelle called Tessa. "Listen, I have to run out and see a patient. He's the one whose blood I want you to test. Can you meet me at his apartment? Ok, I'll text you the address. See you in a few."

Tessa wasn't a doctor, far from it, but she had an amazing ability to puzzle through mysteries and come up with a viable solution. If Isabelle didn't know better, she would think Tessa's father was the famous doctor turned scientist instead of the crazed tyrant hell-bent on destroying mankind with his army of hybrids.

Isabelle grabbed a supply of pain medicine that was currently waiting on FDA approval. It was on the last test before getting the go-ahead, and she was sure it was going to go through. It was stronger than ibuprofen but not as addicting as Oxy. When she developed the drug, she'd taken it herself so she felt no qualms about giving it to Dane.

Her GPS led her to the apartment complex. Tessa was leaning against her black Harley, already waiting on her cousin. Her auburn hair was streaked with bright red and was longer than the last time Isabelle had seen her. Her green eyes were bright, and her one dimple was deep from the grin on her face. Isabelle often felt plain in her presence.

"How did you get here so fast?" Isabelle asked as she walked past her toward the entrance.

"I was already in the neighborhood. So what's up?"

Isabelle explained her findings to Tessa as they rode the elevator to the third floor. "He called asking for pain medication and he sounded really bad."

They found apartment 314 and knocked. When there was no answer, Isabelle knocked louder, "Mr. Abbott, it's Dr. Sarantos."

Tessa reached for the doorknob and turned. Unlocked. She pushed the door open a few inches and peered inside. "Shit." She opened it all the way to show Dane's unconscious body on the floor.

Isabelle knelt down and felt for a pulse. "He's alive; pulse is strong. Actually, it's too strong for him to be unconscious. It's beating like he just ran a marathon. Here, help me get him to the sofa."

They swapped places so Tessa could grab under his arms, and Isabelle took his feet. Tessa was surprisingly strong for a woman her size. Isabelle pulled out her stethoscope and listened to his chest. She then took his blood pressure. "One eighty over one hundred."

Isabelle pulled a syringe and vial out of her bag and stuck the needle in the rubber covering. She pulled the plunger back filling the tube halfway. Pressing the plunger slightly, a small amount of the clear liquid shot forth, pushing any air out. She stabbed the needle in the bend of Dane's arm and pushed the plunger all the way in.

"What is that?" Tessa asked, watching the process with curious attention.

"A pain medicine that isn't on the market yet. It should help him to rest easier."

"I really don't think he needs that Belle. And since when do you administer something not yet approved?"

"Since I found my father's journals and started studying his formulas. I knew he was smart, but my

God, the man was a genius. You've been gone a long time. Things change, dear cousin. People change."

"Yes, I know he was brilliant. I mean he did make another one of me after all."

"Dammit Tessa, quiet." Isabelle was amazed at Tessa's nonchalance around strangers, even passed out ones, about being the famous 'Montague baby'.

Dane began stirring, moaning, and crying out. "Dane, can you hear me?" His response was more moaning. Isabelle brought out another vial and injected him again.

"What was that one?"

"Something to lower his heart rate. Until I find out what is causing his symptoms, I'm afraid the best I can do for him is to make him comfortable."

Isabelle watched his face as the medicine made its way through his bloodstream. His thrashing about calmed as did his moaning. She felt his pulse once again, and it slowed to normal.

They both sat quietly and waited for him to come to. Twenty minutes later, Dane opened his eyes. "What the…" He sat up and looked at the women. "Dr. Sarantos, what happened?"

"I'd say you passed out, Mr. Abbott. I gave you something for pain, so you should be feeling a little better." She picked up the bottle of pills she had brought with her. "I'm going to leave these with you in case you need them later. Take one for pain every eight hours, but no sooner. They're pretty strong."

Dane frowned at Tessa. "Who are you?"

"Her assistant." Isabelle noticed Tessa didn't offer her name.

"Mr. Abbott, how do you feel?"

106

"Better. Thanks, Doc. I'm sorry you had to drive all the way out here."

"Think nothing of it. I'm just glad you're better than you were. I will get back to the lab. Tessa and I need to continue testing your blood, but don't hesitate to call again if you get worse." Isabelle stood and headed to the door. Tessa follow her outside.

"I will meet you at the clinic." Isabelle watched her cousin make a phone call before straddling her bike.

Chapter 19

Tessa was bent over a microscope, studying Dane's blood cells. Isabelle was pacing the floor behind her. "Well?"

Tessa raised up and looked at her cousin. She was right; shit was fixing to get real. Was her cousin ready for the truth? Belle needed to know what she was in for, same as Dane. If she never met her mate, she would never go through the pain and agony of the change. If she did though, Tessa wanted her to be prepared.

"Belle, we have to talk." Her cousin flinched at the nickname, but she didn't care. "I know what this is. It's the same abnormality that's in my blood. In your blood. Have you never tested your own blood before?"

"I've never been sick so no, I've never needed to." Isabelle stopped pacing the floor and was staring at her. "What do you mean abnormality and how do you know I have it? What exactly is it?"

"Here, sit down." Tessa pulled out the stool beside her and patted it. "You're really going to want to."

Hesitantly, Isabelle sat next to her. "So spill it, Tessa. What do you know that I don't?"

She hated it when Isabelle used her haughty tone of voice. Just because Tessa didn't have a medical degree didn't mean she wasn't as smart. She had spent more time in the lab with her uncle than Belle did going to the university. She was blessed with the one-on-one training of an expert. Therefore, she felt more qualified on this particular subject than her degreed cousin.

108

"What I'm going to tell you will sound absurd, but please just hear me out. Isabelle, we are not fully human. We are…" Isabelle jumped up from her stool.

"We are not Unholy!" The doctor was wringing her hands, pacing back and forth.

Tessa stood and grabbed her hands. "Stop. Isabelle, no! I didn't say that. You have to let me finish. Of course we're not Unholy. We come from a line of shapeshifters dating back thousands of years."

"Shapeshifters, you mean like werewolves? Tessa, they are a myth. Purely fiction."

"I assure you we are not a myth. But not werewolves, no. We come from the Gargouille line. Gargoyles to be more modern."

"You mean we turn into those stone creatures? You are right; this is absurd."

"No, you and I won't turn into anything. Listen, let me start at the beginning. Full-blooded Gargoyles date back hundreds of thousands of years, if not longer. Males of the species have claws, fangs, impenetrable skin, and wings. Females don't get wings. Half-bloods like you and I are children of Gargoyle males and human females.

"Dane is also a half-blood and, as far as we know, will get the full package when he transitions. Instead of the change happening as it should, when he matured, it happened later in life, when he met his mate."

"So what you are telling me is that our mothers had sex with some creature that is a shapeshifter and you and I are part shifter?" Isabelle laughed and shook her head. "I don't believe this. Did you drink some tainted water while you were off on your last adventure? You really are mad."

"I'm not and I can prove it." Tessa waited until she had Isabelle's full attention. Once she did, she allowed her fangs to elongate from her gums. Instead of scaring her cousin with a horror movie growl, she gently touched the tip of one with her finger. Isabelle's eyes widened but instead of backing away she reached out and touched the fang herself.

"Holy shit!" Isabelle sat back down on the stool, holding on to the lab table for support.

Tessa held up her hand, and her claws extended. "For some reason, unlike the males, we don't get the special skin. The original female shifters lived long lives, but there are few left that we are aware of. Female half-bloods get an extended life cycle, enhanced hearing and eyesight, and extra strength. That my dear cousin is the extent of my parlor tricks. The guys get all the cool stuff."

"What do you mean the cool stuff? That right there is beyond believable." She was pointing at Tessa's sharp claws.

Tessa was waiting on the reality of what she said about their parents to sink in. "Like I said, the males get special skin and wings. They are almost impossible to kill, *and* they get to fucking fly. How unfair is that?"

"Fly? You mean like a bird?"

"Yep. Totally unfair."

Tessa gave her cousin time to digest all she had told her. It was a lot to take in, but she needed to know. "Listen Belle, the reason I told you is twofold. One, you should be prepared for your own change. I take it you haven't experienced it yet, or you would have known what I'm talking about. The second is that we have to help Dane through his transition."

Isabelle stopped and stared at her. "Hold up. You said our human mothers. If our fathers are these shapeshifters, that means Jonas isn't my father. If he's not, then who is?"

"Jonas Montague is your father, Belle. His real name is Jonas Victorious Montagnon. In the old days, he went by Victor. He is one of the original Gargoyles, and he's alive."

Nikolas was excited. He finished reading the novel and began research on the infamous author. Dr. Jonas Montague, deceased, was survived by one daughter, Isabelle Montague. After deeper digging, Nikolas found that the daughter had moved to Greece and married a native. A boating accident claimed the life of her husband, and Isabelle Sarantos moved back to the states. Now he just had to find her.

Nik was going to check out every book ever written by Montague. That required him going to the library. Sure he could probably download them, but there was the little problem of one cute librarian he was curious to work through. If she affected him again like she did last time, he would know she was his mate. What were the odds of that? Julian could probably tell him without deciphering, but he knew it was a long shot.

Nik took the steps to the third floor. He let his senses fill. There it was: that hint of honeysuckle. Okay, a hint was good. He could handle a hint. He pulled open the door, and the scent became stronger. Avoiding the desk, he headed in the opposite direction to a row of computers. So far so good.

The lingering essence was causing his cock to come alive in his jeans. He sat down at a computer and pushed his chair under the desk. *Put it out of your mind stud. You can do this.*

"Excuse me." There was that heavenly voice, the one that sounded like an angel had descended upon the earth, if you believed in that sort of thing. Don't turn around. Do Not Turn Around. He turned around to see that cute button nose squinched up like a rabbit.

"How are you feeling?" She pushed her glasses up only to have them slide back down. She was dressed in a long, colorful skirt topped with a bright orange t-shirt. Even though it was October, she wore sandals. Nikolas could see the bright orange nail polish on her toes peeking out from beneath the skirt.

"Fine, thank you." He couldn't stop staring. Was she truly his mate? Could this be the one he was meant to bond with, live with, have babies with? Love?

"Well, I'm glad. You really worried me. If you tell me what you're looking for, I can probably find it a lot faster than you can." She didn't sound cocky, just sure of herself.

"How long have you worked here?" Nik was trying to determine her age without being rude. She appeared to be late twenties.

"I've been here since I was sixteen. Started part-time, then when I graduated college, I got put on full time. So twelve years."

Twenty-eight. Perfect. "I see. Okay then..." he glanced at her name tag... "Sophia, let's see if you can help. I am looking for every book ever written by Dr. Jonas Montague."

The surprise on her face showed only for a second before the cute grin was back in place. "Oh my, now there was an interesting man. Not only was he a brilliant scientist but an excellent writer as well. I so enjoy his fiction. Follow me."

Nikolas was glad Sophia was not paying attention to him, but rather the rows of books she was walking through. The nausea was barely lurking in his throat. He couldn't say the same for the hard-on in his pants. "All those stories about shapeshifters and vampires just seem so real. I've only read a couple of authors who could make you believe in the unbelievable, you know? Here we go." She reached up to pull down a thick hardback. Under the pretense of helping, Nikolas leaned over her, grabbing the book at the same time. The need to touch her was stronger than his willpower not to. His body was more alive than any time he could remember in five hundred years.

Sophia glanced over her shoulder, her eyes never leaving his. Did she just shiver? She whispered, "This one is my favorite. He writes as if he were alive during the Renaissance era. I just don't recall a famous scientist also writing fiction. Non-fiction, sure, but his stories..."

"Are you one of those romantics who wishes she would be swept away by a creature of the night?"

Nikolas was smiling down at the cute librarian, but his synapses were misfiring. He felt as though he would pass out. Shit, is this what Rafe felt? Instead of trying to get himself under control, Nik allowed the feeling to wash over him, filling him with an intensity like he had never experienced.

"Creature of the night? Oh my, no! I prefer shifters." Sophia blushed. Fuck, she was so pretty.

"Shifters huh? So if I told you I was a shifter and wanted to steal you away, you'd be okay with that?"

She gave him a sideways look that was a cross between lust and a mischievous grin. He could smell her scent; she was feeling the pull too. Sophia took another book off the shelf. "What do we have here?" She flipped the book over and scanned the blurb then opened the book to read the inner jacket. "This doesn't look like fiction."

"So what is it?" Knowing it was only going to make things worse, he leaned over her shoulder and glanced at the book. Her scent was infiltrating his nose, making its way into his system. He would be smelling honeysuckle for days. "What the fuck?" He pulled the journal out of her hands and started flipping through the pages.

"What is it?" Now she was looking around his arm, leaning against him. The warmth from her chest was seeping through his shirt. Was that a nipple poking his back? *Concentrate Nicky boy. Focus!*

"I'm not sure; it looks like a journal. I want to check this out. Sophia, load me up with every book written by Montague. Please." She nodded and pulled an armful of books off the shelf. Nik took the books from her and followed her to the checkout desk.

114

"If you'll just swipe your card, Mr. Stone, you'll be all set."

"How did you…"

"Nikolas Stone, everyone knows who you are. Now, do you have a card?" She was squinching her nose as she grinned. He would never look at a rabbit the same way again.

Nik pulled his wallet out of his back pocket and dug out his fake twenty year old card. "Uh, not sure this will swipe." He handed her his paper card that showed a young boy's handwriting scrawled on the signature line. Her fingers brushed his as she took the paper from his hand. Electricity flowed between them.

If she felt it, she didn't let on. "I'll make you a new one. Hang on a sec." She pulled out a new card with a magnetic strip on the back, typed in his name and handed it to him. "Here you go."

He swiped the new card and put it in place of the old one in his wallet. "Thank you, Sophia. I'll get these back to you in a couple of days."

"You're going to read all these in a couple of days?"

Nik grinned at her, "Yep." His *bunny* grinned back.

Chapter 20

Nikolas mentally patted himself on the back for being around Sophia without dragging her to the back corner of the library and having his way with her. He opened the car door and tossed all the books onto the passenger seat with the exception of the journal. Someone put a fiction jacket on it, maybe to disguise it? This journal seemed out of place like it had been bought at an estate sale and then donated. He still found it odd that it was camouflaged. He opened the first page and began reading.

Italy, January 1822

If she only knew the truth. How can I tell my dear Caroline what I am? What would she say? Never has one so fair come across one of our kind but the pull I feel to her is unlike anything I've ever felt. How can someone so frail be destined to be mine? I do not understand why the fates would do this to her, to me. Surely we are not meant to be bonded.

"This isn't a journal; this is a diary. Holy shit. 1822? That's over two hundred years ago." Nik continued reading.

March 1822

Caroline continues to brighten my otherwise dreary existence. Father is getting suspicious. I tried to tell him there is nothing to our relationship, but the way she lights up when she sees me and I her, it's going to be hard to continue the ruse for much longer. I cannot continue to shirk my duties. The others are getting suspicious as well. We do not get sick. How do I convince them I'm lovesick? With a human, no less. I know I need to let her go, but the pull to her is too strong. I need answers. I have searched the archives, and there is nothing there about human bonding.

"Well hell. Looks like we're in the same boat but Jonas Montague, a shifter? If that's even what he was."

May 1822

I told her. I told Caroline what I am. She was pressuring me to get married before we make love. I cannot be around her any longer without succumbing to my desires. I cannot marry her with her not knowing the truth of who I am. My dear, beautiful love, she just laughed. Until I phased. And bless her, she laughed again. I could see the fear in her eyes, smell it on her, but she just grabbed my face and kissed me. She asked me what I am, and I told her. Gargouilles are depicted as monsters, dragons even, but we are protectors, warriors. We have been looking after humans since time began. The chimeras used on building facades portray us as ugly, evil. It breaks my heart, but my sweet Caroline explained it away. 'People have believed in fairy tales for centuries. Look at Beauty and the Beast,' she said. 'I bet the Beast was really a shifter!'

Nikolas thought about Caroline. How lucky Jonas was to find someone so understanding. His thoughts immediately went to Sophia. She laughed and blushed when talking about choosing a shifter over a vampire. Would she truly?

A tapping on his car window found Nik looking at a police officer. He rolled down his window. "Yes officer, how can I help you?"

"Mr. Stone, your parking meter expired. Either add more money, or I'll have to write you a ticket."

"Sure, no problem. Thank you, officer."

He rolled his window up and started the engine. Jonas and Caroline would have to wait.

Kaya had driven around for half an hour trying to get Rafael Stone out of her head. What a kiss! Not only had she initiated the kiss, but she had rubbed against his erection. Her hands had wanted to grab hold of his cock and stroke him through his pants. She barely managed to keep them fisted in his hair. The magnetism between them was almost beyond her control.

She pulled into a parking space at Dane's apartment complex and shut the engine off. If he was going to be out for a few days, she was going to put someone else on the case with Jorgenson. At this point, they should probably have all hands on deck. She needed leads instead of the dead ends they were hitting.

Kaya knocked then waited. The door opened, and Dane's large body was filling the frame. "I told you I'm contagious. Does that not matter to you?"

"Hello to you too. Right now? No, it doesn't matter." Dane still didn't move to let her in. "Are you going to make me stand in the hallway?" He didn't look contagious, but he did look, ashen. That was as good a word as any.

He finally stepped back and allowed her in. "I would offer you something to drink, but I drank everything in the apartment. I only have water left."

"I'm fine, but thanks anyway. I wanted to ask you about the lead you mentioned. Right now we have absolutely nothing. What did you have?" Dane's eyes shifted as he hesitated in answering.

"Spill it, Abbott." Dane was now pacing back and forth like a caged animal, apparently irritated.

"Like I told you, it didn't pan out."

"What was *it*? If you're going to be out, I'm putting Craven on the case to help Kyle. We have eleven murders and a missing delegate. Dane, I need what you have, whether you think it's viable or not."

He ran his hands through his hair then rubbed his neck to loosen the tension. It was something he did when he was frustrated. "What's up with you, Abbott? Is there something you should tell me?" She didn't have time to babysit, but she also worried about him as a friend.

"I'm just not myself right now. I have this condition that's making me ache all over. At first I thought it was the flu, but the doctor says it's something else. What, she doesn't know."

Dane continued pacing, seeming more agitated as he wore his carpet out. "Dane, stop. Listen, I'm sorry you don't feel well, really. Give me the lead you have and take the week off. We'll handle this."

Dane walked out of the room then came back holding a piece of paper. "Here. It's a possible location for Gordon Flanagan."

"What *the* fuck? Didn't pan out? Did you already check the location? And where the hell did you get this?" This wasn't just some tip that could be checked out whenever. This was big.

"I promised I wouldn't say, Kaya. Nobody with half a brain would want credit for finding him. And no,

I haven't had time to check it yet. I've been lying on the floor dying." He was getting agitated again.

She was ready to ream his ass for withholding something of this magnitude. "Since when do doctors make house calls? Just who are you seeing anyway?" Suspicion came with the territory, even with her own employees.

"Dr. Isabelle Sarantos. She was referred by a neighbor, so I called her. She specializes in infectious disease."

"You really think you're contagious? I guess I should get out of here. You're not off the hook for withholding this information *and* lying about it, but I'll cut you some slack since you're sick. Don't come back until the doctor clears you, hear?"

What if he was contagious? Could she have already contracted what he had in this short amount of time? If she had, it was probably too late to do anything about it today.

Dammit Dane. This shit's big. You don't sit on something like this. Pulling her phone out of her pocket, she dialed Kyle. "Jorgenson, Kane. Do you have anything new from the hotel? I still think there had to be inside help there. Listen, I need you to take over the investigation for Dane. He's going to be out a few days, and we don't have time to wait. I have an address I want you to check out. I know this is huge, that's why I'm pulling Craven from the drug sting so he can assist you. Right, do you have a pen? Okay, here's the address…"

Kaya hung up, feeling both excited as well as aggravated. Hopefully, this would turn out to be a legitimate lead. She got in her car and headed home.

Rafael stood on the balcony of his apartment, looking out over New Atlanta. He was enjoying a cigar when Nik's Audi came speeding around the corner and pulled into the parking lot. Nikolas was almost yelling for Rafe when he didn't find him inside. "Out here," Rafe said quietly, knowing his cousin's shifter ears would pick up his words.

Nik was holding a book in his hand and talking about Jonas Montague, some woman named Caroline, and babies as he came through the sliding glass door that led to the patio. "Nikolas, slow the fuck down. Do you mind repeating that?"

"Which part?" Nikolas was always high strung, but this was different.

"All of it. Jesus, start at the beginning." Rafael gestured to the cushioned chairs, and they sat down. Nik recounted finding the journal and what it contained. After leaving the library, he went to the park and read the rest of Montague's words.

"Rafe, this is it. What I don't understand is how Montague, *Victor*, hid the fact that he's a shifter and why we didn't know about it. I have never seen his name, or any other Victor, listed in the archives.

"That's a very good question, one I hope to find the answer to. So, Montague was a shifter, and he and his human mate were able to produce children?"

"Yes. He was scared to try because as far as he knew, it had never been done, but Caroline finally won out. The baby and mother both lived, Rafe. He

121

mentions several children, both boys and girls, but that's where this journal ends. I need to find the next one. If I can find his daughter, it's possible she would have the next journal. I *have* to know more."

Is this about a woman?" The look in Nikolas' eyes was the same one that Rafe now saw in the mirror. Hope.

"Not just one woman, Rafael, all women. All *our* women."

Rafe cocked an eyebrow at his cousin. Nik never could bullshit very well.

"Ok, maybe there is a girl, woman, whatever. But if we can mate with humans..."

Rafe allowed him a moment to ponder the possibility. "If he were one of us then he could still be alive. Did you show this to Jules?"

"No, I came straight here. I am headed to see him now. Between the two of us, hopefully we can track down the daughter and get some answers."

"Great job, Brother. I am proud of you."

"Thank you my King." Nik stood, bowed ever so slightly and headed for the lab.

Rafe inhaled on his cigar then blew a smoke ring. He closed his eyes, envisioning Kaya as she was standing between his legs. Her hands curled in his hair as her hips rubbed against his. She wanted him whether she knew it or not. Now he just needed to convince her of the fact. That, however, would have to wait.

He had received a phone call earlier from the Elders, demanding a meeting in person. The original Gargouille established a governing body comprised of Kings from each continent. They had been after Rafael for two hundred years to take his rightful place among them. He was perfectly content to rule from New Atlanta. One more plea, one more wasted trip. This time though, he had questions for them. Questions about his future.

Vincent was restless. He hated sleeping in the woods, but he would wait as long as it took. He had given that reporter the address two days ago. He felt sure she would pass it along to the police immediately. If someone didn't show soon, he would send another anonymous tip. Wanting a change of scenery, he stood and slung the rifle over his shoulder. He was just about to reach the clearing when he heard an automobile approaching. He pulled the rifle off his shoulder and looked through the scope. *Hello, detective.*

Vincent let out a loud whistle. Once the detective turned his direction, he fired one shot. Bullseye.

Vincent walked to where the body had dropped and picked it up, taking it into the warehouse to join Magnus.

Chapter 21

Flying overseas was boring and tedious. Even with a private jet and his own personal staff, Rafael loathed any flight that lasted more than a couple of hours. The Elder Council made their home in Italy, and he had no desire to return for an extended period. He was glad the meeting was scheduled for early morning. He could get this over with and head back to the states.

He stood outside the Elder chambers and took a deep, cleansing breath. These conversations were always the same. Now that it was possible he had found his mate, there was no way under the heavens he was leaving New Atlanta.

As he entered the chamber, all conversations ceased. "Rafael, so glad you could join us." The once warm voice was now laced with ice and fatigue.

"Mother, good to see you as always." He placed a kiss on her cheek. Was she shorter than the last time he'd seen her? Female Goyles didn't die when their mate did, but they often stopped living. Since Rafael wouldn't take his place on the council, his mother was required to serve instead. This did not sit well with her, so she had distanced herself from her son.

He greeted the other members with a nod and took the vacant seat at the end of the table. Xavier, one of the original Elders, spoke to the room. "Now that we are all here, we can get started. Rafael, as you know, it is your duty to serve on the Council since you are King. Your mother, as you can see, is not well."

Rafael's mother held her head high even with being spoken about in such a way. He should feel guilty about leaving her with his responsibility, but he didn't. The Elders rarely met. New laws hadn't been put in place since before his father was killed. His participation was not warranted at this juncture in time.

"Xavier, please let me interrupt here and save us all valuable time. While I understand my mother's health is not as it once was, from what I can tell, the only time you meet is when you bid me to come to you. If you understood that I am not going to join the Council, you would stop having these meetings. Now, more than ever, I am determined to continue in my role as King, living in New Atlanta."

"Why now, has something happened?" his mother asked him with concern on her face.

"Yes, it has. I believe I have found my mate." Rafael knew he shouldn't bring up the subject of Kaya until he had more information, but he wanted to gauge the reaction of those in the room.

His mother was the one to ask the question, "How is that possible? All the females alive have been spoken for."

"I didn't say she was one of ours, Mother. I have met a human who has brought on the changes in me that a mate would. This is why I am here, not to discuss the Council. I need to know if any of you have heard of humans being mates."

Rafael watched each face closely. Most were looking confused and talking among themselves. Only one was looking at him. He spoke directly to Xavier. "We have searched the archives and there is no mention of mating with humans. In fact, there is little mention of mating at all. Why is that?"

125

"This information was to be passed down between the families. We didn't put it in writing because we didn't want the information to fall into the wrong hands." Xavier, being an original, should know.

"I see. Let me ask you this: is it possible that Jonas Montague, the scientist, is a shifter and alive but in hiding?" He watched Xavier for any sign of recognition. He hid it well, but the fluctuation in his breathing for just a couple of seconds let Rafe know he hit the target.

"Why would you ask that?" His mother seemed more shocked than inquisitive. Was she hiding something from him as well?

Rafe responded to his mother while looking at Xavier. "Because he has written books on the subject of shifters."

"Yes, but those are purely fiction. I've read them myself." Xavier obviously knew more than he was telling. He was not controlling his breathing nor his heart rate.

"Then have you read his journal? The one talking about mating with a human?"

This brought about more rumbling in the chamber. Rafe's eyes were locked with Xavier. "I'm sure it's more fiction from a man with a vivid imagination. Rafael, if you have no intention of joining us, I will declare this meeting adjourned."

Could the other Elders not see what Rafael saw? Xavier was standing, whisking everyone out of the room. All except for Rafe and his mother. "Athena, if you would stay, I'd like to talk to you and Rafael."

Xavier waited until the room was cleared. "I apologize for acting so skittish. There are those of the

Council who do not believe as I do, as your mother does. Rafael, we do feel it is possible that we can mate with humans, but the original Gargouille are quite prejudice against humans."

"You are an Original, Xavier. Are you not prejudice against humans as well?"

"No, I am not. If I were, I wouldn't have spent my whole life protecting them."

"Mother, you're being very quiet. How do you feel about this?"

His mother had tears in her eyes. "My son, my King, I have waited hundreds of years for you to tell me you have found your mate and that you are going to be able to continue the Di Pietro lineage. If your mate is human, then the fates have deemed her worthy."

"What about Montague, is it possible he is a shifter and fooled everyone?"

Xavier paused a little too long. "Yes, I guess it could be possible. He created a clone, so the man was a genius."

"Do you know anything about mating with humans? Or are you speculating? If you are withholding information, I will not be happy Xavier."

Xavier's eyes flashed. "Do not threaten me boy."

"It's not a threat, X, it's a promise. Mother? What about you? Are you withholding information I require for my Clan?" Xavier flinched at his disrespect, but Rafe ignored him.

"Of course not, Son." She wiped a tear from her cheek then patted his. "I only want your happiness, Rafael." He gauged her sincerity and honestly didn't know if it was real. He had never seen her shed a tear, not even when his father was killed. Why would her heart have softened now?

"I will not stop until I have unburied any information I need, nor until I have found Jonas Montague." Rafe left them standing in the chamber. They were both hiding something, and he was going to find out what.

Chapter 22

Frey, Lorenzo, and Jasper were recounting the events of Tamian's so-called attack. It would take a few days for the judge to hear the case since this was Friday, but that allowed Tam to sit in regular lock-up before being sent away. Jasper was laughing. "If we weren't shifters I'd have a black eye. That man has a helluva left hook."

As he did every night before taking flight, Frey stood on the heli-pad enjoying the fresh air. Being the pilot, he kept the family helicopter at his estate. Lorenzo and Jasper had enjoyed their time with their cousin: working out, learning about the family on the east coast, getting to know one another. Now they were going to fly together. He was relieved to hear Jasper laughing.

The sun was no longer visible and in its place was the full moon. Frey closed his eyes, drinking in the power from the heavenly orb. Now, he needed to fly. He removed his shirt and phased. The others did the same and soon they were headed toward downtown. First, they would patrol the more heavily populated areas before going to check out the warehouses the family owned.

There was no trouble from the Unholy, which was unusual for a Friday night. Not begging for trouble where there wasn't any, they turned toward the outskirts of town. As they approached the warehouse that was farthest from the city, they noticed a vehicle parked haphazardly. Geoffrey gave the signal to spread out, and they each took a corner of the property.

Once on the ground, the men phased and slowly made their way to the building. Frey whistled giving the signal to stay put. He would go in and check out the interior. What he found made his skin crawl. He had seen some fucked up shit in his many years, but this was beyond comprehension. He whistled again letting the others know they could enter the building.

"What in the holy hell happened in here?" Lorenzo held his forearm against his nose.

"I do believe we have found Magnus Flanagan. Or what's left of him. Jasper, go see if you can identify whose car is outside. I doubt it belongs to him." Frey was pointing at the mutilated carcass at his feet.

Jasper left to do his cousin's bidding as the others looked around. "I have another body over here," Lorenzo said from the other end of the building. "Gunshot wound to the forehead, through and through."

"Fuck!" Frey was clenching his fists. He pulled out his phone and dialed Rafael. Hopefully he would still be in Italy and not headed back to the States.

"Good morning Geoffrey. I guess I should say good evening to you since it's still night. What is it?"

"Lor, Jasper and I took a patrol tonight. We were checking out the warehouses when we found two more bodies at Forest Grove. One sort of looks like Magnus Flanagan. I'm waiting on Jasper to get the identification of the other victim out of his car. Hang on, here he comes."

Jasper was holding a wallet in his hand when he returned. "Detective Kyle Jorgenson, New Atlanta P.D."

"I guess you heard that. Rafe, why the fuck are they using our warehouses?"

"Because they're empty, secluded, and they implicate me. Fucking Flanagan. We have to find him. Right fucking now." The Society had half-heartedly searched for Gordon over the last thirty years. Now it seemed they were going to have to put more effort into it.

"I know I just asked this, but again, why you? Neither you nor the family has ever had any dealings with the man, not directly anyway. We had nothing to do with his wife and child going into seclusion. Do you think there's some way he has found out about us, that we're the ones who take down the Unholy?"

"Anything's possible, Frey. Until we know without a doubt it isn't him, I am going to go with the assumption it is."

"Son of a fucking bitch. You know you can't tell the chief. She'll have this pinned on you faster than you can phase."

"I will have to think on this. I have a few things to see to, but right now I am headed to the family archives to do a little research on my own. If that doesn't take too long, I should be home Sunday. Now, there's nothing you can do for those two so get out of there. We will discuss our options when I'm home."

"Safe travels my brother." Frey hung up and told the other two, "Let's get out of here."

Rafael leaned back in the soft leather seat of the convertible he had rented. Frey wasn't wrong about telling Kaya what they found, but he also wanted to start a relationship with Kaya on a positive note and that included honesty. He called Julian to fill him in on Frey's findings and to give him his orders. Once that was accomplished, he steered the car out of the courtyard of the Council Building and headed toward his family's old country estate. Xavier and his mother probably wouldn't like him snooping around but at this point, he didn't care. Unless his mother had certain books destroyed, it was possible he could find the answers he was looking for in just a few hours.

The albino sat in his shithole of an apartment, viewing the video feed coming from the warehouse. "Gotcha you bastards," he thought to himself. He rewound the feed, spliced, diced, and then saved. He didn't want the chief to see too much of the video, not yet. Opening a secure browser, he typed in Kaya Kane's personal email address. "A little present for you" was typed into the subject line. He attached the video file and hit send. Leaning back in his chair, he lit a cigarette. He took a long drag and sent a text: "It's done".

Chapter 23

"I can't believe you didn't throw up." Julian was listening to Nikolas fill him in on the information he'd found in Montague's journal.

"That's all you got from what I just told you? We're still on that? Fuck you, Jules. I bet when you finally meet your mate you sprout horns or grow warts or something." After more than five hundred years, Nik still let Julian push his buttons.

"No, that is not all I took from it, but it is important. Maybe she isn't your mate. Maybe it was chemical and not psychological. There could have been something in the air such as a chemical used to clean the place." Nik missed the grin on his brother's face as he turned back to his computer.

Nikolas knew Sophia was his mate. The few journal entries he found in the family archives described the reactions to mates when they met. Between Rafe's nearly passing out and his own nausea, he was certain they were onto something. But why now? Why after all these years and two within hours of each other? They needed to find Montague's other journals.

"You're not gonna believe this shit." Jules was squinting at his monitor.

"Why are you squinting? We have better than perfect vision. Is something wrong with you?" Nikolas was not paying attention to the information on the screen.

"Maybe because I can't believe my eyes? I found her. Dr. Isabelle Sarantos nee Montague lives right fucking here in New Atlanta." Julian was writing down her address on a piece of paper. "Here, find this location. I'm going to give Ms. Sarantos a little visit."

Nik took the information and began an address search. "Don't you mean *we* are going to pay her a visit? I did find her father's journal after all. I should be the one to talk to her."

Jules frowned at his brother. "You are too high strung for such a conversation, little brother. I, however, will keep a level head and obtain the information we seek from the lovely doctor." Julian was younger than Nik but was a couple inches taller. He never passed up the opportunity to remind him of the fact.

"Lovely? How do you know she's lovely?" He stopped typing and looked at Julian.

Julian angled his monitor so his brother could see the picture he was looking at. "See, lovely."

"She's all right." Nikolas returned to locating her address. "Here it is. Southside, close to the prison. Are we going tonight?" Once again his brother was frowning at him.

"*All right?* She's beautiful." Julian turned back to the monitor.

"Yes, *all right*. I prefer blue eyes over dark. Now, are we going or not?" Nik was imagining a set of clear blue eyes behind a pair of cute glasses looking back at him. A paper wad struck him upside the head. "What the fuck? What was that for?" He stood, glaring at his brother.

"You have it bad, man. I'm placing my bet now on that librarian. She's your mate." Julian's hands were clasped behind his head as he grinned.

134

"Fuck off. Just because I don't think every woman is gorgeous does *not* mean I'm mated. It just means my tastes are changing. Are we going or not?" Julian was staring at him.

Fuck, he's right. Nikolas really loved women. All women. He could appreciate the beauty that was female no matter her shape or size. Now it seemed his appreciation was for one particular type: slender, average height, smallish breasts, button nose, and geeky. *Well shit.*

Julian brought him out of his thoughts, "A visit this late wouldn't be appropriate. We want to give a good impression when we meet with the doctor. We should wait until morning, don't you think?"

"Yeah, sure. I will pick you up at eight at your house." Nikolas placed Montague's diary on the desk in front of his brother. "Good night, Julian."

"Good night. Be well my brother." Nikolas' retreating form caused Julian to sigh. "Be well indeed."

Julian shut down his computer and grabbed the journal Nikolas left with him. He wanted to read it for himself. After punching in the codes on the alarm, he got in his Corvette and headed home. Surely it was a fluke. The odds of Rafe finding his mate were high. Add to that Nikolas finding his, those odds increased. Jules could calculate the odds in his head given the number of shapeshifters in the family as well as in the city and surrounding states.

As he was pulling into his drive, his phone rang. Avenged Sevenfold's *Hail to the King* let him know it was Rafe. Something was amiss. "Julian."

"Hello, Brother. I want you to drop everything including the search for Montague's daughter. Frey

135

was scouting tonight when he found two bodies in the Forest Grove warehouse. One of them he believes is Magnus Flanagan. The other is one of Kaya's detectives."

"What do you mean *believes* it is Magnus?"

"His exact words were, 'Rafe, in all my years I've never seen anything like it. Dante is going to require dental records for a positive ID'. He did mention seeing security cameras at this warehouse. Where are you with the rest of the locations?"

"I haven't put a camera at that warehouse. It must be left over from whoever owned the building previously. We were able to hit most of the buildings today and were going to finish tomorrow after the visit with the doctor. Rafe, we found Montague's daughter, right here in New Atlanta. I will call Nik and let him know he is flying solo with the doctor, against my better judgment."

"This is fortuitous. Maybe one of our problems is becoming less of that, a problem. Yes, Julian, please finish the install. I'm sure your brother can handle a meeting with Ms. Montague. If there's nothing else, I will speak with you tomorrow. Be well my brother."

"Be well my King."

Julian called Nikolas to tell him he was on his own tomorrow and why. He begged his brother to behave and remember how important the information was. He wasn't surprised when Nik hung up on him. He also wasn't surprised when he realized Rafael called the chief by her first name.

Trevor stepped out of the elevator and all but ran into a pretty lady coming down the hall. "Oh, excuse me there, sweet cheeks." She didn't acknowledge him; she just kept going. He shook his head and continued toward Dane's apartment. He had checked with the pharmacy several times, but a prescription was never called in. Maybe the detective was feeling better, and that hot little number was the cure.

When Dane didn't answer his phone, Trevor got worried and left work to check on him. He knocked then waited. He put his ear to the door and didn't hear anything coming from inside. He knocked again a little louder. Still nothing. Trevor pulled out his cell phone and called Dane's number. Some random song he didn't know was coming from inside the apartment.

He tried the knob finding it unlocked then stuck his head inside and listened. "Dane, it's Trevor." He stepped further into the room and looked around. Medicine bottles were lying on the end table beside the sofa. He picked one up and noticed there was no pharmacy label. Trevor opened the bottle and dumped the pills into his hand. Upon further examination, there was no imprint on the pills stating what they were. "What the fuck dude? You're a cop."

"Dane!" The apartment was laid out exactly as his was, so he headed down the hall to the master bedroom. Either Dane was a slob or something major went down in there. He looked in all the rooms but didn't see the detective. "Maybe the black market dope did the trick. Guess the little lady was out of luck as well." Trevor assumed Dane was feeling better and had gone out for fresh air. He left things as they were and went back to the Morgue.

When he returned, Dante was talking to the Warden from the Pen. Their conversation immediately ceased, and Dante asked, "Trevor, you remember Gregor?"

He held out his hand. "Sure do, how's it going, Mr. Stone?"

Gregor shook his hand then narrowed his eyes. "Why the fuck do you smell so good?"

Trevor pulled his hand back quickly. "Excuse me?"

"You smell like sunshine, like a woman, that's what I meant."

"Sir, no offense but I think you've been around the general population a little too long. I do *not* smell like the fairer sex. I don't smell like sex at all. I haven't had sex in far too long. Now, if you'll excuse me, I'm going over there with the dead. They don't freak me out."

Chapter 24

Kaya was waiting to hear from Jorgenson and Craven. The drive to the address on the note would take a while, but they still should have arrived by now. She discarded her uniform into the dirty clothes hamper and put on a pair of flannel sleep pants and a worn out UGA t-shirt. The University of Georgia, like most everything else, had taken a hit during the bombings but was once again thriving.

A glass of wine in hand, she sat down on her sofa and turned on the television. Rarely did she watch anything other than the news. Not tonight. She wanted something to take her mind off her everyday life. She saw enough of the real world on a daily basis, so tonight she was going to indulge in good old-fashioned fantasy. The *Underworld* marathon was starting in less than an hour, and she planned on watching them all. They contained the best of both worlds: vampires and werewolves.

As a kid, she loved scary movies and all things that go bump in the night. Werewolves were her favorite. She drove her mother crazy pretending to be a shapeshifter, crawling around on all fours, howling at the full moon. Her father would have indulged her had he lived. She was the son he always wanted. Her mother loved Kaya but when her father was killed, it changed her. She went from a loving, sweet woman to a withdrawn introvert. Kaya really should call her. Knowing the conversation would be the same tired script, she put it off until later.

Her stomach growled alerting her to the fact that she hadn't eaten since lunch. Dammit, she was not going to think about lunch with Rafael. Or the kiss. Did he eat lunch like that every day or did he bring it in knowing she was going to be there? Surely he wasn't interested in her, was he? The way he kissed her said yes. His erection said hell yes. She was definitely smitten with him. *Smitten*. Who the hell used that word? Obviously someone who hadn't dated since college.

Kaya didn't think much about dating, not with her job. She took it in stride that she would be alone the rest of her life, but what if? What if she were to let someone in, someone like Rafael Stone? He was a complete enigma as far as the public was concerned. According to him, he would keep it that way if he were seeing someone. Did that mean he would never take her out in public? Would they only meet each other under the cover of night?

Maybe he would take her to eat at Chez Vaison but have her sign a confidentiality agreement first. She laughed at herself. Surely he wasn't *that* private. If he were, did she really care? She was in the spotlight often, and it got tiresome. She could go for a little privacy now and then.

She still had a little time before the movie started so she opened up her laptop and went through her personal emails. When her mother felt nostalgic, she would send Kaya messages with old pictures. Then she would go into her rant about needing grandchildren and Kaya needing a husband. Her computer pinged with a new mail notification. It was from an unknown sender. The subject was "a little present for you". There was a video attached. Her finger hovered over the mouse. She could be opening a

140

virus, but the subject matter had her curious. If it was a virus, she would deal with that later. She clicked the paper clip icon to open the file.

The film was grainy. Three men were walking toward a warehouse. The film pauses then starts with the men walking back out of the building. She replayed the video several times. The taller man looked very familiar, but she still couldn't make out his features. The surroundings were undistinguishable since it was filmed at night. If this was supposed to be a tip, it was a bad one. How had someone get her email address anyway? She forwarded the clip to Wilkes. Hopefully, he could clean it up so they could at least identify the men.

Was someone trying to point a finger at Rafael again? It would only make sense that this warehouse belonged to his family as well. She would call him tomorrow and set up another meeting. This time she would keep her hands and her lips to herself. Glancing at the television, she noticed the movie was starting. She turned her mind from Rafael and the video to Selene and the vampires.

Rafael spent several hours in his old home. When his father moved the family to the Americas, Rafe talked him into keeping the Italian Villa. The property was located on the Ionian Sea, and the view was breathtaking. It was where he was born and raised; where he and his brothers and cousins had grown up together. Eventually, he paid a hefty sum to purchase the property from his father but it was worth every penny.

Even though he didn't want to move back, he was glad to have the option of vacationing there. Rafael was hopeful that one day soon he would be sharing the villa with Kaya.

Priscilla's younger sister, Penelope, and her family lived in the villa, taking care of it in Rafe's absence. As far as his mother knew, it no longer belonged to the family.

Part of Penelope's contract included a non-disclosure agreement. She was never to reveal the true owner's identity, and nobody except Rafe or his inner circle were allowed on the property. This included his mother and the Elders. Penelope's mother and grandmother before her had cared for the villa. When Rafael found loyal people to serve him, he paid them well and treated them like family.

He was disappointed with his time looking through the library. He hadn't truly expected to find any information on bonding, but there had been an inkling of hope. Now he transferred that hope to Nikolas, who would be meeting with Montague's daughter.

The unease of the day seeped deep into Rafael's bones. The weather in southern Italy was still such that humans could take a walk on the coastline and be comfortable. Being a Goyle, he didn't have to worry about that, but the sunshine was always welcome on his skin.

Rafael made his way to a cliff overlooking the sea. The view reminded him of his vision. He looked down at his side just to make sure there was no dark-haired boy standing beside him. The vision had pricked at his soul. He was half a millennium old and in all his years that part of him had remained dormant. Until now. Until Kaya Kane. Surely the fates wouldn't be so cruel as to tease him only to have it be a deception to his heart. No, he had to believe the bonding was possible. Just thinking about her now, about her lips touching his, their tongues dancing together, made him want to be back on the other side of the pond so he could see her, touch her. He was ready to go home.

The wind blowing across the land was like a balm to his soul. It gave him clarity when he thought about how to handle Kaya. If only he could come up with a plan regarding the murders. As King, he felt the need to handle all matters that affected the Clan but his brothers often reminded him they were family, and family had each other's back. He would be in the line of fire soon enough.

With one last breath of the sea air, Rafael headed inside to gather his things. He still had one more place to visit then he would be on his way.

Chapter 25

Kaya was sitting on her front porch enjoying a cup of coffee when her phone rang. "Kane."

"Boss, we just received an anonymous tip: two bodies at an abandoned warehouse." Walter Craven was a twenty year veteran on the force. He was a good detective who was closing in on retirement.

"Shit. Give me the address." She wrote the location down then looked at it again. "Craven, that's the address I sent you and Kyle to yesterday. Did you not go check it out?"

"No, Ma'am. By the time I got to the precinct, he had left without me. Have you not heard from him?"

"No, I haven't. Okay, you go ahead to this location and I'll meet you there." Kaya was pissed. She hung up and dialed Kyle. The call went straight to voicemail. Next she called Wilkes. "Chief, I got your email but I haven't had a chance to look at it."

"That can wait. I want you to find Jorgenson's vehicle. He's M.I.A. I know this is Saturday, but I have a missing detective. Call me as soon as you have the location. Also take down this address. I need the owner's name immediately. Yeah thanks, Wilkes."

Kaya didn't bother pouring her coffee out. She sat the mug down on her kitchen counter and went to her bedroom to change clothes. She would bet money the Stones owned the property.

Kaya was about ten miles away from her destination when her phone rang. "Chief, I got the information you wanted. The good news is Stone, Incorporated owns the warehouse. The bad news is

144

that Jorgenson's GPS has been disabled." Kaya muttered, "Thanks" and hung up. She immediately dialed a number she was becoming too familiar with.

"Stone, Incorporated." The voice was an unfamiliar one but then again it was the weekend. Probably an answering service. "This is Police Chief Kaya Kane. I need to speak to Mr. Stone."

"He is currently unavailable. I will be glad to take a message for him." Definitely a service.

"Tell him his presence is required at his warehouse located in the Forest Grove Industrial Park."

"I will make sure he gets the message."

Kaya hung up and drove. Dammit. She really didn't want to believe Rafael was involved in this mess. She kept telling herself that he was innocent until she had indisputable proof of his guilt. Craven was at the scene when she arrived. He was bent over, hands on his knees. She got out of her car and stopped. The man was heaving his guts up.

"Jesus, Craven, what is wrong with you?" She started toward the building, but he grabbed her arm. "You really don't want to go in there, Boss." He released her arm and stood up, wiping his mouth on the back of his sleeve. "I don't know what the fuck that even is in there."

"Have you secured the crime scene?" If this man was losing his breakfast, she really didn't want to go into the building. She normally didn't have a weak stomach, but she wasn't going to risk it.

"No, Ma'am. Took one look, and I was right back out here. I'll call CSU. I suggest you stay put." He walked away from her and the puddle of vomit. She didn't hang around the area either. She was looking around for something to cover the spot with when she noticed a shiny sports car pulling into the parking lot. A Corvette convertible stopped, and Mr. Stone angled out of the car. The wrong Mr. Stone.

"Chief Kane, Julian Stone." He held his hand out to the pretty cop. He could see why Rafe would be drawn to her, mate bond or not. She gripped his hand firmly and shook.

"I was expecting your cousin, Rafael. Where is he?"

"I'm afraid he is away at the moment. Would you care to tell me why we are here?" He gestured to the building.

"Mr. Stone, I appreciate you driving all the way out here but I need to speak with Rafael since he owns the property." Julian could smell the agitation rolling off Kaya. Was it because she was hoping to see Rafael and was disappointed?

"First, please call me Julian. Second, while I really should let you believe Rafael is the sole owner of our little empire, I too, am part owner in this particular building. Now, why are we here?" He heard the vehicles before he saw them; Dante would be arriving within minutes.

"Very well, Mr. Stone. We have another murder. At least we think it's a murder. The body is such that we aren't certain what happened to it. Since you didn't have security cameras in place at the other warehouse, I'm assuming you don't here either?"

Julian replied as he turned to see Dante walking up, "We are in the process of adding cameras to all our properties." Dante stood in front of him, and they both kept their faces void of recognition.

Dante looked to Kaya. "Chief Kane, what do we have?"

"I haven't actually seen the bodies but from Detective Craven's reaction, the first one is ugly."

Dante disappeared into the building and quickly returned, frowning.

"Chief Kane, I'm not sure even dental records will give me a clue as to who *that* is in there. It is going to take a hazmat crew to gather the remains. I did not see a second body. Are you certain there were two?"

"The tip we received said there were two, but I haven't been in there yet, so no, I'm not certain."

Dante was scowling now. "Mr. Stone, Chief Kane, if you both will excuse me, I will make the call."

Julian cocked his head to the side. The unmistakable sound of a rifle slide carried across the wind. He quickly stepped in front of Kaya, putting her between him and the building. The bullet hit his back, and he tried to play it off with a fake sneeze. Dante turned around. "Mr. Stone, are you catching something?" Julian had to suppress a groan. "Yes, I believe I am. Maybe I will just grab my jacket out of my car."

"Here, let me get it for you" Dante opened the passenger side door and grabbed the windbreaker that was stowed behind the seat. Goyles rarely felt the cold, but they never knew when they would need to hide a "wound". "Here you go, Mr. Stone."

Dante accidentally dropped the jacket just as Julian reached for it. "My apologies."

Julian grabbed the jacket off the ground along with the bullet that should be imbedded in his back. He slid the jacket on, pocketing the evidence. "Thank you."

Dante finished his call to the hazmat crew. "They will be here within the hour. CSU will want to suit up before they enter the building. Whoever did this wanted to make sure the body could not be identified." Julian watched the chief as her mind worked.

"Are you certain there wasn't another body?" Kaya asked Dante.

"I only saw the one. Did Detective Craven not do a walk-through of the premises?"

"I don't think he got past the first body. I will go check it out myself." If the remains were as bad as Dante indicated, Julian hated for her to witness it.

"Chief Kane, are you sure you want to go in there? I mean if it's bad enough that your detective can't stomach it..." The look on her face stopped him.

"I may be a woman, Mr. Stone, but I'm a seasoned officer. I can handle whatever is in that warehouse." With no warning, she turned and made her way into the building.

Julian listened until her footsteps were on the other side of the warehouse before speaking to Dante. "I need to get out of here and find whoever took a shot at us. I didn't have a chance to get a good look at the bullet, but I will take it back to the lab and examine it."

Dante looked around as the CSU and hazmat crews parked and gathered their gear. "Jules, when Frey said it was bad, he wasn't exaggerating, but he said the man looked like Magnus Flanagan. There's no way he could tell by looking at *that* in there. The killer must have come back. It's as if someone poured acid on the body parts that can provide proof of identity. And where the fuck is the second body? I'm telling you brother, someone is out to get us. We need to locate the cop and soon. I will stop by the lab on my way to the morgue to look at your DNA samples. Then I will compare them to whatever I can get off this victim. When the chief turns you loose, please call Rafe and fill him in."

"Will do." Kaya appeared in the doorway looking a little green. "Did you find another body, Chief?"

She shook her head no. Stepping out of the building, she took a few deep breaths through her mouth, obviously tamping down the urge to throw up. Julian had to give it to her; the woman was tough. "Listen, Chief, both Rafael and I want to assist in any way we can. We do not like the fact that our properties are being used in such a way. Here's my card. I need to finish the install of the security systems on our other vacant buildings. If you have no further questions, I would really like to get busy on that."

"Yeah, you can go but Mr. Stone, don't leave town. The fact that your brother isn't available doesn't look good."

"I assure you Rafael can provide proof of his whereabouts, but I will let him know of your feelings." Julian could definitely sense the changes in Miss

149

Kane's body whenever his brother was mentioned. She was feeling something for the King.

Julian waited until he was in the Vette and headed away from the warehouse to call Rafael. *Fuck.* He was upset with himself that he didn't have all the buildings secured. He would rectify that today. With the time difference, he didn't know where Rafael would be, but this couldn't wait.

"Julian, please tell me there isn't more bad news." Rafael sounded troubled.

"I'm sorry, but there is. I just left the warehouse and it's a mess. First, the body that is supposedly Magnus is in such a state that hazmat was called in for removal. Second, the body of Kaya's detective was nowhere to be found. It has been moved. You do not have to tell me to make the security my first priority. I will be doing nothing else until all warehouses and empty buildings we own are wired."

"My plane is taking off now. I will think on this and we will regroup when I return. Thank you for the update."

"Safe travels, my King." The phone disconnected. Julian felt like a disappointment. With the hacking of their computer system and now the failure to secure all the buildings in a timely manner, his batting average was lessening every day. That stopped now.

Chapter 26

Nik came up empty when he arrived at Dr. Sarantos' home. Next up was the clinic she owned. With it being the weekend, her working would be a long shot, but it was his only option at that point. He parked in the spot next to a sleek, black Harley. The lady in the picture didn't look like someone who would ride a motorcycle. Maybe she was with a patient. The front door was locked, so Nikolas knocked and waited. He could hear talking in the interior of the building. He knocked again, and the talking stopped. The lady from the picture was walking toward him, followed by a feisty looking redhead. He would lay odds on who the bike belonged to.

Dr. Sarantos turned the lock and stood in the opening just enough to talk to Nik. "I'm sorry the clinic is closed. If you would like an appointment, please call and make one."

"Dr. Sarantos, I'm Nikolas Stone and I would like to speak to you about your father." The doctor held up her index finger in the "wait here" gesture and closed the door. She turned toward the redhead and whispered something. His hearing allowed him to eavesdrop.

"Tessa, I don't want to talk to him, and I especially don't want to talk to you right now. Not after everything you told me last night. I need time to process all of this."

"I'll talk to him for you. I hate to say this, Belle, but I probably know Jonas better than you do. I spent all my spare time in his lab with him, watching him work, listening to the old stories."

"Yes, you made it very clear just how close you are to my parents. I can handle everything else you said." She wrapped her arms around herself. "But that, that was a little too much. You talk to this man if you want. I don't care."

Nik saw the pained expression on the doctor's face as she frowned and walked away. So the redhead knew Montague too. Interesting. Nik knocked again.

This time the redhead, Tessa, opened the door. "Please come in. You'll have to excuse Dr. Sarantos. She has been up all night with a patient and is extremely tired." She didn't lead him any further than the waiting room where she took a seat. He sat across from her.

"I'm sorry; I didn't catch your name. You are?"

"Tessa. Tessa Blackmore. Now, how may I help you, Mr. Stone?"

"I am very interested in Dr. Montague's written works. I am a collector of sorts and came across a journal of his at the public library. The story was so interesting, but it was incomplete. I was hoping Ms. Sarantos would have a copy of the other journals so I can read them."

Tessa squirmed in her seat. There was something oddly familiar about the woman. Something that called to him on a cellular level. It was nothing like his body's connection with Sophia; this was not sexual. No, this was some kind of psychological recognition.

"Mr. Stone, as you probably know, most of his works have already been duplicated and published. What type of journal are you looking for? Are you wanting to clone someone? A hot woman perhaps? You think one is good so two would be better?"

152

Nik laughed at her humor. She was definitely feisty. "No, nothing like that. What I'm looking for is a work of fiction. I have read every book the man ever wrote, but I'm interested in one story in particular. I believe he was writing a series of books about shapeshifters. Do you know the one?"

Tessa was very nervous now even though Nik could see no sheen of perspiration covering her skin. Interesting. "I do know the one. I'm curious as to how it made its way into the library though. You see, that was one of his last works. The publishers wouldn't release it until they had read the complete story, and since Dr. Montague passed away before the series was finished, it went unpublished."

Wow. He had seen cool under pressure, but this woman took home first prize. Not only was her heartbeat steady, she looked him in the eye without flinching while telling her lie. Was it one she had practiced and recited over and over? Something was going on here and if he heard her correctly earlier, she used the present tense instead of the past when referring to the man. Jonas Montague was alive, and this Tessa undoubtedly knew where he was.

"I would be so grateful if you would ask Dr. Sarantos about the journals, just in case. If they were never published, hopefully she will have the original manuscript, being his only child. I am not going to be able to sleep until I know how his story ends. You wouldn't want me to lose sleep would you?" Nikolas was pouring on the Stone charm and didn't feel guilty in the least.

"I seriously doubt a male like you would lose sleep over a fable, Mr. Stone. But since you're so cute, I will ask the doctor. Now, if you will excuse me, I have somewhere I need to be."

Cute? He wasn't cute; he was handsome. "Here's my number in case Dr. Sarantos finds something."

Tessa took the card from his hand and shoved it into the back pocket of her tight jeans. If he weren't certain Sophia was his mate, he would pay more attention to those jeans. As it were, he truly wasn't interested in what the pants encased. Yep, definitely mated.

He offered her his hand again and appreciated the tight grip. "I hope to hear from you, Miss Blackmore." She said nothing more as she walked him to the door, locking it behind him.

Nik got in his car and stared at the building. So Jonas Montague was alive, and the ladies knew it. He couldn't get the nagging feeling about the redhead to unclench its jaws from his gut. He knew her. Somehow. He backed his Audi out of the parking space and left the lot. Circling the block, he found a hidden spot where he could watch and wait on Tessa to leave. She may not take him to Montague but then again, she just might. While he waited, he called Julian to let him know what had transpired and to see what was going on at the latest murder scene.

Tessa found Isabelle just down the hall, obviously having eavesdropped. "Did you hear?"

154

"Yes, I often wondered where the first one ended up. It all makes sense now. I have the other journals and couldn't make heads or tails of the stories because I didn't know how they started. If what you told me is in that journal..."

"I'm afraid it is, but what worries me is this Mr. Stone. Belle, he's a full-blood."

"Well, that's good isn't it? I mean don't we want to interact with those of our kind? Jesus, what am I saying, our kind..."

"That's just it. The Gargoyles ostracized your father when he mated with a human. Yes, this was hundreds of years ago, but still, I'm sure they don't want anything to do with us. Didn't you read his last journal?"

"No, it's missing as well. I only have those in the middle that speak of his children. Tessa, just how many brothers and sisters do I have out there? He mentioned several boys and girls. How did he hide them all from me, and why did I think I was an only child?"

"You have a few. Jonas thought it best to separate you all in case you were ever discovered. I've been keeping tabs on all of you over the years. That's what I do Belle, I'm a watcher."

"But if you're a half-blood, then is Gordon Flanagan one of them?" Isabelle started pacing the room. Tessa knew it was information overload, but it was essential she go help with Dane.

"That monster is *not* my father. Listen, I know this is a lot to take in and there's more you must know, but I have to go check on Dane. He's going to be changing soon, and they're going to need me to be there."

"They, who's they and what have you done with Dane? I'm his doctor; I should go with you."

"Dane is in a safe place where he can't hurt himself or anyone else. This is what we do, what I do. You're welcome to come along, but only as my cousin, not as a doctor. Can you do that?"

"I… yes. Yes, I can."

"Okay then, let's go." Before Tessa started her bike, she pulled her phone from her back pocket. The caller picked up, but Tessa didn't wait for them to speak. "One of Jonas' journals was at the public library. How could this happen?" She listened to the explanation, but it was not satisfactory. "We'll discuss this later."

Chapter 27

The room was cold and sterile. Where the hell was he? What the fuck happened? Dane tried to sit up, but whatever drug he was given earlier was making it hard to focus. His attempt to sit up failed, and he flopped back down on the bed. The overhead lights were off, but there was a small lamp on the far side of the room casting enough of a glow for him to see.

Voices were coming down the hall toward his room. The door opened, and in walked who he assumed was a nurse. She was dressed in scrubs with a stethoscope hanging around her neck. "Hello, Mr. Abbott. I'm glad to see you're awake. Let's check your vitals, shall we?"

"Who the fuck are you, and where the fuck am I?" Dane attempted once more to sit up, but he was unable.

"Mr. Abbott, there is no need for hostilities. My name is Caroline Wexford. You were brought here to our facility for your own protection. There is a lot I have to tell you about yourself, but first I need to check your vital signs and see how close you are to changing. The good doctor may have done more harm than good in easing your pain."

He watched almost detachedly as she put the cold stethoscope to his bare chest and listened. She flashed a light into both his eyes which caused an instant headache. "Easy with the eyes, Jesus." He closed his eyes and began rubbing them.

The nurse pulled his hands away from his face. "None of that, you'll make it worse." She wrote notes in a metal clipboard then put a thermometer in his mouth. While it was heating up, she pressed her fingers to his wrist, taking his pulse.

"Why am I here?" He mumbled around the thermometer.

"Shush. Keep your mouth closed." When it beeped, she removed it. "Hmm."

"Hmm what? Listen, I'm a detective with the New Atlanta Police Department. I happen to know that kidnapping is against the law and would appreciate some answers here." This time when he tried to sit up he was successful. The nurse sighed at him as if he were a petulant child.

"I know very well who and what you are, Mr. Abbott. I was hoping we could do this later, but I guess now is as good a time as any. Dane, what do you know of your parents?"

"My parents? What the hell do they have to do with anything? Oh shit! Do I have cancer? Is that what's wrong with me?"

"Oh heavens no. Quite the opposite. You, my dear, are special. Do you remember anything about your parents, about growing up?"

Dane thought back to his childhood. He had never met his father. His mom said he was in the Marines and was killed in the line of duty before Dane was born. His mom was loving and took great care of him, giving him anything he could want.

"My dad was in the military, and even though I never knew him, I felt obligated to follow in his footsteps. My mom is alive and well, living in Florida." Another surge of pain ripped through his body. The medicine Dr. Sarantos gave him yesterday had eased the pain immensely. "Please, find Dr. Sarantos. She

158

gave me something yesterday, some type of miracle drug. I feel like I'm dying! Please Miss Wexford!"

"I'm afraid to tell you that you are going to have to deal with the pain. It will all be over soon and then you'll be better than ever."

"What the fuck are you talking about? What will be better?" Dane lay back on the table and once again was thrashing about. The pain was becoming unbearable. "Just fucking shoot me and get it over with, gahhhhhhh!"

The nurse yelled down the hall, "It's time!" That was the last thing he remembered before everything went black.

Kaya picked up her phone for the fiftieth time. Not only was she looking to see if Jorgenson had called, she was also seeing if Dane had checked in. Before she went home from the crime scene, she was going to go see him.

She got off the elevator and saw Trevor at Dane's door. "Hey Chief, what's shaking? You know, for a sick man he sure does attract some hotties."

Kaya rolled her eyes. "Trevor, is he home or not?" She laughed internally at the young man. He was never boring; that was for sure.

"Not. I have been trying him ever since I saw the brunette leave. If I had her coming to my door, I think I'd stay home."

"What brunette, and when was that?"

"Uh, yesterday? Yeah, yesterday. I think."

"So was she coming out of his apartment or just knocking to see if he was home?" Dealing with Trevor felt like herding cats.

"I honestly don't know, but his door was unlocked, so I went in. He wasn't home. If he had been home, she would have been naked. In his bed. Not huffing off down the hall."

"How do you know she would've been naked? You know what? Never mind. When you went into his apartment, was there anything out of the ordinary?"

"Other than the narcotics, no."

"Narcotics?"

"Yeah, you know drugs, pills, dope."

"Were these not prescriptions from his doctor? He said she made a house call. Could it have been the doctor you saw leaving?"

"I've never seen prescription drugs in non-labeled containers, well, not that a doctor prescribed anyway. And I've never seen a doctor dressed in military fatigues, unless they were, in fact, in the military."

"Okay, Trevor, thank you."

"Anything for you, my lady." Trevor bowed at the waist then headed down the hall.

Kaya looked to the ceiling, "Give me strength." She knocked on the door and tried the knob. Locked. Of course it was. If she didn't hear from him by the end of the day, she would ask around the precinct.

Once home, Kaya immediately showered. The remains in the warehouse were worse than anything Rob Zombie could conjure up in a horror flick. It had taken all her willpower, plus some, to keep her coffee from coming back up. She was glad she had skipped breakfast. The stench of death was bad enough, but the horrific odor seeping from that body had been too much. The victim's body was cut open with the intestines strewn outside the stomach. The face and hands were melted down to the bone. By some miracle, rats were not feasting on the flesh. She stood under scalding hot water attempting to wash the decay from her senses. It wouldn't be enough to wash it from her mind though.

She turned her thoughts to Julian Stone. The younger cousin was gorgeous with his dirty blond hair. He, unlike Rafael, was not afraid to be seen in public. Almost every newspaper article featuring the family contained a photo of Julian. The man was built lean, like a runner. However good-looking he was, she felt no spark when she was around him. Kaya hoped the disappointment she felt when Julian introduced himself hadn't been visible on her face. If she could focus near as much on the case as she did Rafael, she might get somewhere.

When the water ran cold, she turned the shower off. She towel dried her hair then combed out the tangles. Pulling on her sweats, Kaya grabbed a glass of wine and settled in for the evening. She was going to spend the rest of the night going through what little evidence there was, and hopefully she would hear from her two missing detectives.

Chapter 28

Rafael never went to Italy without visiting his father's tomb. The family mausoleum was located approximately fifty miles away from the villa. As with his home, he employed caretakers to keep the property maintained as well as secure. Edmondo Di Pietro had been a good father and friend to Rafael, and he missed him still, even after two hundred years. He talked to his father's tomb, telling him all that had happened lately, including meeting Kaya. Nearly an hour later, he was ready to go.

As the crew was readying the plane for takeoff, Julian had called and filled him in on the events of the morning. Rafe sighed and closed his eyes as the jet taxied down the runway. The dip in his stomach as the plane lifted did nothing to help the knot that was already there. He had to find Flanagan and put a stop to his madness. Kaya already doubted Rafael's innocence, even with the proof that he wasn't at the first warehouse. Now, with a second location being used, he had to think long and hard about coming clean with her.

The plane touching down woke Rafe from a troubled sleep. The horrible dream that invaded his subconscious along with Julian's phone call helped him make up his mind to tell Kaya the truth. Well, most of it anyway. If she didn't return his feelings, there was no need to divulge his secrets. He would start with dinner at his place and go from there.

He arrived home to a quiet manor. The sun had yet to make its early dawn appearance. After a quick shower, he headed to the kitchen where he heard the voices of his houseguests talking with Priscilla. "Good morning."

There was a chorus of good morning responses as he poured his first cup of coffee. "Priscilla, could you excuse us, please?" He waited until his housekeeper exited the kitchen. "Okay, fill me in on the details of Friday night." Rafe sat and listened as both Lor and Jasper recounted what they had found at the warehouse. They didn't have much more to offer than Frey had told him over the phone. Julian had already filled the others in regarding Magnus and the missing detective. They were all waiting on Rafael to inform them of his plan. Unfortunately, he couldn't come up with one. Not one that would hide the truth about the Goyles.

"Lor, have you been to the quarry yet?"

"Yes, I spent all day yesterday there."

"Excellent. Jasper, Julian has your paperwork in order. I am hoping to dine with the chief very soon. I will let her know to be expecting your application next week. If either of you wish to borrow any of my vehicles, just tell Jonathan. I have put in a call to Sixx. He will transfer your bank accounts and your investments, if that is needed."

Michael Gentry was one of the more eccentric of the Goyles. He was a genius with numbers, and he headed up the Clan's private equity firm. Any business venture he suggested they invest in was always a winner. However, to look at him, you would think he was in a rock band. With his spiked black hair and leather pants, he could have been the love child of his favorite guitarist, Nikki Sixx of Motley Crue. When the world fell apart, so did the music and movie industries.

It took many years to rebuild what was lost. Art forms that should have been classics remained mainstream. If Goyles could get tattoos, he would no doubt be covered in them. Their thick skin would not allow the ink to penetrate properly.

"Thank you. I would like to borrow one so I can take a look around to see where I want to live, if that's okay."

"Of course. Do you need someone to accompany you? Show you where everything is?"

"I was going to ask Lorenzo if he wanted to ride with me."

Lor took a sip of coffee then replied, "Sorry man. Finley is picking me up, and we're going to his house."

Rafael didn't miss the flash that went through Jasper's eyes. "Yeah, no problem."

"You're welcome to go with us. We're just going to hang out and watch a game."

Jasper wouldn't meet his eyes. "No, you go ahead. I want to look at houses."

"I assume your furniture and vehicles are being delivered to you at some point?" Both men confirmed this was the case.

Rafael hoped the tension he felt rolling off Jasper was not from jealousy. He would have to wait and see. "You know Jas, if you want the best view of properties, you should have Geoffrey take you up in the helicopter." Jasper's eyes grew wide. This obviously excited him. "Do you think he would do that?"

Rafael laughed. "Frey never can find enough excuses to fly the bird, so yes, I'm sure he would love to. Just give him a call."

164

Rafe left the two men to their day and refilled his coffee then went outside to the garden. He sat on his favorite bench and pulled out his phone. He dialed Kaya's number, hoping she was awake.

"Hello?" Her voiced sounded sleepy. If she hadn't been slumbering she just recently woke. "Miss Kane, this is Rafael Stone. I hope I didn't wake you."

"No, I'm up. What can I do for you, Mr. Stone?" Rafael could hear Kaya moving in her sheets. He closed his eyes and visualized her blonde hair spread over her pillow.

"You can have dinner with me."

"Dinner?" She was pushing the covers back and probably sitting on the side of the bed.

"Yes, Miss Kane, dinner. Tomorrow night, six o'clock. Is that too early, too late?"

"Mr. Stone, I don't think dinner is a good idea. You are a person of interest in an ongoing investigation."

Ah, the conflict of interest card. "Miss Kane, dinner is an excellent idea. I need to speak with you and would rather do it in private. So, may I pick you up at six?"

"Mr. Stone, if you have information on the murders I would appreciate you telling me now instead of making me wait and losing precious time." Her feet were now padding across the floor. She was pacing.

"Kaya, please, what I wish to speak with you about is more personal in nature. So I will pick you up at six tomorrow evening. Please wear a dress. I will see you then." Knowing it was rude, he hung up on her.

165

He would not give her time to overthink this any more than she already was.

What the hell just happened? She was having dinner with Rafael. Tomorrow. At six. *Wear a dress.* "I don't own a dress!" She shouted to her ceiling. It seemed her plans for the day had been made for her. She was going shopping. For a dress. What a rude ass, hanging up on her. She should call him back and tell him to shove a dress up his tight, toned, ass. Not that she had noticed his ass. Or his arms. Or his chest.

Who was she kidding? She was going to spend all day stressing over the perfect outfit for her date. She, Kaya Kane, had a date. With the man that made her insides melt with just a phone call. Was it wrong that she was going out with someone who was still involved in the largest case she had ever worked? Her brain told her yes. Her body said, "Who gives a shit? This is Rafael Stone."

She needed to shop for the Ball so she could kill two dresses with one shopping trip. Dammit. If she bought a new dress, she would probably need shoes. She hated buying shoes almost as much as she hated buying dresses. She loved the look of high heels on other women but being tall made her feel self-conscious when she wore them herself. Rafe was a tall man. If she did find a cute pair of shoes with some height, he would still be taller than her. Now that she was rambling to herself, she mentally prepared for her day.

The stores didn't open for a few more hours, so she had time to get a little work done. First she would have some coffee and shower. Then she would do what she dreaded; she would head to the mall.

Kaya found the perfect ball gown in the first store she went in. It was black with a draping crisscross over the chest area. It would show cleavage but not enough to be immodest. The slit up the side of the skirt ended just above her knee. Sexy but not slutty.

Finding a dress to wear to dinner was proving to be harder. She wanted something flirty but not desperate. Not knowing how formal it should be was also a hindrance. Since all magazines mentioned a little black dress, she was on a mission to find one even though hers would not be little. At five-nine, she was anything but small. She wasn't overweight, she just felt like an amazon most of the time.

The number of stores left to visit was dwindling right along with her hopes that she would find something to wear. As she walked past a store that featured younger gothic clothing, a little voice told her to go in anyway. A very spunky salesgirl greeted her. "Hi there, can I help you find something?"

Kaya felt like a fool, but told the girl anyway, "I'm trying to find a dress to wear to dinner tomorrow night. I'm almost out of options so I thought I would just browse."

The younger woman looked her over. "Is this a special occasion? Like, is there a hot man involved?"

Kaya laughed. "I guess you could say that. It's technically a first date."

"Come with me." The salesgirl walked toward the back of the store to a rack of all black dresses. She pushed hangers around until she pulled out a black dress that looked like it wouldn't fit a ten year old. "Try this."

"But that's so, *small.*" There was no way she would fit her size twelve ass in a size two dress.

"Trust me, it stretches and as toned as you are, this is going to be the shit." The girl didn't look abashed at her own language. Instead, she was grinning and pointing toward the dressing room.

"What the hell." Kaya took the dress, handed the girl her package that contained the ball gown, and went into the dressing room. She removed her clothes, again. She took the skimpy article off the hanger and slid it over her head. She smoothed out the front and was blown away. It was perfect. The neckline was scooped, billowing over her breasts. The fabric was soft and flowing and was not as tight as she thought it would be. The length hit right above her knees. Teamed with a nice pair of pumps, this would be stunning if she did say so herself. This was indeed the shit.

"How's it look?" The young woman certainly knew what she was doing. Kaya opened the door and stepped out.

"What do you think?" She kept running her hands down the front, feeling the softness of the material.

"I think your man is gonna eat you alive." She was grinning and wiggling her eyebrows. Kaya laughed at her.

"Yeah, well, we shall see. I'll take it."

Finding a pair of black heels proved to be relatively easy. She found a pair of open toe pumps on sale at the first store she went in. Now all she needed was a pedicure. A mask to wear to the Ball would have to wait until she could find a costume store. With packages in tow, she headed to her car. Placing the dresses in the back seat, she locked the door and returned to the mall to find a spa.

Kaya picked up Chinese takeout and headed home. She had twelve murders, a missing delegate, and two missing detectives on her plate. She was going to spend the evening focusing on all of those things.

Chapter 29

Sunday at the manor had turned into family day. Rafe didn't mind it at all. As a matter of fact, he was thankful for the houseful of men. Having his brothers with him all day was a tradition he enjoyed. He wondered if the ritual would continue when the men found their mates. With the journal entries Nikolas found and the feelings he held for Kaya, he knew in his heart human bonding was possible. He had yet to figure out if Xavier was hiding the truth about it.

There was a video game tournament going on in one room and a billiards tournament going on in another. Julian was off installing security cameras at the last warehouses. Frey had jumped at the chance to fly Jasper around in the helicopter. Scoping a home out from the air was prudent for Goyles. They required privacy and lots of it.

Rafael was lost in thought about his upcoming dinner with Kaya. He wanted to get to know her better and figure out if she was only attracted to him because of the mating bond. He was looking forward to the Policeman's Ball where he could be anonymous. Would she be attracted to him if she didn't know who he was? That would be a true test.

"Rafael. Yo, Rafe, you're up." Sixx was waiting impatiently at the pool table.

Rafe took a drink from his beer then lined up the shot. He sank three stripes in a row then called the eight ball in the side pocket. Perfect shot.

"Next," he said, grinning at Sixx. He had won three out of five. He was eventually dethroned by

Urijah. The kid spent a lot of time in bars, watching out for the humans.

The day was winding down now that they all had their bellies full of Priscilla's cooking. "I'll be on vacation next Sunday so one of you will have to do the cooking." She always kidded with them good-naturedly. She often told Rafael that if she didn't have a houseful of her boys, she wouldn't know what to do with herself.

Rafael asked the men to join him on the patio where they discussed the second murders and the fact that the detective was missing. "Now that Julian has all properties set up and being monitored, hopefully, there will be no more bodies showing up. The missing detective bothers me. Tonight when you are scouting, be on the lookout for his vehicle."

Rafael told them all about his conversation with Xavier. All Goyles knew of the Elder, but few had ever met him. "I will not stop searching until we know what we need to about bonding with humans. Also, I think that X knows more about Jonas Montague than he is letting on. I have a feeling life is gearing up to be even more interesting."

Everyone left for home with the exception of Jasper and Lorenzo. They were both ready to find a place of their own. Rafe couldn't blame them. When you were as old as they were, living under someone else's roof, no matter how expansive, was nice for only so long. Lorenzo called it a night and that left Rafael and Jasper.

"What's on your mind, Jas?" He could tell his cousin was nervous.

"I wanted to ask you about the mate bond. If it's true, that we can bond with humans, do you think the fates will put us with the right person?"

Rafael could feel the trepidation coming off Jasper. "Yes, I do. I have never seen a Goyle mated to someone they didn't like, and I do not think you will be an exception. You will be put with the perfect man."

Jasper gasped. "I'm not..." Rafael stopped him. "It's okay. I've watched you, and I see who catches your attention. I have no problem with your sexual orientation, Jas, and neither will any of the other brothers. Well, unless you are hitting on them." Rafe laughed. Jasper ducked his head, and Rafael could have sworn he saw tears threatening to fall. "Now, I have business to attend to if you are okay."

Jasper nodded. "Yes, my King. Thank you."

Rafael clapped him on the shoulder and headed inside to his office. Being King, there was always something going on that warranted his attention. Tonight he was fielding emails from two leaders in the southwestern states, something about boundary issues. Once he responded with what he felt were reasonable settlements, he shut his computer off. He would go to the office in the morning and bid on the Cromwell job. If the bid was accepted, he would be one step closer to figuring out who the mystery man was.

Rafael knew he would get little sleep. He was too anxious about dinner with Kaya. He decided a late night flight was in order. Julian had called earlier and said there had been a problem with the video surveillance at the warehouse on Industrial Boulevard, so Rafael decided to check it out. He phased in the woods then walked toward the building. What he

172

found made his blood boil. Kyle Jorgenson's car was inside the building with the detective at the wheel. Fuck! So this is where his body had disappeared to. It shouldn't come as a surprise but still, finding bodies that implicated you in their murder was a shock. Rafael did not need this, especially before his date tomorrow. He had to tell Kaya, just not tonight.

He pulled out his cell phone and called Julian. "Jules, you're not going to believe this." Together they worked through a scenario that Rafael prayed would not blow up in his face.

He needed to be fresh for his evening with Kaya, not worn out. He had not called her all day on purpose, even though he picked his phone up several times to do just that. He flew home and prepared for bed as he normally did; he turned the news on while he was brushing his teeth and changing clothes. Tonight he opted for no sleep pants. They would only get in the way when he was stroking his cock and thinking of all the things he planned on doing to one pretty blonde police chief. Once his dick was satisfied, maybe his brain would shut down for the night.

Kaya spent all day Sunday combing over the scarce information she had on Gordon Flanagan. She called in two more detectives since Jorgenson and Abbott were both M.I.A. She sent them to the archives, pulling information on Elizabeth Flanagan as well as anything else they might find on Gordon.

When the documents she read gave her no clues, she headed to the library. Not only did she scour for information on Flanagan but also on Rafael. She was going to have dinner with a man she didn't know anything about other than he drove her body crazy and his kisses made her toes curl. She always thought that was a stupid saying until she encountered the reaction herself.

Nothing she found on Flanagan helped her case. All the data on Rafael certainly helped his case. There was not one negative thing printed about the man. She went home empty-handed, but she felt better about her date.

She checked her phone every five minutes to see if he called or at least sent a text. Nothing. She decided to stop acting like a teenage girl and clean her house, anything to keep her occupied and her mind off Rafael. She cranked some hard rock on her stereo and got busy.

With a clean house and a black screen on her phone, she called it a night.

Chapter 30

Kaya got to work early as she did most days. Still not having heard from Dane and Jorgenson was forefront in her mind. A close second thought was her date tonight. She called a meeting of all her employees, asking if anyone had heard from either of the detectives. Nobody had. She set up a couple of task forces; both whose responsibilities were to canvas neighborhoods and areas looking for Dane and Kyle. Since the GPS on Jorgenson's car had been disabled, and Dane's car was still in his parking lot, they had their work cut out for them.

A knock on her door alerted Kaya to the young dispatcher entering her office carrying a huge vase full of wildflowers. "These just came for you." She sat them on the edge of Kaya's desk.

"Thank you." Kaya knew who the flowers were from without looking at the card. Kim didn't move toward the door. "Did you need something?" Kaya knew the girl was just being nosy.

"No, Ma'am." She reluctantly turned and left for her own desk, or the desks of everyone along the way so they could speculate who the bouquet was from. In all the years Kaya had worked at the precinct, not once had she received flowers. Kaya pulled the envelope off the plastic holder. Thank goodness it was sealed. She picked up her letter opener and carefully slid it under the flap. Once open, she pulled out the card and read it.

There is much beauty to behold in hearts that are wild.

There was no name, no initials, just that beautiful line. Did Rafael find her heart wild? She would have to ask him tonight. Shit, tonight. She knew she should stay at work but now she just couldn't. She was going to take her flowers home and start getting ready.

She put her laptop in its case and grabbed the vase. Kaya knew leaving this early was completely irresponsible, but she couldn't help herself. She had to pass by the bullpen and the dispatcher's desk, but she didn't stop. As she walked by, she told Kim, "I'll be working from home the rest of the day."

Rafael submitted the bid to Cromwell. It was so ridiculously high he almost hated to hit the send button. Now, he could not sit still. There were a couple of hours left until he picked up Kaya. He rehearsed what he was going to say in his head, but it sounded stilted, fake. This was their first official date, and he was nervous as hell. Never had he brought a woman back to the manor. That honor he had saved for his mate. In his heart, he knew that was Kaya and bringing her home tonight was huge.

Unsure of how well the night would go, he asked Frey if Lorenzo and Jasper could stay with him. He confided to his cousin his plan to skirt the truth in finding the body at the warehouse. A conference call with the others had them in agreement that it was the best course of action. After Priscilla had served dinner, she and Jonathan were to remain in their private wing for the rest of the evening. Priscilla's eyes filled with tears when Rafe requested the special meal.

Everything was in place. He just needed to expend some energy, waste some time, and stop thinking so hard. Rafe hated running. Why run when you could fly? Julian was the runner in the family. One day he took off and didn't return for almost twelve hours. He said he just got lost in his head. Rafe enjoyed swimming, but that was too relaxing. What his body required now was to hit something. He found himself in the gym decimating a punching bag.

His thoughts turned from the object of his desire to the current bane of his existence: Flanagan. Why now? What had set the tyrant off this time causing him to commit mass murder? Was it his twin being out in public that had pushed him over the edge? Rafael was certain he was behind the killings, especially with Magnus being one of the victims. Why was he targeting Rafe? Was it coincidence that the bodies were piling up in his warehouses? Never having met the man, Rafe couldn't answer that. If there was bad blood between them, he could understand being set up. As it were, he couldn't figure out the motive.

If Goyles sweated at a normal rate, Rafe would be drenched. Being a shifter had his skin barely glistening. A quick look at the clock told him he had been punching and jabbing for a couple of hours. Perfect. He made his way to the shower where his thoughts returned to his mate. He soaped and rinsed his face then shampooed his hair and ran conditioner through it. Rafe washed the rest of his body taking great care with his cock. He couldn't get in the shower now without getting a hard-on. Thoughts of Kaya's lips wrapped around the head and her pink tongue licking down the length, fueled his soaped hand to stroke longer and faster. Blue eyes looking up at him while she swallowed what he offered spurred his orgasm up through his balls and onto the tile wall.

Hopefully by the end of the night, his fantasy would become reality. He finished bathing, rinsed the conditioner out of his hair, and cleaned his spunk off the tiles.

Rafe stepped out of the shower wrapping a towel around his waist. The overhead fan kept the steam from fogging up the mirror. He pulled his razor and shaving cream out of the drawer. The face staring back at him was one he had seen hundreds of thousands of times. It was so familiar that he rarely looked at his reflection. Didn't really see himself. What did Kaya see when she looked at him, a plain man with too rough features? Or did she find a handsome man that she would be happy looking at every day for the rest of her life?

Rafael knew that his initial feelings for her were based on the mate bond, but for him it also went deeper. The connection was there when they touched, when she spoke, when they kissed. He had to trust she felt it too.

He ran some gel through his longish black hair that would keep it out of his eyes. Did she think his hair too long? Did she like it or wish it were shorter? When she had her hands in it, grabbing and pulling his face to hers, that made him think she did indeed like it. After shaving, he slapped some lotion on. Not that it was necessary, he just liked the way it smelled. He never thought about what scent a woman might like, but since he met Kaya, everything he did, every decision he made tonight caused him to wonder. He

178

brushed his teeth and put on deodorant. Now for his clothes.

Fuck. Rafael was second guessing his decision to dress up. He would be more comfortable in jeans, but he truly wanted to see Kaya in something sexy. Of course, that was just going to make keeping his hands to himself impossible, but what the hell. Tonight would tell the tale. Did she want him? He pulled out a charcoal grey suit and silver button up shirt. Black dress loafers completed the ensemble. Standing before the floor length mirror, he adjusted the lapels of the jacket. Hopefully, Kaya would appreciate what she saw.

Chapter 31

5:50. "Shit, this is such a mistake." Kaya checked her hair in the mirror. She made sure she had her keys and cell phone in her clutch.

5:52. "Oh, God. I'm gonna throw up." She didn't know why she was so nervous. It wasn't like she'd never spent time with the man, just not much and not on a date.

5:57. The doorbell rang. "I can do this. It's just dinner, and he's just Rafael." She looked one last time in the mirror before answering the door. The man standing in front of her took her breath away. He had been wearing slacks both times they met, but the suit he wore was molded to his body perfectly. He was now clean-shaven. His beard had been sexy but this Rafael was heart stopping. The man was exquisite. "Would you like to come in?" She stepped back so he could enter her living room.

Rafael wasn't moving. His eyes traveled the length of her body and stopped at her feet. Slowly they made their way back up her legs, lingered on her hips, then continued up to her face. He held out a small package without saying a word.

Kaya took the box from him. "Thank you, but you shouldn't have. Oh, and thank you for the beautiful flowers. They were from you, weren't they?" He nodded, still looking at her legs.

"Make yourself at home. Would you like a drink? I'm just going to open this. Is it okay if I open this?" She realized she was rambling, but the man's silence was unnerving. Did he not like her dress? Was it too juvenile, too trashy? He was probably used to more sophisticated women who knew what to wear to please a man. Her hair was down but maybe he didn't like it that way after all.

She pulled a steak knife out of a drawer, and she slid it between the folds of the paper, being careful not to rip it. The box inside was long and skinny, like a jewelry box. Kaya opened it to find a bracelet with one silver charm: a heart. She pulled the bracelet out of the box and held it up to the light. There was an inscription on one side of the charm: *Bella Mia*. When she turned around he was standing in the doorway, leaning against the frame with his arms crossed over his chest. She wished she could read the look in his eyes. "Rafael?"

"Hmm?" He was again staring at her feet. Kaya glanced down to make sure she hadn't chipped the polish on her toes.

"It's beautiful." Her heart was pounding in her chest. She didn't know for certain, but she was pretty sure the inscription was Italian for *my beauty. Oh God, don't cry. Don't you fucking cry, Kaya Kane.* She attempted to put the bracelet on her wrist, but her hands were shaking too badly. Rafael took the bracelet from her and snapped it in place. She felt herself being wrapped up in strong arms. Rafael was holding her against his body, one arm around her waist, one around her shoulder with his hand under her hair.

She took a chance and looked up. This look she recognized. It was the one she saw the first time they kissed. His eyes were hooded, and he was staring at her lips. "I have never seen a more beautiful woman in all my years." So maybe he did like the dress.

He softly touched his lips to hers. "We need to go now or we won't be leaving at all." Unwrapping her from his arms, he placed his hand on one of her cheeks and brushed his thumb across the bone under her eye. "Stunning," he whispered.

Wow. Kaya didn't know whether to be flattered or scared out of her mind. Either way, she followed him out of her house. He held her hand as they descended the steps, then opened the car door, helping her in. She looked around the interior, knowing the Jag was top of the line. She couldn't wait for the ride.

When he was seated on his side of the car, he turned to her. "I promise to try to be on my best behavior tonight. However, I do believe I should have asked that you dress in sweat pants and a hoodie. That dress is going to prove my downfall."

He cranked the engine and backed out of her driveway. "Thank you, I think," she laughed softly. "You look quite handsome yourself, Mr. Stone. Not that you don't usually, but I really like the color of the suit. It darkens your eyes."

"No my dear, that is all you." Rafael kept one hand on the steering wheel while he reached over with the other and entwined their fingers together. He rested them on his thigh, rubbing his thumb across the back of her hand.

"So where are we going?" She was curious to find out where the rich and famous dined on dates.

"My home." He was looking at her when he said it. "I want to show you where I live, who I am. I need for you to see me, Kaya. The real me. Not the one you've caught a few glimpses of. And please allow me to apologize. I should have taken the time to show interest in your home as well. I was momentarily mesmerized."

"Apology accepted. Did I thank you for the flowers? They were beautiful. Wildflowers happen to be my favorite."

"Mine too. It is getting late in the year, and the blooms are dwindling. That's another reason I wanted to dine at home tonight. I want to show you my garden before the cold weather sets in."

"You have a garden?" Kaya didn't know why that amazed her. The man was an architect and designed beautiful structures so it would only make sense he loved other beautiful things as well.

"Don't sound so surprised. It is my favorite place on earth with the exception of the Isles of Greece. I am a peaceful man, and I look for those places or things that offer me serenity. There is too much chaos around us, so I cherish those moments that the stillness of my garden bestows."

Kaya was staring at the profile of this man she knew nothing about except what was written about him. Once again his words surprised her. When was the last time she enjoyed something simply because it *was*? He was certainly right about the chaos. It consumed her life, ate up her time, devoured her faith in humanity.

"It's my turn to apologize. I have a lot to learn about you, and I promise to be less assuming." She squeezed his hand. His eyes met hers as he lifted her knuckles to his lips.

"Apology accepted. We both have a lot to learn, so we will use tonight to start our quests for knowledge."

Rafael turned into the same driveway as when she had followed him. Instead of punching in a code, he spoke her name into the security panel. The gate slowly opened, and he continued on down his drive. Hi-tech indeed. "Why is my name your passcode?"

Rafe was grinning. "Each person allowed onto the grounds has their own passcode. They choose what they wish to say, however it is simply voice recognition. I could have said *Rumpelstiltskin* and it would have allowed us in."

"Oh." For a second, she was flattered. She felt a tug on her hand. "Hey, don't look so sad. Since I met you, I have only used your name to gain entrance. You have me entranced, Miss Kane." There was that look again.

"*Oh.*" Now she was thrilled.

Chapter 32

Rafael came around and helped Kaya out of the car. She paused, looking around the estate, taking in the vastness and beauty that was his home. She didn't realize this could be her home as well. If he got his way, she would be living here sooner rather than later. He led her up the steps to the front door. "Normally I go through the garage, but for your first visit, I thought the grand tour was in order."

The front door was pulled open by Jonathan. "Good evening Sir, Miss Kane."

"Kaya, this is Jonathan. He and his sister Priscilla take care of everything you see. I only live here." He shook his old friend's hand, and they both laughed.

"It's a pleasure to meet you, Jonathan."

Rafe showed Kaya the manor, pausing in each room to allow her time to take it all in. "Before it gets too dark, I'd like to show you around outside." Her sexy heels were going to make walking across the grass a bit difficult. "I have a suggestion, let's do this barefoot." He pulled off his shoes and socks by the backdoor. She toed off her heels.

The swimming pool had yet to be enclosed. Rafe held her hand as he explained the design of the structure that would allow them to swim indoors during the colder months. What he didn't tell her was that he had only planned to enclose it since he met her.

As soon as they reached the archway leading to the garden he paused. "This is what I want to show you, Kaya." Other than a few of the Clan and Jonathan and Priscilla, nobody else was given the privilege of witnessing the beauty that was his garden. While Jonathan kept it growing and flourishing, it was Rafe himself who designed it.

He kept his eyes on Kaya as she took it all in. He needed her to love this place as much as he did. She stopped and touched leaves. She bent and smelled blooms. She walked the path that meandered throughout this heaven on earth. When they got to his favorite bench, he pulled her down to sit beside him.

The look of awe on her face and the tears shining wet in her eyes told him everything. He gently took her face in his and leaned his forehead to hers. Closing his eyes, he cherished this moment. He would never forget it. A tinkling of chimes behind them stirred him back to reality. Her hands were on his wrists, thumbs lovingly stroking his skin. She placed her lips to his whispering, "Thank you."

Rafe leaned back and placed his arm around her shoulders, once again enjoying the serenity. He spoke softly, reverently. "This is where I meditate. I come here as often as I can to this very bench and allow myself to just be. Sometimes I am left to my own thoughts. Other times the cosmos has its way of speaking to me."

"I get it now. I understand why you are this private person. Rafael, if I lived here I would never want to leave." One lone tear escaped down her beautiful face. He caught it before it plunged to her lap where her hands were clasped together.

"If you lived here, neither of us would ever leave. I would have to turn the business over to someone else, and you and I would make many dark-haired little boys who would run through these gardens until the moon shone in the sky."

Kaya gasped. "What did you say?" Her eyes were wide, the emotion he couldn't read.

"Love, I was kidding. You are just so enticing, and I would be hard pressed to leave our bed." Her face was paling. "Kaya, what is it? Did I say something wrong?" *Don't fuck this up before you even start Rafe.*

"No, I'm sorry, I just…"

"You what? Kaya, talk to me, what is it?" Rafe was worried now. Was the mention of children too much too soon? Did she not want children? Did she have a child? Oh gods, what if she bore one and had lost it? There was nothing about a child in the research he did on her.

"It's nothing, really. Now, didn't you promise to feed me?"

Rafe knew better than to press. He would wait until a more appropriate time to bring it up again. "I did indeed. Let's go introduce you to Priscilla. You've already met her cooking."

Once inside they put their shoes back on and went in search of sustenance.

Kaya felt like a fool for freaking out. Of course, Rafe would talk about dark-haired boys. What man wouldn't want his child to look like him? There was no way he could have known about her dream. She walked with him through the house to where the delicious aromas were coming from. If this meal was half as good as lunch, she was going to need those sweat pants Rafael mentioned.

The older lady, Priscilla she presumed, looked just like a housekeeper slash cook should look. Like someone's mother. "Oh, there you are! Miss Kane, it is so good to meet you. Please, may I get you something to drink?"

Rafe was laughing. "Kaya, this is Priscilla. She runs the house if you haven't already figured that out. I'll get our drinks." He kissed Priscilla on the cheek and grabbed a piece of cheese off a platter on the island. She smacked his hand playfully. "You stop being rude. Now go on into the dining room. Everything is all set for you."

"Would you like a glass of wine or maybe you'd prefer something stronger?" Rafe was holding a bottle of the same Riesling she bought.

"Have you been watching me, Mr. Stone? I'll take the wine, please." She was grinning at him, but it really was disconcerting that he would have the same cheap brand that she drank.

He poured Kaya a goblet of wine and himself a tumbler full of Scotch. "A toast. Here's to the first night of many in what will be a beautiful relationship." They touched their glasses together and took a drink. She took a couple more sips trying to get some alcohol in her system to calm her nerves. Rafe sat his glass down and pulled a chair out for her. The table was full of several different types of meat, vegetables, salads, and breads.

Priscilla came in with the last bowl and set it in between them. "There you are. Miss Kane, I hope everything is to your satisfaction. I didn't know what you liked so I made a little of everything." The older lady was blushing. She was so cute. "Thank you for going to so much trouble, Priscilla. I really do appreciate it. With my schedule, I don't get a chance to cook very often."

"Think nothing of it. Now, will there be anything else?"

"No, thank you, Priscilla. You and Jonathan enjoy your evening."

She bowed and quietly slipped out of the room. Wait, she bowed? Kaya wondered if Rafael insisted on it. Jonathan didn't, did he? No, the relationship between the three of them was more along the lines of family. She could see the love in his housekeeper's eyes as she looked at Rafael.

Kaya asked him about his business, and he proudly spoke of not just the drawings he created but also the planning and building that went along with it. He boasted of his team as if they were family. He said it was one thing to put something to paper but to have someone be able to take those drawings and make them come to life, that was truly where the credit was due.

Never once did he brag on himself or act better or pretentious. He was a man who enjoyed what he did for a living. While he did speak vaguely about the various charities he donated to, he didn't do it to boast. No, Rafael Stone was a passionate man, and he didn't mind showing it. While she was listening, she had to remember to eat. She would find a bite of food dangling from the fork as she sat enchanted by his words.

The only subject Rafael shied away from was his parents. He briefly spoke of them with tender words then changed topics.

When they were finished eating, he stood and grabbed his glass. He refilled his Scotch, poured her more wine then held out his hand. He led her out onto the patio. "Stay here." He disappeared back into the house, and soft music that sounded like John Legend started playing from hidden speakers. He rejoined her and put his arm around her waist. Random spotlights emitted a faint glow around them. Rafael took a sip of Scotch then gazed up at the sky.

"What are you looking at?" She looked up as well and was amazed at all the stars. Having lived most of her life where the stars weren't very visible because of the many street lamps, she was in awe.

"Perseus. It's my favorite of all the constellations."

"Why is that?" Kaya never thought about them as anything but groups of stars.

"He was a hero. He beheaded Medusa and saved the fair princess."

Kaya wondered if Rafael saw himself as the hero. Had he ever saved the fair maiden or was he just another man? Would he be her hero?

Chapter 33

"May I have this dance?" Rafael set both of their glasses on the outside bar and held out his hand. She placed her hand in his and he pulled her close. She wasn't a very good dancer, but she soon found out if the man leading you was, you could just follow along. The song was jazzy but sexy, slow and seductive. It allowed the dancers to sway to the tempo or grind to the back beat. Oh, how she wanted to grind.

All night the intensity between her and Rafael grew more palpable. Every look, every touch, felt like a live wire was connecting them, growing stronger and tighter with each moment. She allowed her hands to play in the soft curls at the edge of his collar. She loved his hair and told him so.

"I love yours too. I know why you wear it up for work, but I hope you'll always wear it down when we're together." Rafael leaned in and inhaled.

She should find that weird but instead she knew why he did it. Not as boldly, she breathed in the aftershave at his neck. It was intense yet subtle. How could that be? The same way the man could be an alpha and still hold himself in reserve to appreciate the simpler things like flowers and solitude.

His hand that was on the small of her back dipped lower, softly caressing her cheek. The other hand wound itself around her hair once again. With the four inch heels she was wearing she was only a few inches shorter than Rafael, bringing them almost eye to eye. Her lips parted, caressing his chin. She continued up his jawline until she got to the soft spot under his ear. With each touch of her lips, the hand fisting her hair tightened just a little more. When she nipped his earlobe with her teeth, her head was pulled back, and his mouth was crushing hers. She didn't make him work for it. She opened for him, searching for his tongue with her own. Their bodies were moving in sync with the music floating on the air. The grinding of their hips matched the rhythm of the drums.

Kaya felt Rafael's hand leave her back and move toward the front. Slowly he caressed each spot along the way until he reached her breast. He kept his hand underneath, rubbing his thumb back and forth. When he rubbed over her already aching nipple she moaned into his mouth.

Rafe was about to lose control. If he didn't claim this woman soon, he was going to phase and then he would really be in a mess. "Kaya," He breathed into her mouth. He wanted their first time to be special, perfect, but he was too close. He was ready to pull her dress up and take her right there. He must back off and get himself under control.

He tried to pull away, but this strong warrior had a mind of her own. She wasn't ready to let him go. "Kaya." She continued to lick and nip at his neck. Reaching behind his head, he grabbed her wrists. "Kaya, stop." She looked confused. "Love, if you want to do this properly we need to go into the house. Otherwise I'm going to take you here, now, and it will not be gentle. Your decision." He could see her warring with herself. He could smell her arousal. She wanted him just as much as he did her.

Thinking she would choose the bed, she surprised him when she grabbed his hard cock and began rubbing him through his suit pants. "Are you sure?"

"Yes, Rafael. I don't want to wait." He slammed his mouth to hers again while he yanked her dress up over her ass. Feeling bare skin, he nearly came right then. Had he known she wore no panties, he probably would have already been inside her. She was fumbling with his belt while he was pulling his shirt from his pants. Before his pants could slide down his legs, he was grabbing for his wallet. He pulled out a condom, tearing the wrapper with his teeth, the foil flittering to the ground. He rolled the sheath on, stroking his already rock hard length. "Kaya, are you certain?"

"Yes dammit, I want you." He spun her around and bent her over the table. Stretching her arms out in front of her, he held both in place with one large hand. Rafael nudged her legs apart with his foot while rubbing his fingers through her folds. Holy fuck but she was wet. He pumped two fingers inside her pussy, rubbing along that spot that made women come unglued. And she would, but not yet. He teased the spot a few more times.

Kaya was pushing back against him, arching that beautiful ass higher. One day. One day he would shove his cock in her forbidden hole but not this day. Tonight was about the already primed and ready-to-go slick piece of heaven. He removed his fingers and placed them in his mouth, savoring the flavor of her juices. He then grabbed his cock and lined up the engorged head with her cunt and with one thrust he was in up to his balls. She pushed back and groaned. Fuck! Rafael remained still. Dizziness threatened to take over. His cock filling Kaya's core consumed his mind, his soul.

"Keep your hands where they are," he demanded as he let go and wrapped one arm around her waist to keep it from crashing into the edge of the table. His other hand was gripping her throat, not hard enough to cut off circulation but with enough pressure to let her know he was in control.

"My sweet Kaya, my beautiful woman, how do you want it? Tell me what you want me to do with my cock." He held himself back. Over the years, he had learned to control his baser needs, but this was Kaya. This was his mate. He was ready to let the beast loose. She reached back for him, and he smacked her on the ass. A groan escaped her as she put her hand back on the table. His woman liked that.

"Hard. I want you to fuck me, hard." She was panting and curling her fists. Her wish was his command. "Move your hands to the edge of the table and hold on. Hold the fuck on."

Rafe began to move torturously slow, giving Kaya time to adjust to his size. When he felt she could take him, all of him, he gave her what she asked for. Never had Rafe enjoyed the kind of raw, carnal sex he was having now. If she wasn't feeling his dick in her womb, he would be surprised. He released her neck and moved his hand to between her legs, circling her clit. "Are you with me?"

"Yes, oh yes. Oh God Rafael, Oh my God!" She was rocking back into him, her ass and thighs meeting him thrust for thrust. "Oh God, fuck me harder." He moved his hands to her hips, bent over her back, and pistoned into her pussy relentlessly. The heat was tangible, and the sparks were flying. He felt his fangs nipping his lower lip. He would not bite her, not yet. He felt her pussy clench around his dick as her orgasm hit. Feeling her inner walls tighten around his cock shredded the last bit of control in his grasp. With a fiery release, he yelled her name to the stars.

Kaya couldn't move, couldn't breathe. Her knuckles were probably white from her grip on the table. Any previous sexual act was long forgotten. What in the name of all that was holy just happened? That was so far beyond the scope of anything she could ever have imagined. She felt soft kisses being placed on her shoulder, strong hands now gently rubbing where they, just a few minutes ago, gripped tightly. She would probably have a bruise.

"That was beyond unreal," she finally managed to say. She tried to turn her head to look at Rafael, but he was intent on her back. "Rafael, look at me."

"Not yet." He was keeping his face hidden.

"Please, Rafael."

She heard him sigh and stood up. "I'll be right back." He turned away from her as he was removing the condom. He tied a knot in it and pulled his pants together with the other hand. He disappeared into the kitchen leaving her with her bare ass in the air.

"What the fuck?" She said out loud. "Was it that bad?" She pulled her dress down and grabbed her wine, downing all that was left. She wanted a refill. She wanted the whole bottle.

Rafael returned with his pants intact, carrying a wet washcloth. "Here let me clean you."

She grabbed the rag and muttered, "I'll do it myself."

He grabbed her arm and pulled her to him. "That was the single most wonderful experience of my life, Kaya Kane. You were amazing." He gently took the warm cloth from her hand and wiped between her legs. "I just needed a minute to compose myself."

The loving look on his face stole her breath. He was telling the truth. She grabbed his face and pulled him in for a kiss. "Thank you."

He raised his eyebrows in surprise. "For what? I am the one who should be thanking you. Here, let's sit down." He led her to a cushioned glider and pulled her down into his lap. "Kaya, that was not how I envisioned our first time being. I wanted more for you, so much better than just a quick fuck over a table. I'm truly sorry. And embarrassed." She couldn't believe the honesty coming from this man. A little piece of her heart floated out of her body into his.

"Hey, look at me." She made sure he was focused on her eyes. "You gave me the choice, remember? You told me you didn't want down and dirty." She grinned, hoping to lighten the mood. "I wanted fast and furious, Mr. Stone, and you gave it to me. Boy did you give it to me. Next time, we will do slow and steady, or however you want it, okay?"

Rafael didn't respond with words; he just leaned closer and answered her with his mouth.

Chapter 34

Rafael absolutely hated lying to Kaya but until she knew what he was, he couldn't let her see how she affected him. He never had trouble controlling his phasing, but the intensity of the sex fucked with him. One thing was for certain; his woman was a goddess. If she could get him that riled up their first time, he could only imagine what they would be like in a bed.

His phone began ringing, and he thanked the gods that it hadn't been earlier. "I apologize but I have to take that." She stood so he could get to his phone.

"Rafe..." "Godsdamnit! Where?" He looked at Kaya. "There's no need. Chief Kane is here now. I will pass this along myself, and she can handle it from there. No, don't touch anything. We'll be right there." Rafe thumbed off his phone and hung his head.

"Rafael, what is it?" Kaya was touching his arm. It might be the last time she ever touched him freely.

"That was Julian; you met him Saturday. After the murders at the warehouse, I thought it prudent to install security systems on the other buildings since we have no immediate plans to use them or tear them down. Julian went to install the last camera and found a body. It's bad."

"How bad?" He wanted to reach out to her but wasn't sure she would appreciate it.

"Maybe you should sit down."

"Rafael, just spit it out."

"It's your detective, Jorgenson."

"Goddamnit, I sent him out there!" She grabbed Rafe's glass of watered down scotch and tossed it back. "I don't have my car. Come on, you gotta drive me."

She didn't wait on him to follow; she just took off through the house to the front door.

Kaya was already in the Jag by the time he reached the car. She was on her phone calling for CSU and the medical examiner. When she hung up, she asked, "Won't this thing go any faster?"

"I wasn't sure how you would feel about me speeding." He accelerated a little, still hovering close to the speed limit. Kaya dialed her phone. "This is Chief Kane. Detective Kyle Jorgenson's body has been found, and I am headed to the scene. Please alert those on patrol that I am traveling west in a black Jaguar XK convertible with the emergency flashers on."

Rafe turned the flashers on and put the Jag in the wind.

By the time they reached the warehouse, several cruisers as well as the ME's van were there. Someone had set up temporary lighting outside. Dante and Julian met them at the car. They both knew Kaya, so introductions weren't required. Julian held out his hand, "Chief, I'm the one who found the body. I've already given my statement to Detective Craven." Kaya shook his hand and turned to Dante. "Well?"

"Detective Jorgenson has a single GSW to the head. CSU is still looking for the bullet casing though it appears he was shot somewhere other than here. His body is in his cruiser yet there are no bullet holes in the vehicle. Rigor mortis puts time of death approximately 24 to 36 hours ago."

Kaya was walking toward the warehouse when Rafe picked up the unmistakable sound of a rifle slide. "Gun!" he yelled right before he threw himself at Kaya. Not knowing who the intended target was, he didn't take a chance. He felt the hit to his shoulder just before he took Kaya to the ground.

"Kaya, are you okay?" He knew that any damage she had incurred was from him landing on her in the gravel parking lot.

Dante told Julian, "Cover the King."

"I'm fine, just find the motherfucker." All of this was said in whispers so the humans couldn't hear them.

Kaya still hadn't responded. "Kaya, baby, talk to me."

"Rafael, what the fuck was that? I'm fine except I can't breathe. You're heavy. You can get off me now."

Rafe didn't move. He watched as the others all scrambled for cover. "I'm not moving until I know there won't be another shot." He did however slide to the side a few inches so that all his weight wasn't on her.

When there were no more shots fired, Rafe finally stood up and helped Kaya to her feet. He had to get away from her before she saw the wound healing. Dante was now at his back. "Chief Kane are you all right? Do you require medical attention?"

Kaya brushed the gravel from her knees and looked at her arms. "No, I just have minor scratches." Her officers were all headed her direction. There was a moment of chaos as they tried to figure where the shot came from and where the bullet landed. Luckily, Rafe had been able to pocket the evidence before standing up.

Kaya looked at him. "How did you know? That shot had to have come from those trees over there, and you knew." The look on her face was one of skepticism as well as distrust.

"I heard it." That was the truth.

"You heard a gun from this far away?" Her hands were on her hips. He really shouldn't but he loved when she did that.

"Yes, I did. I have exceptionally good hearing." Truth again but he could tell she wasn't buying it.

"Mr. Stone, if you would come with me, I will look at your shoulder." Dante was running interference and trying to patch Rafe up at the same time.

"What's wrong with your shoulder?" Kaya tried to get around him to look, but he held out his hand. "Nothing, just a scratch."

She wasn't having it, "Let me see."

"Oh my God, you were shot!" Kaya was no longer scowling. "You saved my life."

"Really, it's just a little nick. I'll be fine."

"Mr. Stone, I really should look at that." Dante knew the wound would close up quickly, and Kaya didn't need to see it happen.

"Yes, go." Kaya looked as though she were going to cry. He reached out and touched her arm.

"Hey, I'm okay, I promise. Let me get patched up. You still have a job to do here." She nodded, and he waited until she turned to her officers. He followed his brother to the van. He unbuttoned his shirt and lowered it off his shoulder so Dante could put a bandage on it.

Julian appeared beside them and glanced at Rafe's shoulder. "I found where the shot came from as well as the casing. I examined it as thoroughly as I could without touching it. It's appears to be from an L115."

"Isn't that British?" Frey was the expert, but Rafael knew a little about weaponry himself.

"Yes it is. The scent of cigarettes was strong, like the shooter was chain smoking. I did find one discarded butt that happens to be in my pocket. There was no sign of the shooter. I followed his scent, but it disappeared into thin air. He is either really fast, or I'm losing my touch. I'm pretty sure it's the same shooter from Saturday."

Rafael froze. "Excuse me?"

"I might have taken a bullet when I met Miss Kane on Saturday."

"And you're just now thinking to mention that fucking fact?" Rafe was almost yelling.

"My apologies, but I'm telling you now." Julian had his hands up in the defensive position.

"First the murders and now attempted murder? Rafe, we have to assume at this point someone is after us." Dante placed the final piece of tape on his shoulder and pulled his shirt back up.

"Whoever it is must be watching us. They knew someone would eventually find the bodies so the shooter must have been waiting. Were the shots meant for us or Kaya?"

"That is the question of the hour. I finally have all the security cameras in place. Fin and Uri are on around the clock shifts monitoring the feed. So far they have seen absolutely nothing. Our killer is either lucky or better than we are." Julian was scanning the area as he spoke. "Your woman does not look happy."

202

The three of them turned at once to see Kaya looking at Rafael.

Chapter 35

The albino watched through binoculars as the intended target stood up. Why was the bitch with Stone? Did she not see the video he sent her? If she did why was he still walking free and not behind bars? Flanagan would not be happy. Maybe she needed a little prodding. He pulled out his cell phone and sent her a message. "Did you see the video?"

Kaya couldn't shake the feeling that she was missing something. She had to believe that someone other than Rafael was using his warehouses as a killing ground. She wouldn't even entertain the possibility that he could be involved. Not after tonight. He threw himself in the path of a bullet and then he called her baby. Oh God. Another piece of her heart fluttered away. She watched the imaginary item float over to where he was standing with his cousin and Dante.

Seeing them all together was a shock. The medical examiner looked more like Rafael than Julian did. Holy shit. Her cell phone pinged, somewhere. Looking around, she saw it lit up on the ground where Rafael had tackled her. She retrieved her phone and saw a text from an unknown number. She didn't have time for spam.

An hour later she was ready to go home. Shit, she didn't have her car. She could either ride with Rafael or have one of her men drive her. That would be the smart thing to do, but her heart was telling her to go with Rafael. He was leaning up against his car when she walked out of the warehouse. He didn't move, just watched her intently.

"Do you mind giving me a ride home?" She was ready to get out of her dress and heels.

"I don't mind at all." He rounded the car and held open the door for her. She slid into the seat then toed the shoes off her feet and leaned her head back. The stress of the last couple of hours was taking its toll, and she needed a drink.

"Are you in any pain? I would apologize for any damage I may have caused to your beautiful skin, but it's better than you being shot."

She turned her head to look at her hero. Perseus. "I'll live, thanks to you. I just want a hot bath and a cold drink." She couldn't stop staring. Something just below the surface was tugging at her subconscious.

"I know you've had a long day. Do you want to continue our date or do you want me to take you home?"

"As much as I would love to go home with you, I have phone calls to make and paperwork to go over. Duty calls and all that."

Right at that moment, Kaya wished she weren't in charge. For the very first time in her career, she wanted to be a woman with a regular nine to five job. One where she didn't have the weight of the world, or at least New Atlanta, on her shoulders. She would give anything to be going home with Rafael and letting him show her if he could do slow and gentle.

Rafael took her hand and brought it to his lips. Oh yes, she had no doubt he could do slow and gentle.

After a silent ride to her home, Rafael pulled into her driveway and parked. Once out of the car he walked her to the door. She surprised herself when she asked him, "Would you like to come in?" She needed to get busy, but she wasn't quite ready to let him walk away.

"I would love to." He followed her in and began looking around. The house was old but in good repair. The few pictures she displayed were of her and her father when he was alive. Any picture of her mother was put away long ago. There were pictures of herself getting awards over the years, but those were also stowed away in a chest. It was sad, really. Photographs were the reminders of happy times. Did she have nothing to celebrate since her father died?

"You have a lovely home. Is this where you grew up?" Rafael was holding a small ceramic black cat.

"Yes, it is. My mother moved out when I joined the force. She had stayed for me while I was growing up but when I became a cop, she couldn't take it. She left me the house and moved on. I like the neighborhood, and it's fairly secluded. My neighbors keep to themselves."

Rafael put the trinket back where he got it and moved closer. "Kaya." That one word sent a shiver up her spine. If she gave in now she would not get any work done, and those phone calls couldn't wait until morning. She had given herself to him tonight, and it had been mind-blowing. She had no regrets.

"Rafael, thank you for a wonderful evening. Well, mostly." She closed the distance between them and took his hands in hers. "I would like nothing more than to get comfortable with you, open a bottle of wine, continue where we left off. I just can't. I'm sorry."

"Do not apologize for doing your job, Love. It's who you are. And I love who you are. I am disappointed that our time was cut short, but there is always tomorrow. I want to see you again, continue getting to know each other. I want to see where this goes. Please tell me you want that too." He was whispering in her ear, the intoxication as potent as a bottle of wine.

"Yes," was all she could manage with him standing so close.

"Yes," he purred in her ear then nipped her earlobe. "Then I will take my leave. I would love to see you tomorrow, but I will leave that up to you. Call me if you are free and I will come get you, yes?"

"Yes. Okay, that sounds good and Rafael?" She waited until he was looking in her eyes, "I love who you are too."

He pulled her hands to his lips and brushed kisses across her knuckles. "Goodnight, Miss Kane."

"Goodnight, Mr. Stone."

As badly as Kaya wanted a glass of wine, she grabbed a bottle of water instead. She applied Neosporin to her scrapes before she slipped into her sweats. She heard her phone ping with an incoming text. It was the same number she didn't recognize from before. This time she opened it.

"Did you watch the video?"

Another text: "Check your email."

She had watched the video from earlier. Was there another? She had a bad feeling about this. Her gut instincts or woman's intuition, whatever you wanted to call it, rarely led her down the wrong path. Who was texting her, and how did they get her number? Was it the same person that called her at work and sent her the previous email?

She called the lab at the station. Wilkes wouldn't be there but, hopefully, the third shift guy could help. "Danny, this is Chief Kane. Is there any way you can find out where an anonymous text is coming from?" She listened as she turned on her computer. "Okay, thank you." He would try. Seriously, with technology as advanced as it was, they should be able to track down whoever was sending her messages.

She opened her email program and saw there was a new video. There was darkness, then movement. A man walking toward the camera. What was he wearing? As he closed in she could tell he was in fatigues and combat boots. No shirt. He walked into the warehouse then a few minutes later he exited the building. The camera zoomed in. Kaya was looking at Rafael. She rewound the video and looked closer. That was the warehouse she had just left. She looked at the date stamp on the video. Last night. Oh my God. Rafael lied to her. Rafael was her killer. She was falling in love with a killer.

She ran to the bathroom and dropped to her knees, throwing up everything that was on her stomach.

Chapter 36

Rafael knew something was wrong. He could feel the emotions rolling off Kaya. After taking his car home, he flew back to her house, wanting to be close to her. What the fuck was going on inside? Her heart rate was accelerated. She was crying and, fuck, was she throwing up? Fuck! He couldn't stand being out here when she needed him. How could he explain knocking on her door so quickly and having changed clothes at that?

He quietly dropped to the ground and listened. The water turned on, and she brushed her teeth. The water turned off. She was walking through the house. Now she was talking. "Dane, Kaya. Listen, I know you're sick but I really have to talk to you. I hate to leave this shit in a message, but I need you. Jorgenson's dead. I sent him to that address you gave me and now he's dead. We have another body that could be Magnus Flanagan. I also know who the killer is. I hope you're feeling better, because I really need you. Please, call me."

Jealousy charged through Rafe like a parade of bulls. "She *needs* him?" He made himself calm down and think rationally. Of course, she needed him as a detective. If he found out she needed the kid for anything else, he would rip his balls off. With his claws. Wait, she knew who the killer was? How the hell did she know that when he just left her. He had to get closer.

Quietly, he made his way to the window outside her living room. Her curtains were cracked just enough for him to see her. Kaya was sitting on the sofa with her laptop open on the coffee table in front of her. She was watching a video of some sort, rewinding then playing again. When she froze the video at one point, she started crying. Rafe looked at the laptop. He was staring at himself coming out of the warehouse. *Oh, fuck me, motherfucking fuck me. She thinks I'm the killer.*

He knelt down, placing his fists to the ground so he wouldn't be tempted to punch something. He had to think. *FUCK!* How in the name of all that was holy did someone get a video of him? Was that all that it showed or did it show him phasing as well? Did he go inside and tell her the truth? Did he take the chance on exposing himself and his kind? Would she accept it or would she arrest him?

Her front door opened, and Kaya headed to her car. She undoubtedly was going to the station. In her hand she held the laptop and the damning evidence. If he stopped her it would be bad, but if he let her go it would be worse. Fuck it. "Kaya!" he yelled out to her before she could open her car door. He jogged toward her, but the look on her face stopped him in his tracks. She was staring at him as if he were a complete stranger. A stranger dressed exactly as he was in the video.

"Please, Kaya, let me explain. It's not what you think; I promise. Just give me five minutes, and if you aren't convinced, I'll put the handcuffs on myself."

"You lied to me. You lied and made me look like a fool. I let you touch me."

"I didn't lie, I just withheld information. Please, Sweetheart, let me explain."

"Don't you *sweetheart me*, Mr. Stone. Withholding information is lying by omission."

"I did it to protect you. Please, five minutes. That's all I ask."

"Fine, start talking."

"Not out here. What I have to tell you, show you, should be done in private."

"Do you take me for an idiot? If I let you get me alone, I'll be vulnerable. At least out here the neighbors have a chance of seeing you kill me."

She thought he was capable of such atrocities? At that moment, Rafe felt pain, real pain, and it was straight through his heart.

"I would never hurt you, never. I am not a killer. No, that's not true, I have killed before." She blanched and reached for her gun. She dropped everything in her arms and pointed her pistol at him.

"You just admitted you're guilty. Rafael Stone, you're under arrest..."

"Stop, Kaya, STOP! I did not kill those men. When I said I have killed, it was in self-defense. I have never murdered a human in cold blood and never would. I am a protector. What I have to tell you is going to be hard for you to believe. You're going to think I am making it up, but I assure you it is the truth. After I tell you, I promise to leave you alone.

"Kaya, I am Rafael Di Pietro, King of the Gargouille. I come from a long line of shapeshifters. I protect humans from the Unholy." He paused to gauge her reaction so far.

She was laughing. "You expect me to believe you are some sort of supernatural being? This is rich."

"I can prove it. I do not want to do this in the open. If humans knew my kind existed, it would cause chaos and panic."

"You're crazy, Mr. Stone. Now, I would appreciate you doing what you said and handcuff yourself..." He didn't give her time to finish. He dropped his fangs and extended his claws. He held his hands up for her to see then he retracted his claws but left his fangs.

"I am telling the truth. I also have special skin and wings, but I really do not want to risk showing my wings out in the open." She was still pointing her gun at him, but her mouth was open.

"How, how did you do that? Is this some type of sick joke?" Her hands and the gun were shaking.

"I assure you, this is no joke. This is who I am. What I am. I am a Gargoyle and like you, I live to protect the innocent."

"Wait, you said your name is Di Pietro? *Fucking hell*. I saw the resemblance in you and Dante tonight. How are you two related?"

Rafael knew he was throwing the Clan under the proverbial bus, but he trusted his instincts and his instincts told him to trust Kaya. "He's my brother. He is the only one who uses the family name. I have several brothers and many cousins living in and around New Atlanta. Our Clan rules the Americas with other Clans serving under us."

"And you're the king? Like King of the Vampires king?" She wasn't laughing now.

"Vampires are a myth, but yes I am King. My father before me was King, and if I ever have a son, he too will be King." He briefly thought back to the little boy in his vision.

"Let's say I do believe you are what you say you are. What then? Do you kill me to keep me from

212

talking? And what about the warehouse? You were there. You were there and knew my man was dead. Why didn't you tell me? Why lie and pretend you didn't know?" She lowered her gun but kept it cocked.

"I would never harm you much less kill you. If you accept nothing else I tell you tonight, you have to accept that. You are mine. I would do anything to keep you from harm. I would die for you. Oh fuck."

The sound of a rifle once again breached Rafael's hearing. Without thinking, he phased and in the blink of an eye wrapped Kaya in his wings. For the second time that night, he took a bullet for his Queen.

Chapter 37

Kaya was dazed. One minute she was looking at the man from the video, holding a gun on him. The next, she's being taken to the ground. Again. Gargoyle King. Clan, brothers, wings. Wings? She was enclosed in…wings. Holy shit! He had fucking wings! He was telling the truth. Oh my God. Oh My God! He was a shapeshifter. Holy hell. "Rafael…you can let go now. Rafael?" He wasn't moving.

"Shhh, Love, be quiet," he whispered in her ear. At least this time when they landed on the ground she was protected from the gravel.

"He's gone," he said as he rolled off her. She looked up just in time to see his wings disappear behind his back. "Holy shit." She sat up and just stared. "We had sex." That was all she could say? She just found out the man she was falling in love with was not human, and she stated the obvious.

"Yes, we did, and it was the best sex of my life." He was holding his hand out to help her up. She let him. "But you're… you're… not human."

He looked stunned, like she had pulled the trigger. "I'm sorry if that appalls you, but you need to get inside." He turned his back on her. Oh my God, he was bleeding. He had been shot. Again.

"Wait, you're bleeding. I should take you to the hospital." She picked up her weapon she had dropped when he tackled her. She turned back to him to see his retreating self. "Wait, where are you going?"

"I told you I would bother you no more after I said what I needed to say. I am a man of my word, Miss Kane."

214

Kaya didn't want to be Miss Kane. She wanted to be Kaya, his love. "Please don't go. Let me at least look at your wound. Please."

Rafael stared at her. The pain in his eyes told her everything. This man, shifter, whatever he was, cared for her. Deeply. "Please."

"Okay." He waited on her to grab her purse and computer bag then followed her inside.

"Let me get my first aid kit, I'll be right back." When she returned, he was standing exactly where she left him, looking lost. "Come sit down." He followed her to the kitchen where he sat in one of the ladder back chairs she pulled out for him. He sat sideways to give her access to the wound.

"Uh, Rafael, there's no bullet. Where did it go?" She examined his back, noticing the bandage from earlier was gone, and there was no visible wound, no sign he had been shot previously. "What the hell?"

"Our skin is such that it is nearly impenetrable. Surface scratches are pretty much the extent of any damage. The bullet is out in your driveway. I have a feeling that whoever is after me is using armor piercing rounds since they are indeed nicking the surface. Most bullets just bounce off." She was wiping an antiseptic over his skin as he spoke. He never flinched. "Can you feel that?"

"The medicine you are applying? Yes, I feel it, but it doesn't sting if that's what you are asking. Really, Kaya, it will heal itself in a matter of minutes. That is why Dante was so eager to tend to me earlier. It just wouldn't do for humans to watch my wound magically heal right before their eyes. What would they think?"

"And when you said earlier you heard the gun, you really did. Do you have super hearing? Is that how you knew? And this time too?" Kaya ran her fingers over his back, looking for evidence of his wings.

"Yes, our senses are enhanced." Rafael shivered at the touch of her fingers.

"Are you immortal, I mean can you be killed?" She couldn't believe she was having this conversation with him. It felt like she had slipped into an episode of the Twilight Zone.

"No and yes. I'm not immortal in the sense that I will live forever. Being King means I will always have a target on my back. Eventually, someone will come along and try to take my head. I can be killed by beheading and certain poisons."

"Is that what happened to your father?" She saw the pained look in his eye, and she wanted to kick herself for being so callous. "I'm sorry; I shouldn't have asked that."

"No, it's all right. My father was in a battle a couple hundred years ago with a shifter who wanted the throne. He thought if he killed my father he would become King. He blindsided my father and took his head. Fucking coward. His plan might have succeeded had he worked through all scenarios. He didn't."

"But if you're King, does that mean that you…" He nodded without looking at her face. She deserved to know the truth about him even if she thought less of him for it. "Yes, I defeated him and took the throne that was rightfully mine anyway."

Kaya was silent as she absently wiped at where the bullet should have embedded in his skin. "Back to the warehouse, why were you there?"

216

"After the first murders, I had Julian install security systems in all the warehouses. He did not have time to get one installed at that particular building. When I was clearing my head last night, I thought it prudent to do a fly-by on that location. Unfortunately, it had already been used as a dumping ground. I am sorry I didn't tell you earlier, but I just didn't know how or what to say. Telling you the truth about myself now has been difficult enough."

"There's another video. It shows three men at a warehouse. Are they your men?"

"I'll have to look at the video to be certain, but if it happened Friday, then I'm pretty sure who it will show."

Kaya moved to stand in front of him. "You have to admit it is a lot to take in for someone like me. Have you ever told another human what you are? Does anyone other than your kind know?" God, this was so hard to believe, but she had seen it with her own eyes. He shifted right in front of her and saved her life. Again.

"Yes, there are humans that know. Jonathan and Priscilla are human. Their family has been serving mine for hundreds of years."

"I thought you had servants because you are rich." Kaya knew the wealthy employed people to look after their households. "Priscilla and Jonathan are really nice and Priscilla seems to be very fond of you."

"She is like a mother to me. She adores you, that's for sure. She's hoping... Anyway, I do pay them well for the services they provide, but first and foremost they are family."

217

"I need to know about you, Rafael. Everything. Where do you come from, how old are you, are you married, have a girlfriend, kids, dogs?" She wanted more information. Could they even be together as a couple?

"My family originated in Italy. I am 573. I am not married nor have I ever been. I hope I have a girlfriend. I have no children as I have never been married, and dogs don't really like our kind."

"You have a girlfriend?" Kaya's heart sank. Why then did he ask her out? Was he trying to cover his tracks with the murders?

"Kaya, look at me. The term girlfriend seems so, I don't know, childish. But if that's the label you choose, I will gladly call you my girlfriend should you not turn me away after this night."

Oh, he was talking about her. Was she going to turn him away? No. She knew in her heart she couldn't watch Rafael walk out of her life. "How does this work? I mean, are your kind and mine compatible? Have shifters ever dated humans?" She saw him frown at her question. Uh oh.

"To tell you the truth, we are looking into that ourselves. Until you, none of my kind had ever felt the pull to a human, not that we knew of. Upon further research, we are finding there is the possibility it has happened before."

"What do you mean the pull?" So maybe she wasn't crazy. The intensity she felt in his presence, could that be the pull he was referring to? She felt like an addict and he was her drug.

"Our kind has one mate for life. When we meet that person, we feel a pull, a connection, and when we get together and commit to each other there is a bond. There are so few Goyle females left that most of us have gone our whole lives believing we would remain alone."

"What happened to all your women?"

"The females of our kind are a little different. For some reason, they don't get wing or the special skin. They are gifted with long lives, but they are susceptible to some human disease. Most, however, have died during childbirth."

"That's horrible. Why would they risk having children if they knew they could die?" Kaya wasn't feeling the maternal instinct right at that moment.

"For the family, for the species. When they died it was usually after having their tenth or eleventh offspring. It was done out of duty."

"Okay, I can see that. Back to this bond. Are you certain that's the pull you felt with me?"

"Kaya, when I met you, even before that, when I spoke to you for the first time on the telephone, you affected me. My body was in turmoil from your voice alone. That type of connection only happens with our mate. When you came to my office, I nearly passed out from the intensity of being so close to you. Did you feel anything when we met?"

How could she tell him what she felt without sounding like a wanton, desperate woman? "Yes, I felt something. It was strong, too. Are you telling me you don't have a choice in your mate? That if you go your whole life without meeting this one person, you have to live alone?"

"I don't have to live alone but I choose to do so. We are attracted physically to others, just as I'm sure you find human men enticing. We just don't feel the deep-rooted connection that bonds us to them for life. Some of the men have casual sex, but it isn't fulfilling."

Kaya really didn't want to know the answer to the question on her lips, but she asked it anyway. "And you, do you have casual, unfulfilling sex?" She couldn't look at him. If he said yes, it was going to rip her heart out.

"Love, look at me. No, I do not have casual sex. I have spent the last thirty odd years helping to rebuild our city, so it's been quite a while since I've lain with a woman."

"Thirty years is a long time to go without."

"Maybe for a human, but I'm over five hundred years old. Thirty years is but a blink of the eye to me. Besides, I have wanted no one until you. Further information on bonding with a human is necessary, but Kaya, I do believe you to be my mate. I feel it in the marrow of my soul. You and I are meant to be together. For eternity."

Chapter 38

Isabelle was having a hard time standing and observing. She wanted to help. As a doctor, it was in her to offer some type of relief from the pain, and Dane Abbott was in some serious pain. Tessa was the only one in the room with him, smoothing his hair back, offering soothing sentiments that obviously weren't working. It was like watching a woman giving birth with no epidural. You might have been through the process yourself, but the words of encouragement tended only to piss the patient off. Dane was pissed.

"Who the fuck did this to me?" He yelled at Tessa.

"I'd say your mother and father since that's who did it to me as well. Now calm down you big sissy and fucking breathe." Tessa's bedside manner left a lot to be desired. Surely Isabelle could do a better job of helping than her brash cousin. "It's hard to watch, isn't it?"

That voice. Isabelle knew that voice, but it couldn't be. Standing next to her, looking like she hadn't aged a day, was her mother. "Wha..." She couldn't form a word much less a question.

"Hello, Isabelle." Those eyes. Those were the eyes she had stared at every day when she was a little girl until one day they were gone. No goodbye, no explanation, just gone.

"Caroline, is that really you? Or are you just another sordid piece of this ever changing puzzle Tessa dropped in my lap?"

"It's really me. I'm sure you have a lot of questions, and I have the answers. Would you like to go somewhere and talk?" The woman acted as though she'd never left Isabelle alone with her father all those years ago.

"No, I prefer to stay here with my patient." She turned back to the glass separating her from Dane.

"Honey, there's nothing you can do for Dane. Tess has it under control."

"Tess? Boy, I guess I've missed out on the mother-daughter portion of my life huh?" Jealousy was a wasted emotion, but she couldn't help feeling that way toward her cousin. First her father, now her mother? Just how much time had Tessa spent with them? The better question was why?

"Why Tessa? Why not me? I'm smart; I'm a doctor. What is she? Does she even have an education?" She knew she was being a bitch, but her feelings were hurt, and she didn't care to let it show.

"Yes, you are a doctor and that is who we need you to be. The half-breeds are all coming into their transitions, and we would like for you to be there for them. We have spent the last thirty years tracking our people, keeping tabs on them. They are going to require a doctor who knows what they are and why they are different. That, my dear, is you.

"As for Tessa, she is a watcher. She tracks the offspring and helps them through their change. Many of your siblings have already gone through it. For those that haven't, Tessa keeps an eye on them and hopefully gets to them before their first time and helps ease them through it. We are tracking those who change to see if they have children and if those children are shifters as well. So far, there have only been a couple who have had children. We also haven't figured out the trigger.

Gargoyles are lucky. They are born with the inherent ability to phase at maturity. Half-bloods, not so much. We all have our roles to play."

Isabelle turned to look at her mother. "But Tessa said... never mind. How is it that you look my age? And what exactly is your role, mother?" Her mother flinched but quickly recovered.

"When a human woman bears a shifter child, the aging process slows drastically. It all but stops. And my role is just that: mother."

"How old are you? And how many children do you have?" Isabelle was feeling light headed. This had been a day for the books. She wasn't sure how much more she could take.

"I'm 245 and I have seventeen children. Victor and I decided you would be the last since I almost died during labor."

"I have sixteen brothers and sisters? Tessa left out a few." How long had she been awake? Almost forty-eight hours now. Surely she was hallucinating. A loud roar made her realize she was indeed lucid. She looked in on Dane and Tessa, and she couldn't believe her eyes. Standing in front of her was not her patient, but a monster with fangs, claws, and wings.

Kaya hung up the phone and sat down on the sofa beside Rafael. There was no family listed for Jorgenson in his file, so she didn't have to make the hard speech tonight. If she found a relative, she would call them. For now, she needed answers. She had shown him the first video, and he confirmed the three men were his cousins. She didn't appreciate being lied to, not only once but twice, but again, he explained it as hiding the identity of his species.

"So tell me about what you do. You said you fight the Unholy." She was having a really hard time keeping her hands to herself. Rafael was sitting on the couch in fatigues with no shirt. His broad chest and ripped abs were an artful masterpiece. She wanted to run her hands over every indention, every inch of olive skin.

"Have you ever wondered why your men rarely ever see the Unholy? We take the worst cases and lock them away ourselves. There is a sub-level for those monsters that don't deserve to see the light of day. Those creatures who would massacre your officers without blinking."

"Wait, you can't do that. You cannot decide who gets locked away, King or no King." Kaya spoke before she thought about it.

"Would you rather we let them run loose, killing wildly with no moral compass to stop them? Slow them even? Are you prepared with an army of your own to stop the worst of their kind? Kaya, we have been slaying the dragons since the beginning of time. We just happen to be facing a man-made dragon at present. Do you think you could really stop the worst of the Unholy?"

"It's just hard for me as an officer of the law to think there is a different type of justice being handed down than the one I promised to uphold. So what happens now?

"What do you mean?" Rafael was keeping his hands to himself, arms folded across his chest. This was the first time they had been together that he wasn't touching her in some way. She missed the connection. Screw it. She placed her hand on his thigh. The muscle jumped under her fingers, but she kept her hand where it was.

"Is there some sort of mind swipe you do that will make me forget what I know about you?"

She felt movement and looked up to see Rafael's chest shaking. Then he did something she would never forget. He tilted his head back and laughed out loud. The sound filled her with joy.

"Oh, Love. You watch too many movies. We don't have that capability, although it would be nice." His smile was brilliant. She removed her hand from his leg and placed it on his cheek. He closed his eyes and leaned into it. She stroked her thumb over the rough stubble. Was it just a few hours ago that his smooth face was rubbing against hers? Thinking back to earlier caused her body to tingle. His nostrils flared, and his eyes flew open.

"What? What's wrong? Please tell me you're not going to tackle me again."

Rafael grabbed her wrist and pulled her hand from his face. "It's been a long night. I should probably go and let you digest what I have told you. Should you wish to see me again, please let me know. If you decide not to, I'll abide by your wishes."

"Just tell me one thing. Did you only have sex with me because of this mate thing?"

"Kaya, you are beautiful, smart, sexy, driven, and strong. What man wouldn't want you? I admit, the bond drew me to you, but Love, I enjoyed every second of being with you. If I had my way, you would be in my bed from this moment forward. I cannot imagine not having you in my life, but it's your decision. I don't want you to feel like you have to be with me."

"But I do have to be with you." Kaya leaned her body over Rafael's and kissed his lips. She sat back and removed her sweatshirt then pressed her bare breasts against his chest. She pulled his lower lip into her mouth and sucked. Running her tongue along his jawline, she nipped at his jaw, remembering his reaction the last time. She was hoping for the same result. He turned his body so that one leg was along the back of the sofa, and the other was bent with a foot on the floor. This allowed her to rub against his growing erection.

She couldn't remember the last time she had gone down on someone, but she needed to have this man, her man, in her mouth. She kissed under his chin, in the curve of his throat. Working her way down she licked each nipple, biting one then the other. A growl came from his throat. She continued down his body, kissing, licking, biting, until she got to his waistband. She unbuttoned his pants and lowered the zipper carefully. She tugged his fatigues off his hips. His cock was ready for her. She wrapped her hand around it, watching Rafael's face as she did. He was studying her, his nostrils flaring. That intrigued her. He said his senses were enhanced. Could he smell her arousal? Could he tell how much she wanted him without touching between her legs?

She licked the head of his cock, eyes still locked on his. She ran the flat of her tongue from the base all the way up to the tip. When she got to the end, she swallowed him down as far as she could. Gripping the base, she bobbed up and down, each time taking him a little farther. When Kaya felt she could take him all the way, she moved her hand to his balls. His chest was rising and falling faster. Each of his breaths more ragged than the last. Knowing she was the cause of his arousal had Kaya turned on. The moans coming from her matched those Rafael was letting loose. She sucked him to the back of her throat and swallowed. Rafael growled and grabbed her hair. The pain to her scalp sent a delicious burn straight to her core. She continued a rhythm of sucking, licking and swirling.

"Fuck, that's good. Suck me down." Rafael's eyes were still connected with hers. "I'm so close, baby."

Kaya wanted to give this to him. Wanted to take this from him. She needed it. She went back to the rhythm that had his hips pumping down her throat. "Mmm." *That's it Rafael, fuck my mouth.* His thrusting into her mouth had her groaning louder. He was obviously enjoying the slurping and moaning. She added her hand and used the saliva from her mouth as lube.

"Kaya, oh gods. Fuck! I'm coming!" He yelled her name as his warm liquid coated the back of her throat. She swallowed everything he gave her. When he was no longer grinding his hips into her face, she licked the head one last time.

Chapter 39

Rafe was ready to propose. Right then and there. Watching Kaya's lips wrapped around his cock, then swallowing his come was better than he imagined. She gave something of herself to him with that selfless act. She could have stopped at any point, but she continued until he came. She did that for him. Was it possible she still wanted him even knowing what he was?

She slid her body up his, slowly, languidly. Her heavy breasts stroked his thighs as she moved farther up. Fuck, she was so sexy, all that blonde hair falling over her shoulders. Her blue eyes were filled with lust. She wanted him. That knowledge alone had his dick hardening again, for her. She licked her lips, and he pressed his mouth to hers, wanting to taste himself on her tongue. Goddamn that was so fucking erotic; his spunk mixed with the mint from her toothpaste mixed with her natural essence.

Their tongues swirled together, each demanding control. She was rubbing herself against his now hard erection. Rafael wanted to please his woman, return the favor. He circled her in his arms, one hand sliding down her back under the band of her sweats. Christ, did the woman never wear panties? He grabbed one cheek and squeezed, kneading the flesh. He slid his other hand down, gripping the other cheek. Massaging her toned ass, he pulled her cheeks apart, dipping one hand between her legs. Fuck she was so wet.

He wanted his tongue to replace his fingers. He began lowering her sweat pants when his phone rang in his cargo pocket. "Fuck me." He did an ab curl sitting up, pulling her up into his lap. "I'm so sorry, Love. I have to get that."

He dug his phone out of the pocket on the side of his pants and thumbed it on. "Rafe."

"My King, I am sorry to disturb you, but we have a situation at the Pen. I need all hands on deck. Dante told me to leave you be, but Rafael, I need you." Gregor never called Rafe unless he was in dire straits. "I'm on my way."

"I have to go. There is something going down at the prison, and I am needed."

"But you're King. Don't you have, I don't know, minions to take care of problems?"

"Sweetheart, I do not ask of my men that which I will not do myself." He stood, pulling her to her feet along with him. "I hate to leave you in such a state, but I promise to make it up to you. You should rest, yes?"

"Yes, but I won't. I'll be worried about you. Let me go with you. I am a cop after all." There was the rub. Before now, he admired her for what she did. Now that he knew she was his mate, he wanted nothing more than to shelter her and keep her from harm. His Kaya was a stubborn woman, and he was going to have his hands full going forward.

"No. Absolutely not. Kaya, I have to go, but please promise me you'll stay here. This isn't human business." He kissed her on the lips, hard. "I'll call you."

He knew better than to order her around, but she was in no way going anywhere near the Pen. He made his way through her house and out the back door to the cover of night. Without looking back, he phased and took to the skies.

229

He could feel when his brothers took his flank. He didn't have to look to know they were there. The soft flap of their wings filled the night as they rode the wind as one. Frey met them and filled them in on what was going down. "We have a breach in the lower level security. One of the Unholy got loose and went crazy. Gregor managed to detain him, but the others are still fighting amongst themselves."

"Do we have a plan?" Rafe knew Frey would have scoped it out and come up with the best solution.

"Yes, we split up into four teams, coming in from each of the corridors that are still blocked off. The stairwells leading down are clear. Luckily the fighting has been contained to the lower lever."

"Why don't we just let the fuckers kill each other?" Sixx asked the question that was on everyone's mind.

"Because Dr. Henshaw is stuck in the middle of the shit storm. We need to get him out before they find out he is hiding down there."

Gregor met the men at the back entrance to the upper level. Frey divided them into four squads, and they made their way down below. The plan was to detain as many as they could without killing them, but if push came to shove, they would shove back. Harder.

As always, Rafael was the first one to rush headlong into battle. He always had been. What he told Kaya was truth. He would not sit back and let someone else put their life on the line while he watched from the sidelines. He was strong and fearless and could fight with the best of them.

Pure pandemonium was underway. Rafe and his brothers spread out, taking down anyone who got in their path. When the Unholy caught on to the fact that they were not alone, they stopped warring with each other and turned on the Goyles. Fangs and claws extended, they let it rip. Literally.

During the cloning process, the Unholy had received fangs and claws but their skin remained as that of a human. The Unholy used their claws to thrash back at their attackers, but the Goyles were able to overpower them and put them back behind bars. It took a couple of hours and quite a bit of bloodshed, but Rafael and his brothers came away practically unscathed. The one casualty in the combat was the doctor. He was already dead when they got to him.

Tessa listened to her cousin and aunt verbally spar back and forth while she helped Dane through his transition. He was resting comfortably now that he had phased a few times with a little guidance. She felt sorry for Isabelle, having been kept in the dark all these years. Now she knew the truth and could begin to heal mentally and play her part in their world. They needed her now more than ever.

Isabelle got the last word in with her mother then walked away. Tessa was glad she insisted they take separate transportation. The doctor could go home and lick her wounds while Tessa stayed with Dane. The door opened, and her aunt came in. "How is he?"

"Very well. His last phase was almost painless; he's just worn out. His boss called again. Do we have a plan for her?"

Caroline shook her head. "Not until we speak to Dane. It's up to him if he wants to continue his life as a detective."

Tessa nodded looking at Dane. "Are you going to tell him the truth?"

"Not yet. I think he's been through enough for one day. We have to figure out the trigger, Tessa. If we knew what brought on the change, we could prepare them all for what's going to happen."

"I'm working on it. As a matter of fact, I think I'll go catch up on some sleep so I can start on that first thing." Tessa brushed Dane's hair off his forehead then stood. She grabbed her helmet but stopped at the door. "She'll come around." Not waiting for a response, she left the building. As tired as she was, she needed the feel of the engine rumbling between her legs while flying down the highway to ease her tension.

Tessa, unlike Isabelle, was blessed with the knowledge that her mother was alive and well. Even though Elizabeth was hidden away from the world, namely Gordon Flanagan, she was above ground and breathing, and Tessa could visit anytime she wished. Tessa also knew the trigger, but was keeping it to herself. That knowledge was not something she wanted to share just yet.

Her thoughts were brought to the here and now by a lone set of headlights behind her. Tessa knew these roads well and didn't hesitate to test the waters. Without signaling, she leaned the bike low, taking the exit ramp quickly. Lights flickered then appeared behind her again. At the bottom of the ramp, she leaned once more, taking the right turn then straightened and opened the throttle wide. The car fishtailed at the bottom of the ramp, corrected, and continued after her. *Fuck a duck! Who the hell is after me now?* Thankful it was the middle of the night and there was no traffic, Tessa wove her way through back streets and side roads until she was able to shake her tail. She stayed hidden until she felt it was safe to move on.

Chapter 40

Kaya had Rafael pinned to the stone wall. She should arrest him; he was guilty. The need to fuck him was overriding all sensibility. He could overpower her at any moment, but he was standing still, allowing her to have her way with him. She grabbed the collar of his shirt, pulling his face down to hers. This time it was her that crushed their mouths together. Kaya couldn't get enough, never enough. It was like she needed his breath to sustain her. He was fisting her hair as she was trying to climb his body. God, she had to have him, now. She didn't care that they were in public. Rafael pulled back and asked, "Where is he? Who's watching the boy?"

Kaya was then sitting on a park bench watching her little boy play on the jungle gym. He slid down the slide, laughing as he landed on his bottom instead of his feet. He jumped up, brushed the dirt off his shorts, and did it again. Her heart was full as she watched her son enjoying life. A shadow fell over her head, and as she looked up, she was grabbed around the neck, being pulled from the bench by an Unholy. She couldn't breathe. She clawed at the thick hands holding her but she was too weak.

She focused on her child, sliding down, landing and laughing. He looked to his momma to see her laughter only she wasn't laughing. *No baby NO! Stay where you are.* She couldn't speak. Her air was being cut off. She looked back to her son who was now a Gargoyle. His little body sprouted wings. He was flying in a rage toward his momma's attacker with fangs bared and claws outstretched. Her attacker released her neck and went after her child.

"NO!" Kaya sprang up in bed, grabbing her neck. Chest heaving, she felt the tears slide down her cheeks. Oh God, would that be her son? If she and Rafael had children, would she have a little Gargoyle? Could she watch her baby become a shifter?

"You're getting ahead of yourself, Kane." She didn't know if she could have Rafael's baby with her being a human. Did she even want to? After the way he left her last night, not allowing her to go with him, she wasn't sure. Yes, she was a woman, but she didn't become chief by being a delicate flower. She may be a rose, but by God, she bore the thorns too. And just because his brother ran the prison did not mean they controlled her.

Shaking off the dream, she headed for the shower. She thought back to the video and what was on it. If Rafael and his men were patrolling as he told her, then someone else could know about him and his kind. Why send her the video? Were they trying to frame him for the murders or alert her to the fact that he was not what he appeared to be? What about the attempts on his life? Someone really wanted him dead. Thinking about the shootings, Rafael wasn't shot until he covered her. "Oh my God, they aren't after him; they're trying to kill me." She sank down in the tub while the water beat down on her head.

She really shouldn't be surprised. After all, she was the chief of police. It was her job to put away scum. As soon as she got to the station she would see who was recently let out on parole. Regardless of who the arresting officer was, it was ultimately her responsibility to put people behind bars. Once all the hot water was used up, she got out and dried off. Without Rafael to save her skin, she would have to be more diligent about watching her own back. How would she know if a sniper were hidden in the trees or across the street? *Shit.*

Maybe she would work from home today. Any reports she needed to file could be done tomorrow. She could find the list of parolees online. The ME's report could also be sent via email. The medical examiner. Dante was a shifter. Gregor and Julian Stone were shifters. Geoffrey Hartley and the two men in the video: shifters. Who else was one of Rafael's kind that she had met and never knew?

She watched the charm bracelet slide up and down her arm as she combed through the tangles of her wet hair. *Bella Mia.* How could she have become his this quickly? The mating pull, as he called it, was the only explanation. Kaya was losing her heart to Rafael a little at a time and she hoped the feelings he had for her were genuine.

She dressed in jeans and a thermal, just in case she had company. She never wore a lot of make-up so there was no use in starting today. She made a pot of coffee then sat down to get busy.

Rafael called a meeting at the manor. The men wouldn't mind getting up early if Priscilla was going to feed them. He had gone to enjoy the solitude of the garden before the others arrived. Footsteps on the walkway alerted him to Nikolas who handed him a cup of coffee before sitting next to him. They both sat quietly, enjoying the peacefulness.

Nik finally broke the silence. "I think both the daughter and the redhead, Tessa, know more than they are telling. Especially Tessa. I can't quite figure her out. She was too coolheaded. It was as though shifter blood was running through her veins. Soon after our conversation they both left so I followed. They drove to a large house over by the University. I checked the ownership, and it's registered in the doctor's name. The weird thing was she didn't seem to know the place. Tessa had to point out which door to go in. I want to go back when it's dark to check it out."

"Very good. Let's finish this conversation inside. I'll be up in a few minutes." Nikolas took his empty cup and left his cousin in peace. Rafael enjoyed the solitude for a few minutes longer then joined the rest of his Clan.

Once they were all seated around the table with their plates full, Rafael asked Nik to repeat what he'd told him about the doctor and Tessa. When he was finished Rafe said, "If Montague was a shifter, he could be alive and the girls could know where he is. If what Nik feels is true about this Tessa, it's possible that she and the doctor both have shifter blood being related to Montague. We need someone to get closer to the doctor, see if we can get information on the lost journals. Gregor, what do you think about interviewing the doctor for your physician's job at the Pen?"

"It's an excellent idea. We have an opening so asking her to apply would not be far-fetched. Nikolas, text me her number and I'll give her a call."

Rafe let the men finish their food before he approached the next subject. "I have something to tell you and it's not pretty." He pushed his plate of untouched food away from him. "Last night there was an incident. Another shooting." He waited for the chatter to die down before he continued. "I am almost certain someone is after Kaya. Before I get to that, I have to start at the beginning. Last night, I brought Kaya over here for dinner. Things went well, and let's just say I'm positive she's my mate. Those details I will keep to myself.

"Julian placed his call and we drove to the warehouse, as you all know. Afterwards, I drove her home and we talked for a few minutes, but I left her so she could do some work. I came home, dropped off the car, and flew back to her house. When I got there she was upset. Someone sent her a video of me at the warehouse the night I found the detective. She was ready to arrest me. She had been sent a video of Frey, Lorenzo, and Jasper as well, but it wasn't a clear picture.

"I had to make a decision; tell her the truth, or allow her to think I'm a killer and put me in cuffs. When I tell you she's my mate, I believe that with everything I am, so I told her the truth."

"How much of the truth?" Gregor was stony faced as usual, this time for good reason.

"All of it. Now before you call for my crown, hear me out. Her gun was drawn. She was ready to shoot. I showed a little fang and claw and gave her time to digest it. That's when I heard the slide of the rifle so I phased and took a bullet."

"Wait, you phased, as in fully?" This was coming from Frey who was looking as surprised as Gregor.

"Yes. That's when I knew without a doubt that she is my mate. I didn't have control over the shift. I really didn't have much choice in telling her everything considering I had her wrapped in wings. So I told her about us and explained the bond. I trust her or I wouldn't have told her."

"I trust her too. I've worked with her for years, and she's a good woman and a great cop. It will be nice to have her in the know. Easier to explain things that I just happen to figure out quickly." Dante crossed his arms over his chest as if to say that was the end of the discussion. He did have the respect of all the men so it wasn't surprising when they all just nodded and murmured, "Okay."

"We need to figure out who is trying to kill her, and why, *and* who the fuck got us on video. Has there been any movement at the warehouses?"

"So far no, but it would probably be wise to add extra security to Miss Kane's house if hers isn't sufficient," Julian reported.

"I agree. I will check it out the next time I'm there. Frey, I want you to set up around the clock security detail for Kaya. Until we figure out who's behind this, I want her covered. Coming and going."

"Is she okay with this?" Frey asked.

"I didn't ask. She's my mate. I don't care if she doesn't want it, she is getting it. I don't have to tell you all how important it is that we find this fucker. Julian, if I get you Kaya's computer do you think you can find where the videos came from?"

"Yes, I can figure it out. How long it takes depends on how well he triangulated the feed."

"Good. Then if you all will excuse me, I am going to shower and head to her house."

Chapter 41

Isabelle was sipping a cup of tea, trying to enjoy the quiet morning. All the questions from the past few years were now answered. Well, most of them anyway. The missing journals, the strange experiments, and the blood samples with odd chromosomes were all explained in one conversation. Those answers only brought more questions, though. Where had her mother been? If Gordon wasn't Tessa's father then who was? Was Dane really her brother? Where and who were her other siblings? She could ask her mother for answers, but she wasn't sure she wanted to. Of course, the obvious person to ask was Tessa.

She didn't want to see her cousin right now either, not really. Tessa could have told her the truth all along, but like the rest of her family, she decided to keep the truth from her. Since Tessa had already been through the change, she must know who her mate was, but why did she not want Caroline to know the trigger? There was a knock on her door, but she ignored it. She didn't want to deal with anyone right now. She just wanted to relax and wallow in her own jealous misery.

"Isabelle?" Tessa was coming through the house searching for her.

"My door was locked for a reason. What did you do, pick the lock?" It wouldn't surprise her if she had. Nothing her rebellious cousin did would ever surprise her again.

"No, silly, I have a key. I thought you might want to talk some more, you know, now that you watched Dane go through his transition."

"You mean since I was blindsided with the fact you're nice and cozy with my mother who looks my age." Isabelle stood and walked past her, not bothering to be hospitable. She poured more hot water into her cup and added a teabag. Standing at the kitchen counter, she silently dunked the bag up and down in the water.

"Hey Belle, don't be mad. It wasn't my decision to keep your mother's *condition* from you. If it were up to them, you still wouldn't know. I think you can help us better by knowing the truth of who and what we are."

"And just who is *them*? My parents? If you tell me nothing else, tell me the truth now, Tessa. Is my father really alive?" She stopped with the teabag and waited.

Sighing, Tessa sat down at the kitchen table, stretching her boots out in front of her. She leaned back and hooked her elbow over the top of the chair. "Yes."

"Yes? That's it, yes? Not yes Isabelle, he's alive and well, and he and your mother have been hiding out in the South of France creating more little half-blood monsters?"

"Yes, Isabelle, he is alive and well and he and your mother have been living their lives away from the Goyles. They are not having more children, and I take offense that you just called me a monster. You are a half-blood. Are you calling yourself a monster?"

Isabelle pulled the teabag out of her cup and took a sip of the hot liquid. "Tell me this, cousin, how many brothers and sisters do you have? If Gordon isn't your father, who is? Please tell me Jonas is not your father, and you are not one of my many siblings I didn't know I had."

"Of course I'm not your sister. You know that Elizabeth is my mother. After she married Gordon she met one of your father's nephews, another full-blood. She was his mate. The passion mates feel for each other is explosive, sometimes to the point of being volatile. My mother had an affair, and I'm the product of that tryst. Long story short, Gordon was already becoming a tyrant before I was born. When I was cloned, Jonas made sure they had an exit strategy in place.

"My biological father took my mother and me, and we disappeared. Jonas took my brother and disappeared as well. The bombing at the clinic was the perfect cover for his assumed death. He has lived with your mother ever since, just in secrecy. As for my siblings, I only have Tamian."

"How can Jonas be a Gargoyle if they don't age? Last time I saw my father he looked sixty something."

"Do you remember the Mission Impossible movies? You know, with that old guy, Tom Crash, Tom Cross..."

"Tom Cruise?"

"Yeah him. In the movies, they used biometric scanners and a latex polymer to make them look like other people. Of course, some of that was smoke and mirrors, but who do you think developed that polymer that was used in the masks?"

"Let me guess, my father." What hadn't the man created?

"Yes, your father. Any time he was in public he was wearing a prosthetic. Belle, he looks as young as your mom does."

"Did you already know about Dane when we went to his apartment? Is that why you were there so quickly? And why don't you want Caroline to know that you know the trigger?"

"Yes, I've been watching Dane for a while and like I already told you, your father was kicked out of the Inner Circle for mixing with humans. If one of our mates happened to be a full-blood, that wouldn't go over well with them. I'm afraid they would try to keep us separated somehow."

"You've transitioned. Who is your mate? You have to know."

The phone ringing broke up their discussion. "Hello?"

"Dr. Sarantos?" A very deep voice was on the other end of the line.

"Yes, who is this?" She watched Tessa come out of her chair, eyes wide.

"Gregor Stone. Dr. Sarantos, I'm the Warden at New Atlanta State Penitentiary, and I have recently had an opening I would like to speak with you about."

"Mr. Stone, I have a job. I own my practice, and I have no interest in working for you." Tessa was waving her arms and shaking her head no.

"You haven't heard the offer. Please, at least hear me out. Allow me a few moments of your time and then decide."

"Isabelle, you can't. Your family needs you." Tessa must be using her super hearing to eavesdrop on the conversation. Screw them. Her family hadn't needed her for the past thirty two years; they could continue on without her.

"All right, Mr. Stone, I will listen to your offer. When would you like to meet?" She turned her back on her cousin who was now cursing like a biker. Hmm, fitting.

"Are you available this afternoon? It is crucial we hire a doctor soon, and whether you agree or not, I want to get the ball rolling."

"This afternoon is fine, Mr. Stone. Is one o'clock good for you?"

"That is perfect. I will see you then." They said their goodbyes, and Isabelle hung up the phone.

"What the fuck are you doing, Belle? Did you not hear me tell you we need you now? Your brothers and sisters are going to require a doctor who knows about them and can help them through the change!" Tessa was throwing her arms around dramatically.

"Oh, I heard you all right. I also heard the rest of what you said. I haven't accepted the position yet, but I do think it would be an interesting change of pace. I have been feeling stifled and bored. I am at least going to meet with the man."

"Then I'm going with you. Do you even know the kind of monsters they put away there? Jesus H! You think I'm a monster? Belle, you haven't seen anything yet. Have you ever come across an Unholy? *That's* the kind of monsters you're going to be dealing with there, not your family."

"How do you know who they keep in the prison? It doesn't matter. Come with me or not. I don't care. I'm at least going to see what the Warden has to say." Isabelle left her cousin standing in the middle of the room while she went to shower.

Dane was phasing with little trouble. He had stayed awake most of the night trying to come to terms with his new body and all he'd learned. Caroline stayed with him, talking him through each change. He preferred the cute redhead until he found out she was his cousin somewhere down the line. Even though he shouldn't be, he was shocked to learn that Dr. Sarantos was his sister.

"Dane, I assure you, Isabelle was unaware of your relationship until last evening. Our family is divided on how to handle the shifters who are coming into their own. The full-bloods do not know that any of you exist. Oh, they may have met you, but they don't know that it's possible for humans to mate with shifters. My husband and I want to keep this knowledge hidden if possible. The Gargoyles turned their backs on Victor when he rebelled against them to be with me.

"We would love for you to work with us in some capacity. Tessa has her hands full with your brothers and sisters, especially since we don't know what causes the shift. So far, there is not a common thread that we can find. If you decide to continue in your current position, we will support you. You will be better equipped to battle the Unholy."

For Dane it really wasn't a hard choice. Being a cop was all he knew, and he was good at his job. He enjoyed it and if being a shifter gave him an added advantage in catching the bad guys, then all the better. "So the Unholy, do you know how that happened?"

Caroline sat down beside him. She had tears in her eyes when she told him, "Unfortunately, yes. Gordon Flanagan and his men came across one of my sons, Gabriel. He was in the beginning of his transition. When Flanagan saw what Gabriel was, he abducted him and kept him drugged. For months, we searched for him to no avail. Finally, when the scientists had no further use for him, they threw his lifeless body in the river. The fact that he managed to pull himself out of the water and find his way home was nothing short of a miracle.

"When he came back to us, he was a shell of the man he used to be: traumatized to the point of deep depression. The scientists had talked around him, thinking he wouldn't be alive to tell what he overheard. They used Gabriel's blood in their clones. We believe that because he was between human and shifter, his blood had anomalies the scientists didn't synthesize properly. Instead of creating a strong shifter, they ended up spawning monsters. The Unholy are stronger and faster than humans, but they cannot control their shifting. Once they transition the first time they usually cannot change back.

"We did the best we could by him. His girlfriend, Rebekah, tried to help, but Gabriel pushed her away. Isabelle was just a toddler. For a while, Gabriel wouldn't have anything to do with any of the family except for her, but even she couldn't save him. Eventually Gabriel disappeared. We haven't seen him in almost thirty years."

That was all Dane needed to hear to know he was making the right decision in returning to the precinct. He would take a couple more days until he was sure the phasing was under control, and then he'd call Kaya and get back to work.

Chapter 42

Kaya looked at her ringing phone. Rafael. "Hello?"

"Good afternoon, Miss Kane. Do you feel like company?" He sounded hopeful, and she wasn't getting anything accomplished.

"If you are referring to yourself, then I would love some company, Mr. Stone. How soon can you be here?" There was a knock on her front door.

Kaya pulled back the curtain to see Rafael grinning at her. She unlocked the door and took in his appearance. He was dressed in faded jeans and an untucked button-up shirt. The sleeves were rolled up, showing his muscular forearms. She liked him in dress clothes, but she loved him casual. He didn't give her time to say hello. Grabbing behind her neck, he pulled her mouth to his and kissed her like he hadn't seen her in days, not hours.

When he finally pulled his lips away, he leaned his forehead to hers. "Hello, Love." Those two words left her breathless. There it was again. She should probably protect her heart, but the way this man had her body pulsing was beyond anything she could ever imagine.

"Do you want to come in or are we going to stand in the open?" She looked behind him. "How did you know I wasn't at work?" They both disconnected their phones.

"Because you're being watched." He pulled her into her living room. "Speaking of open doors, I want to talk to you about your security system among other things. Can we sit, please?"

249

She led him to her sofa, and they sat side by side. She turned to face him, angling her knee between them. He pulled her leg across his lap and began massaging her calf. "Kaya, I want you to allow Julian to upgrade your security system. Until whoever is after me is caught, I want to add a security detail to you as well."

"That would be much appreciated. You probably thought I would argue with you but honestly? I'm scared. And I don't think the shooter was after you. Think about it. Both bullets hit you after you covered me. I think I'm the target."

"I am not happy you were the target, but I am glad you figured it out on your own. I know you are a strong, smart woman, not some damsel in distress. I agree with your assessment, I just didn't want to scare you. And make that three bullets. Julian took one at the warehouse on Saturday."

"You must be mistaken. He didn't tackle me."

"No, he was more subtle. Remember the sneeze? That was actually a grunt covering the blow to his back."

"Holy crap. And the jacket?"

"Was to cover the wound. We all keep extra shirts and jackets in our vehicles for incidents such as that. Now, I have a favor to ask. Can you do without your laptop for a few hours?"

"I can, but I shouldn't. Rafael, that's Government Issue." She could get in a lot of trouble if anyone found out he had access.

"It'll just be for a couple of hours, I promise. I want Julian to see if he can find out where the video originated. If we can find the sender, we may be able to locate the shooter."

"What makes you think Julian can find it better than my department?"

"We have a state of the art tech facility at our disposal, and we have a Julian. Kaya, I trust you to keep this to yourself. If the government ever finds about us and our abilities, it wouldn't bode well for anyone."

"Rafael, your secret is safe with me. Who would believe me anyway?"

"So, you'll let us have your laptop?"

"Yes, as long as I get it back today."

"I promise." Rafael dialed a number and put his phone to his ear. "Jules, you can have it. You have three hours." He hung up, and there was a knock at the door. "That would be Julian."

"You're pretty sure of yourself aren't you?" She wasn't annoyed, not really. Not when he was trying to find out who was trying to kill her. She pulled her leg from his lap and stood, going to the dining room table to retrieve her computer. He followed behind, stopping in the opening to the kitchen. "No, I'm pretty sure of you." The look on his face was filled with another emotion she couldn't recognize. Maybe someday she would be able to read all of his looks.

"Here you go." She handed him the laptop bag. He carried it outside and handed it off to Julian, who was waiting on the porch, scanning the surroundings. "Miss Kane, I will have this back to you soon. Would it be convenient for me to upgrade your security at that time?"

"Yes, that's perfect. Oh, and thank you. Rafael told me you took a bullet for me. You saved my life."

Julian didn't immediately respond. He seemed to be thinking about his answer then finally whispered, "It was my honor." He looked to Rafe. "I'll just be going."

"Wait, he doesn't have my password."

Rafael shut the door and took Kaya's hand, leading her back to the sofa. "Trust me, he won't need it. Now, there's one more thing we should talk about." He waited until she was seated and once again had her leg stretched over his. She really liked sitting like that. "As I already explained, once Gargoyles reach maturity, we stop aging. When that happens, we have to either remain in isolation as I choose to do, or change locations and start over. One of my Clan, Jasper, recently came to me from out west. He is going to put in his application with your department tomorrow."

"That shouldn't be a problem. I'm down two detectives so the added personnel will be welcomed." Rafael grabbed Kaya's ankle and directed her leg behind him on the sofa so he was between her legs. "Good, because I'm tired of talking."

He released the button from its hole and slowly unzipped her jeans. Each tooth being released from its counterpart made the anticipation almost unbearable. He pulled her pants down her legs. She raised up making it easier on him then watched as he tossed her jeans onto the floor. Every movement he made was graceful yet powerful.

In this position she was wide open to him. He was staring at her pussy like he was looking over a

252

menu filled with all his favorite foods. Without taking his eyes off her core, he asked, "Do you even own panties, Miss Kane?"

"Yes, I just prefer to not wear them. Uh, Rafael..."

"Shhh." Slowly, like a big cat stalking his prey, he placed his hands on her inner thighs. He pushed her knees to her chest so that her legs were even farther apart. "Absolutely perfect." Rafael lowered his mouth to the inside of her knee and nipped at the tender skin. He alternated legs, kissing and biting his way closer to where she wanted him to be.

"Rafael, please." He placed his thumbs on either side of her wet lips and pulled them apart, massaging just inside. He let his tongue tease her clit while his thumbs tormented her. "More, oh God, more." She pressed herself into his face, trying to coax him into going faster.

"The first introduction of my face to your pussy should not be rushed. You will get what you need; I promise. In giving you what you need, I am going to take what I want and that, Bella Mia, is time. I am going to take my slow (lick) sweet (lick) time (lick) worshiping at the altar of my Queen."

His tongue, along with his words, were sparking a fire in her nerve endings. His thumbs were replaced with first one finger, then two. Those digits were like the rest of the man, thick. His two fingers filled her up almost as much as his cock had. His mouth lavished her aching clit. He alternated between licking and sucking. Her blonde curls didn't deter his feast. The moans and growls coming from her lover were proof enough that he was enjoying himself.

Kaya leaned up and pulled her thermal over her head, tossing it in the vicinity of her jeans. Her hands found her breasts where she pulled on her nipples. Rafael was looking at her, eyes dark. She really wanted to close her eyes, but she was frozen in place. It was like he cast a spell on her, forbidding her to look away. With their gazes locked, he continued stoking the fire.

She wanted to touch him. Removing one hand from her breast, she reached out with a fingertip, touching his tongue as it licked her clit. She dipped that wet fingertip inside herself, pumping in rhythm with his fingers. She pulled her finger out and stuck it in her mouth, tasting her own juices. Rafael growled like a feral animal. Kaya gasped when she noticed his fangs. Holy shit! The fact that her lover was sucking on the tenderest part of her body with teeth sharper than knives protruding from his mouth should scare her. Instead, it prompted her orgasm to rip through her body, the nerve endings exploding back inside.

The lack of heat from her thighs brought her back to reality. She looked to where Rafael should be, but instead, he was across the room, chest heaving. The wave of her orgasm that was crashing into the rocks turned tide and rolled back out to sea when Rafael growled, "Kaya, RUN!"

Chapter 43

Tessa and Isabelle arrived at the security gate outside the Pen. Isabelle rolled her window down. "Dr. Isabelle Sarantos to see the Warden."

The guard bent over and peered in the window at Tessa. "Identification please, Dr. Sarantos. Who's this?" he gestured to Tessa. "I'm her body guard." She shoved her driver's license into his hand.

"Stay here." He went into the guard shack and typed something into a computer then picked up the phone.

Tessa smiled at the guard as he looked at her, probably calling the Warden to get permission for her entry. He came back to the car, returning their I.D.s. "Follow the drive all the way around to the back. You will be escorted to Warden Stone's office."

He raised the security barrier and allowed them to proceed. Tessa mentally made notes of everything she saw. The building was a tall monstrosity with guard towers situated at all four corners of the property. Thirty foot tall chain linked fence was topped with razor.

Isabelle parked in a designated visitor spot and turned the engine off. She hadn't spoken one word since they left the house. Now she turned and looked at Tessa. "I have one question. I take it Alexi wasn't my mate since I didn't transition when we were married. If he and I had a child, would that child be like me or human?"

Tessa stared at her cousin. "Belle, *did* you have a child with Alexi?"

255

"No, of course not, I'm just curious as to how all this works."

"Honestly, I have no idea. You and a couple others are the only ones who have married someone that wasn't your mate, and as far as I know, neither of them have children."

"So, for those of us who have no idea what we are and get married to someone who isn't our mate, what happens when we meet our mate while married? Does everyone have an affair like Elizabeth did? Is it that strong of an attraction?"

Tessa winced when Belle mentioned her mother. "It depends on the person I guess. My mother was married to a monster. She lived her life in constant fear so when she met my father it was a blessing. If she had never met him, she probably wouldn't be here. I definitely wouldn't be here."

Their conversation was interrupted by a knock on the window. A security guard was waiting to escort them inside. They both exited the car and the guard said, "Dr. Sarantos, Miss Blackmore, please follow me."

Once inside, Tessa made note of the number of guards and where they were situated. The Warden's office was located down an interior hallway. They were ushered to a waiting room filled with standard hardback chairs and asked to please wait. They both sat, looking at nothing in particular. Isabelle turned and whispered, "I would appreciate if you would stay out here. I amused you by allowing you to tag along, but what the Warden wishes to speak to me about is really none of your business."

"Sure, whatever you want." Tessa didn't care to come face to face with *the* Gregor Stone anyway. The guard returned for Isabelle, "The Warden will see you now." Isabelle rose and followed him into the inner office.

Tessa glanced around, taking in her surroundings. She heard voices coming down the hall, one of those voices she knew as well as her own. Tamian. She walked to the door and peeked around the corner. Her brother was in handcuffs coming down the hall. The guard leading him stopped when he saw Tessa. "Excuse me, Ma'am." She stepped back into the waiting area, and Tamian was escorted in then pushed into a seat.

Tamian glanced at Tessa, frowning. *Andrea, what the hell are you doing here?*

Tessa reached out with her mind. *"Hello, Brother. Forget why I'm here. Why the hell are you here? I saw the arrest on TV. This is bullshit. I'm going to get you out of here."*

"No, you can't. I'm supposed to be in here."

"You are the last person who belongs in here, Tam. Don't worry, I'll get you out."

"No Andi, you don't understand..." The inner office door opened, and Isabelle appeared along with the guard from earlier. She turned back toward the office, "Thank you, Warden Stone, I'll be in touch." She walked past Tessa and asked, "Are you ready?"

Tessa looked at Tamian. *"Don't worry, Brother, I'll get you out of here and Tam, don't EVER call me Andrea."*

"Andi no. Andi! ANDREA!" Tamian was shouting out loud. Just the distraction she needed.

When they were once again in the privacy of Isabelle's car, Tessa asked her, "Well, how did your

257

meeting go? I'm sure the Warden was as charming as ever."

"It went well. How do you know Mr. Stone? I didn't realize the two of you had met, or I wouldn't have rushed you out."

"I don't know him; I just bumped into him once." Literally. "So, are you going to take the job?"

"It's a big decision, one I have to think about. It's not just me I have to consider."

"You're right; you have the family to think about."

"Yes, family." Isabelle slipped into silence and drove them back to her house. Tessa had no idea what was going through her cousin's head. She only hoped she made the right decision.

Rafe was doing everything within his power to gain control of his inner beast. Gods, Kaya had to be scared out of her mind. Here he was, fangs out, yelling at her to run. His eyes were closed so he could concentrate. Unholy... think about Unholy. Anything but the beautiful woman who just rocked his fucking world by doing nothing more than tasting her own essence. Godsdamn Kaya. He didn't know how much more he could withstand.

"Rafael." Her soft voice was right in front of him. Her hands were on his biceps, gently caressing him.

He opened his eyes to see his woman braving his rage. "Kaya." His voice was tormented, even to his own ears.

"Rafael, look at me. See me. I am not running. You will not hurt me, I know this. I understand though. If I had fangs of my own, they would be out now. I would want to bite you, mark you as mine. Maybe that is not what happens with your kind but I feel so connected to you that *I* want to bite *you*."

"Kaya, you don't know what you're saying. To my kind, the bite completes the bonding. That is why I disappeared last night. You didn't know what I was, and I couldn't get my fangs to retract. I was so close to biting you that I had to retreat into the house. I know you felt disillusioned. I heard you talking to yourself. But Love, you have to know that what you were thinking was so far from the truth. Having sex with you sent me over the edge. I was so close to hitting bottom that I panicked."

Kaya pulled his face down to hers and ran her tongue over the tip of one of his fangs. Fuck! She didn't realize how sharp they were. He could smell the blood in her mouth. Instead of gasping or crying out, she stuck her tongue out and removed the blood with the tip of her finger. She stared at it like it were a scientific experiment and then she surprised him. Looking in his eyes, she stuck her finger in her mouth and sucked.

Rafe's cock was throbbing in his pants. It had been hard when he was going down on her, but seeing Kaya lick the blood caused by his fang had him hardening to the point of passing out. "Kaya." He groaned out her name.

"Rafael." She placed her hands on his face. "Will you hurt me? Truly cause bodily harm to me? Or are you feeling the effects of the bond to the point you want to mark me? Because let me tell you, I trust you with my body, with my life, my soul. Normally I'm a rational woman. What this is between us doesn't make sense. We've known each other a few days. Had you asked me before we met if I thought love at first sight was possible, I'd have said no. But now?" She shrugged a shoulder.

"What are you saying?" Rafe was feeling light-headed. All the stimulation was too much to take, even for King of the Gargouille.

"I'm saying I'm falling for you. In my brain, I know it's too soon. In my heart, it's not. I want you in my life, and I feel if I don't have you I will stop breathing."

Rafael's heart was overfull. This time a week ago, all hope was gone at finding a mate and having children to carry on the Di Pietro name. Now, it was so much more than that. This woman loved him, he knew it as well as he knew his own name.

The look in her eyes was all the confirmation he needed. The doorbell rang, and his fangs retracted. "Get dressed, Love. That would be Julian."

Rafe waited until Kaya had snagged her clothes from the floor and disappeared into the bathroom to redress. He peered out the side window to see his cousin waiting patiently on the front porch. "Julian, please come in."

Chapter 44

Kaya checked herself in the mirror then went back into the living room. Julian handed the laptop to her. "I found him. The man who sent the email is Vincent Alexander. I had to dig past some extensive firewalls. I have Nikolas doing a background search on him, but so far, he's a real piece of work. Juvenile records were sealed, so it appears Mr. Alexander has been trouble from a young age, if he is indeed the real Alexander.

"I have multiple addresses and aliases. Most addresses are no longer valid, but a couple of them are. I have a team spread out, and they are searching his locations as we speak. He won't be hard to spot since he's an albino. At this time, I can't categorize him as an Unholy, but there is something off about him. He may be a clone."

"You can't just go around searching people's houses without a warrant." The law she'd upheld for years was always forefront in her mind.

"Kaya, the man is trying to kill you. I know you don't want to hear this, but when dealing with Unholy, we don't always abide by your laws. We do what we have to so that the streets of New Atlanta are somewhat safer than they would be otherwise." Rafael was pacing the floor. "I need to get out there, help search."

"My King, please, stay here and guard Miss Kane. We are patrolling the area and will continue to do so until this Alexander is found."

"Julian said he isn't an Unholy. If that's true, we have to get a search warrant. I'd say the judge will agree we have probable cause seeing as he's tried to kill me, but he's going to want to know where the evidence is. I haven't spoken to CSU about the bullet casing that was found. I need to get to the office and do my job instead of hiding out here."

Julian pulled a plastic bag out of his pocket. "The bullet that hit me was from an L115 sniper rifle. The casing I found that hit Rafael was also from an L115. Several of those particular rifles have been found in one of Alexander's apartments. I use the term apartment loosely."

"You took a bullet? Mr. Stone, that is tampering with evidence." Julian looked bored. "Okay, I'll overlook that. But gentlemen, we really have to follow the rules so that when you do capture him we can put him away. If the court finds out the evidence was not gathered in the proper manner this Alexander will walk, and we will be right back where we started."

"Not if he's in the Basement." Rafael turned to Julian. "Go find him. You have two hours until I join the search."

"What about the security upgrade?"

"I will protect Kaya for now. You go find this fucker."

"Yes, my King. Miss Kane, again it was a pleasure." The younger Mr. Stone left to do Rafael's bidding. Kaya wasn't sure she could do this, not and be chief too.

"Rafael, I made a promise to uphold the law and what just happened, well that's not the way I do things. If you are going to continually usurp my authority..." Rafael didn't let her finish. He pulled her tightly to his chest and kissed her softly. Ever the dichotomy this man.

"Kaya, I rarely break your human laws, and when I do, it's only for the greater good of humankind. The laws we break are so that you don't have to. If my breaking the law and keeping you safe means that we cannot be together, then so be it. It would kill me for you to walk out of my life; but I would rather watch you from afar, knowing you're alive and well, than sit back and do nothing while this monster continues to target you."

"What is the basement? Is it exactly as it sounds?" She wasn't certain she wanted to know.

"Yes, it's the lowest level of the Pen where we put the Unholy to keep them away from the other inmates."

"I don't know what to say. I need to think. I am almost certain I cannot walk out of your life, but where does that leave me in my job? If I continue to act as chief and knowingly allow you to run shod of the rules, I would be lying. I need time."

"I honestly don't understand your dilemma. Did you not become a police officer to get the scum off the street?" Rafael backed up but was still holding her hands.

"Yes, you know I did. But I also took an oath." She tried to pull away, but he wouldn't let her.

"As did Dante. He's a doctor for the gods' sake, but he also has to make hard choices when it comes to dealing with the Unholy. Kaya, these creatures are the worst of the worst. They are bred for killing and nothing else. Do they deserve to walk free because my men didn't obtain a piece of paper stating we have the right to put them in the Basement? We make those hard choices every day, but it is always for the greater good, the protection of humans."

Kaya looked into the eyes of the man standing in front of her. She had a choice to make, and if she were honest with herself, it was an easy one. "I'm hungry. Are you hungry? I don't think I have anything to cook, but I can call for delivery." She pulled her hands free and went to the kitchen to find the various menus for local restaurants.

"Why don't you come back to the manor with me? There is plenty of food there, and I would feel better about your safety."

"As wonderful as that sounds, I want to stay here and think. If I go with you, I have no doubt we will be doing anything but thinking. You are a hard man to resist, Rafael Stone." Hard indeed.

"Are you kicking me out, Miss Kane? I'm wounded." Rafael smiled like he was teasing, but she could see the hurt in his eyes.

"No, I'm not kicking you out. I am asking you to give me time alone to think." She already knew what her decision would be, but she wanted to make sure. With him in the room, his body was all she could concentrate on, not their future.

"I will give you time, but I will be close by. Until Alexander is caught, either I or one of my men will be watching you at all times. Kaya, promise me you will remain diligent. Promise you will call me when you leave and when you arrive at work. And please, if you need anything in between you will call me for that as well." Rafael was once again holding her in his arms. His mouth was warm against her ear as he pleaded with her to keep herself safe. She put her arms around his neck and laced her fingers through his gorgeous hair. She leaned away from him so she could see his eyes. "I promise," she whispered against his lips.

She couldn't resist. The invisible bond between them was such that she could not contain herself. Her lips found his, and when he exhaled into her mouth, she inhaled, breathing his life essence into her own body. She would keep that small part of him with her while they were apart.

Chapter 45

Rafael hated leaving Kaya but mates or not, he couldn't make her want to be with him. Technically, they weren't truly bonded and wouldn't be until he bit her with her permission. That didn't negate the fact that she was his. He tried to understand where she was coming from with regards to her job. Did she not understand everything he did only made her job easier? If only it were night and he could take to the skies. Flying helped clear his head better than almost anything.

Lorenzo, Jasper, Deacon, and Sixx were assigned to the areas around the apartments. Nikolas was helping Uri and Finley monitor the security feeds. Dante and Mason were meeting him to sweep Kaya's neighborhood. Gregor called to update him on the meeting with the doctor. He asked Rafe, "What exactly do you feel when you're around the chief?"

"At first, it was like a chemical imbalance, sort of like vertigo. Remember when you phased the first time, and it took a few seconds to get your bearings? Sort of like that. Now, gods, it's like I require her to breathe. If I'm in the same room with her, I have to be touching her because if I'm not my claws are aching to burst through my skin. As cliché as it sounds, she completes me. Until I met Kaya, I didn't realize I didn't feel whole. Why do you ask, do you think you've met yours?"

"I'm not sure. I felt what you're describing once, but it was a while back. I just thought I was sick."

"Gregor, we don't get sick, not like that."

"I know, but I didn't know how else to justify the feeling. Then this morning I felt it again, first when I called Isabelle and then again when she came to visit."

"Do you think it's her?"

"No, it was weird. There was something when she walked in the office and then again when she left. But when she was sitting across from me, I didn't feel anything."

"If you meet your mate you'll know it. Our dear Nikolas is either going to avoid the public library like the plague, or we will never see him again."

"I have my hands full enough with the Pen without adding a woman to the mix. I don't need the distraction."

"The way I see it, if Kaya chooses me, it will only make me stronger, not weaken me."

"What do you mean if she chooses you?"

"She is the chief of police and has a code of ethics she lives by. Some of our methods do not fit into that code. Her brain is overruling her heart right now. I have to give her time and hope her heart wins out."

"For your sake, I hope so too. Keep me posted on this Alexander character, and I'll have a special cell prepared for him, just in case."

"Thank you, Brother." Rafael hung up just as Dante and Mason rolled up on their bikes. He knew without looking that Kaya was standing at the window. Instead of turning toward her, he said, "Mason, protect her with your life. Dante, let's do this."

The next few hours were uneventful and frustrating. Rafe wanted to find the man who was trying to kill his Queen. He had faith that the bond would win, and she would rule by his side.

Kaya spent most of the day fielding phone calls. The weekend dispatcher was getting calls regarding men in fatigues roaming the neighborhoods. Kaya explained it away as a military drill. Her neighbors were calling about the motorcycles and extra car in her driveway. When Katherine Fox was shut down at the precinct, she called Kaya at home. Kaya hung up on the pest. She wanted to yell at all of them, "They're out there looking for the bad guys! They're keeping us safe!" but she couldn't do that.

Even if she and Rafael didn't pursue their relationship, she knew. She now knew there were those out there behind the scenes helping her do her job. Those of his kind had been doing this for thousands of years, and humans like her had known. Wasn't that what everyone hoped for? Some type of superhero hiding behind a mask that secretly saved the day? Hollywood was full of the pretend heroes that kids emulated at Halloween. So what was wrong with Rafael and his Clan being real heroes?

Nothing. Nothing at all. As a matter of fact, having Rafael at her back would mean putting away more criminals. She could use his resources since his were obviously more advanced. This time her cell phone rang. "Kane."

"Hey boss, it's Dane. Listen, I'm sorry I'm just now calling you back, but I was pretty bad. I just got out of the hospital."

"What the hell, Abbott, the hospital? Are you okay now? Wait, we called all the hospitals and none had record of you being there."

"It was a private clinic, and as a matter of fact, I'm better than ever. I plan on being back on the job tomorrow. I was hoping you'd fill me in on what I've missed."

"Dane, Jorgenson's dead. I sent him to the address you gave me, and someone shot him." Kaya told her detective all that had transpired since she saw him at his apartment with the exception of Rafael being a shifter. She couldn't leave out the fact that he had been present at the warehouse. There were too many witnesses that saw him save her life.

"Holy shit! That should've been me. I was supposed to check that out. Dammit, Kaya, I just..." Dane was silent. Kaya knew how he felt. She's the one who sent Jorgenson out there. But as officers of the law, they all knew the risk they took every day.

"Have you contacted his family? I don't remember him mentioning a wife or a girlfriend."

"I'm still digging. There was nobody listed as an emergency contact in his file. Dane, I'd really like to know where you got that address. I know you said you promised you'd keep that to yourself, but that tip led to Kyle's death. It could have led to yours. Do you think your source was setting you up?"

"No, I think whoever she got it from was probably using her to get to us. I'll call her and find out where she got it. You said you knew who the killer is."

"About that, I was given a false lead, and when I followed through I figured out it was bogus." If Dane was on his game, he would hear the lie for what it was. When she called him, she had been frantic, panicking almost. Now she was nonchalantly blowing it off. She didn't miss that he used "she" for his informant. Kaya had no doubt it was that reporter.

"So, what's this Rafael guy like? The papers must have it wrong if he saved your life huh?" Yep, definitely off his game. He must have listened to her messages while still sedated.

"He's complicated." Kaya didn't know if she was allowed to talk about Rafael with him being so private. "Back to you, are you sure you're ready for duty? The doctor's gonna release you?"

"Yeah, she released me. Listen, do you want me to come get you tomorrow, you know, as your bodyguard?"

"Shut up, Abbott. I can drive myself. See you tomorrow." She hung up before her detective could offer any more smartass remarks.

She wanted to talk to Rafael and get some clarity on their relationship. He told her if he found someone to share his life with that it would be in private. Was she going to have to pretend she wasn't in love, that she didn't have someone to share her life and her bed with?

The rumble of the bikes in her driveway meant Rafael was back. She glanced around the curtain to see him walking up the steps. She turned the locks and opened the door. He walked right in and kept going to the kitchen. She followed him to see him sitting at the table.

270

"What are you doing?" She was really confused. Did something happen? She wasn't used to this Rafael, the one who wasn't loving and kept his hands to himself.

"I'm sitting down. We have to talk. I cannot do that if we are sitting next to each other, because I have a constant need to touch you."

Kaya sat down across from him. "Okay, talk." She placed her arms on the table, crossing one over the other. She knew what he meant though. It was all she could do to keep from reaching out and touching him. It was like there was an invisible force constantly pulling them toward each other.

"We haven't found Alexander. We have eyes on all of my warehouses and any other property I own in case he gets ideas about those. Julian is on his way now to upgrade your security system. Mason will be guarding your house tonight and will escort you to work tomorrow. I will have someone escort you home as well."

"And where will you be?" She really didn't like the look on his face or the tone of his voice.

"I'll be giving you space. Kaya, I will not pressure you, ever. I want you to have time to decide with no interference from me if you want me in your life. I will be watching you, though. I will not stop until Alexander is no longer a threat to you. If you need me for anything, if you feel threatened, whatever, just call, and I'll be here." Rafael stood. "I really want to kiss you right now, but I'm not going to. The way I feel, if I kiss you, I'm not going to stop there. So I will just say goodnight, Miss Kane."

271

"Rafael…" Kaya blinked back the tears she felt in the back of her eyes. She didn't need time. She was sure, but maybe one more night would give her even more clarity. "Goodnight, Mr. Stone."

Chapter 46

For the first time ever, Rafael felt completely lost. The unknown was part of life, but having his mate within his grasp, only to lose her, would be more than he could withstand. He was ready to claim her and put her in his bed, never letting her leave it. If he didn't find Vincent Alexander before... he wasn't going to allow himself to even entertain that thought.

As he drove the Jag back to the manor, the sky clouded over, and a light rain began to fall. That was perfect for when he hit the skies. His claws ached with a demand to tear something apart. Rafe had to have release. He needed his mate. Since that wasn't an option, he was going hunting. It had been a long time since he had sought out Unholy to decimate. Kaya would probably be appalled if she found out. He would just have to hope she never did.

He didn't go in the house. If Priscilla saw him, she would know something was wrong. He took the hidden staircase that led to the roof of the garage. The sun was no longer an issue since the clouds had covered the sky. He stood unmoving, allowing the mist to dampen his skin and hair. He drew in a breath and phased, launching himself upward and heading where Unholy usually congregated. He knew going in alone was asking for trouble, he was King after all. He didn't have an heir to take over like his father had when he was killed. If he perished before he could produce an heir, Sinclair would be next in line.

He circled higher and higher, allowing the cooler air to fill his lungs. When that didn't help calm his mood, he retreated lower, scanning the streets for those monsters that Gordon Flanagan called his army. Rafe knew for every Unholy he took out, Flanagan created two more.

Something was wrong. There was no brawling in the streets, no claws meeting flesh. He continued through the various quadrants where he was sure to find confrontation. When he saw nothing happening below, Rafael flew to one of the buildings he owned and landed on the rooftop. He pulled his cell phone out of his cargo pocket and called Nikolas. "Nik, status report."

"Nothing to report. Everything is eerily quiet."

"Yeah, out here too. I've been over every quadrant, and there's no movement at all. Alert your brothers. Something is very wrong, I feel it. I'll call Mason." Rafe hung up on Nikolas and immediately dialed Mason's number.

When his younger cousin answered, Rafael asked, "Mason, is all well? There is something amiss with the Unholy, and I am checking in with everyone." He didn't want the younger Goyle to assume he was picking on him.

"Yes, my King. There has been no movement since Julian left. Chief Kane has showered and is now in her bedroom."

"You do know that is my mate you are watching?"

"You have my word that I would never disrespect her or you. I am not looking in on her, only listening. She has made several phone calls to her coworkers updating them on the events leading up to and including Jorgenson's murder. Dane Abbott is

274

coming back to work tomorrow, and she likes pepperoni and green olives on her pizza. Thin crust."

"Thank you, Mason. Hopefully one day soon that woman you are guarding will be your Queen."

"I hope so, Brother. I truly hope so."

Rafael flew to the manor after checking back in with Nik. He was given the all-clear by each team. He took a quick shower then went in search of food. Priscilla was in the kitchen covering several dishes to put in the refrigerator. "Oh, Rafael, there you are. I was getting worried about you."

He kissed his old friend on the cheek. "Please, leave the dishes out and I'll make myself a plate." He wanted to be alone right now.

"Nonsense, I'll be glad to do it." She began uncovering the dishes.

"Priscilla, I need your help with something." Jonathan was standing just inside the kitchen. He was much better at gauging Rafael's moods than his sister. She just wanted to mother him all the time. "Can't it wait? Rafael's hungry."

"No, it cannot wait. Now, Priscilla." When Jonathan was stern, she listened. She glanced at Rafael then gave in. "Okay, but you leave everything out, and I'll come back later to clean up." She patted his arm then followed her brother to their wing of the manor.

Rafael dished out the food then nuked it in the microwave. He stood at the counter, eating without truly tasting anything. He had popped open a beer while waiting for his plate to heat up. Having a Goyles' metabolism, it would take a case of beer before he even felt a slight buzz. He still enjoyed a good Scotch, but his tastes had changed over the years and craft beers were his drink of choice at the moment.

Rafe rinsed his plate and put it in the dishwasher. He grabbed another beer and made his way to the patio. The sky had cleared and was now cloudless. The moon was almost full, and the stars were visible. He took a pull from the bottle and glanced up at Perseus. Rafe wanted to be Kaya's hero. He walked shoeless down to the garden, enjoying the feel of the damp grass on his bare feet. He sat on his favorite bench, not caring that it was still wet from the rain. Taking a few cleansing breaths, he closed his eyes and allowed his mind to clear.

Kaya rarely went to bed before eleven, but tonight she did. She was ready for tomorrow. She hadn't really needed the extra time to decide whether Rafael was where her heart was, her future was. If he hadn't been so adamant earlier, she would have told him then. Maybe *he* needed time to think. Whatever his reason, she hoped that tomorrow they could start their life together. She turned her computer off, brushed her teeth, washed her face and double checked the new security system.

Usually she wore very little to sleep in but with Mason standing guard outside, she felt she should cover herself. She pulled on some sleep pants and a t-shirt and slid under the covers. She glanced at her cell phone just in case. No messages. What the hell. She sent Rafael a quick goodnight text then closed her eyes.

"Momma wake up. Momma! Momma you have to wake up!" Kaya felt herself being lifted. She tried to open her eyes, but everything was black. Her arms wouldn't move. They didn't feel like they were tied, just that she had no control over them. Sleepy, she was so sleepy. The house phone was ringing. She couldn't reach it. Her cell phone was going off on the nightstand. Why couldn't she get to her phones?

Kaya woke to that little voice she had come to know was her son. *"Momma, that mean man has you. I don't like that man, Momma."* Kaya opened her eyes to see a very pale, very blond man walking out of the room. *Oh my God! That's the albino. That's Vincent Alexander.* Kaya tried to yell, but no sound came out. Why couldn't she talk? Her eyes were getting heavy again. No, no, no! You have to stay awake! As hard as she tried, she couldn't hold her eyes open.

Rafael found himself once again standing on the cliff overlooking the sea. This time the sky was gray and lightning flashed in the distance. The water was ferociously crashing over the rocks. He felt a tug on his hand. Looking down, he saw his little boy. His frantic little boy. "Papa, Papa." He squatted down until he was nearly eye level with his child.

"Yes, my son, what is it?"

The strong winds were blowing his dark hair about as he implored, "Papa, you have to help her. That mean man has her."

"Who, has who my boy?"

277

"Momma. That mean man has Momma. Papa, you have to help her."

Rafael came out of his trance to Jonathan yelling his name. "Rafael, Jesus Rafael!!! His cell phone was ringing at the same time. He took off running toward his servant. "Tell me she's ok."

"Here, Sir. When you wouldn't answer your phone, Geoffrey called me."

"Frey, tell me you have her! Tell me she's okay!"

"Rafael, I've been calling for an hour. Where are you?" Frey forewent the formalities. "Mason called me when he couldn't reach you. Said it was too quiet in Kaya's house and when she wouldn't answer either of her phones he wanted permission to go inside and check on her. I gave him permission. Rafe she's gone."

Rafael dropped to his knees and roared.

"Rafael...RAFAEL...MY KING!!!" Frey yelling into the phone got Rafael's attention.

"Frey, I'm going to kill that sonofabitch. I'm going to tear him apart with my claws and my fangs, and then I'm going to shove his parts down his own motherfucking throat. Do you hear me?"

"I hear you, but for now we need to go. Nikolas knows where she is. You were right to have them monitor all the office buildings. She is being held in the basement of the State Street Towers. Rafe, there are Unholy everywhere. We have been fighting them for the last hour while we were trying to get hold of you."

"I'm on my way." Rafe didn't bother taking off his shirt; he just phased and launched himself into the sky. He heard Jonathan say, "Bring her back safely, my lord."

278

Rafael still clutched his phone in his hand. He called Nikolas. "Tell me what you see, Nik."

"About an hour ago, Vincent Alexander took Kaya out of the back of a nondescript white van and into the lower level of the building. I pulled the plans, and the place should be empty. It's the one we gutted and renovated a few months ago. We were still waiting on the final electric inspections to pass before we began leasing the offices.

"The internal security feed was cut earlier this afternoon, so this was premeditated. Mason, Jasper, Sixx, Gregor, and Deacon are on their way there now. Getting there is an issue seeing as there are Unholy everywhere. I've called in Clan from other cities to come fight. Rafe, even the police are involved in this. We're doing the best we can to keep the public out of it, but it's difficult. Right now you just need to make a beeline for State Street and get your woman. We'll worry about the rest."

Rafe hung up and flew faster than he'd ever flown before, not caring if humans saw him or not. Gordon Flanagan had been busy. Rafael had never seen this many Unholy, dead or alive, in one place. Knowing his brothers would take care of them, he continued on to Kaya. Arriving at the State Street Towers he headed to the back of the building where he landed amidst more fighting. Sixx and Gregor cleared a path for him. "Go get her, we've got this," Gregor said as he slashed his claws at an oncoming Unholy.

Rafael opened his senses and found his mate. He ran full out until he got to the door.

Chapter 47

Kaya still couldn't talk. She must have been injected with something because her neurological system wasn't working. All she could do was watch. And wait. If the man wanted her dead, she would most likely already be dead. Obviously he was waiting, and she was afraid she knew who and what he was waiting on. The man didn't speak. He texted someone several times, but he never spoke, not even to her. She couldn't answer if he did.

Her captor was watching a couple of computer monitors. Kaya couldn't tell what was on them, but whatever it was made the albino happy. The air was stagnant with smoke. He lit cigarette after cigarette, watching the screens and checking his phone. Not once did he look at her. For that, she was grateful. He lit another cigarette when something on one of the screens sparked his interest. He stood abruptly, knocking his chair over backwards. He took one last drag and flicked the butt to the floor. Smoke escaped his nostrils on the exhale.

He turned toward Kaya with a syringe in his hand. Oh God, he's going to kill me, just like those delegates on the loading dock. This is it. I didn't get the chance to tell Rafael that I love him. Oh God, no! Don't let it be too late! The albino stuck the needle in her neck and depressed the plunger, filling her system with something that made her insides catch on fire. "No!" she yelled. What the hell? "Why are you doing this Vincent?" Her voice was still a little squeaky from lack of use but it was coming back. "What do you want with me?"

When he looked at her confused, she finally got a chance to take in his features. He wasn't a true albino. Vincent's eyes were a bright green. It was like he had been kept out of the sun his whole life. He looked toward the door then back to her, frowning. "Please let me go. Save yourself. You know he's going to come for me, and he's going to save me. I can't be held responsible for what he does to you, Vincent. Please, save yourself."

Kaya's pleading had the opposite effect. He smiled at her with an evil grin, turning his somewhat handsome face into something twisted. A wretched sound came out of his throat. Was he laughing? She watched in horror as the albino phased in front of her. Leathery wings burst through his t-shirt, ripping it apart. He turned away from her just as the door crashed open and a monster charged Vincent. No, not a monster: Perseus.

Her hero in fighting form was breathtaking. She couldn't stop the tears that slid from her eyes. Kaya was both relieved and terrified at the sight of her lover. Not because of his physical characteristics. She feared the albino would harm Rafael.

It was like witnessing a plane crash. Kaya knew she was seeing what would end in death. A lot of it. Yet she couldn't look away. More people flooded the room. Men she'd seen with Rafael were fighting their own opponents. Unholy. Rafael had been right; Kaya had never seen one this close. He'd kept the monsters away from her for all these years. She was aware of the blood being shed all over the large room. Fangs were bared, claws gouging and ripping. Rafael slashed his way through several Unholy while calling out for

Kaya. She couldn't yell loud enough over the den of fighting for him to hear her.

After what seemed like an eternity, all of the Unholy were defeated. The rest of the men backed away as Rafael squared off with the albino. His wings were gone, but his claws and fangs were bared at her captor. "Where is my mate?" Rage was pouring off Rafael as he demanded answers.

Rafael was close to losing it. He couldn't see Kaya anywhere and then he heard the most precious sound in the world. "I'm here, Baby." Rafael stepped to the side of Vincent so he could peer around him. Kaya had been hidden by his wings. He froze when he saw Kaya sitting unbound but making no attempt at escape. His eyes snapped back to Vincent as he demanded, "What have you done to my mate you crazy fuck?"

The albino didn't answer, he just retracted his wings then bared his own fangs and continued watching Rafael.

"Are you all right? Did he hurt you?" Rafael never took his eyes from the man who was now assessing his opponent.

"I can't move. He injected me with something. But I'm unharmed. Please get me out of here." Kaya's voice was weak and her face was streaked with tears. Rafael never wanted Kaya to be a witness to what happened when they took down the Unholy, but this is who he was, who his people were. Better for her to find out now and be able to walk away if it was too much to handle.

"I will, Bella Mia. You just sit tight, and this will be over soon." Rafael cringed at the sound coming from his competitor. "So you're the sick bastard that tried to take out my mate. You failed. You won't get another chance." Rafael was surprised Vincent was a shifter and not a clone of some sort. "You're one of us, huh? Who's your daddy? He sure as hell isn't mine. My father wouldn't sire such a foul creature as yourself." The pale man just grunted. He had yet to say a word. "What's the matter, cat got your tongue?"

The man growled as he slashed his claws towards Rafael's face. Rafe barely dodged the long arm. "Aww, daddy issues? I bet the only man to make a freak like you would be Flanagan. But your last name is Alexander. Do you even know who your daddy is?" He jumped, missing the sweep of Vincent's leg. Whoever he was, he had trained extensively. Rafe was glad he'd spent time in the dojo with Frey.

Rafael punched with fists then slashed with claws. Vincent was just as quick to phase, blocking and striking back. Rafe raked his claws down the albino's chest. He quickly retaliated with gashes of his own down Rafael's arm.

"I guess since you're not gonna talk, I'll put an end to your suffering." Rafe stopped toying with him and let his beast loose. After a roundhouse kick to the head that the albino couldn't block fast enough, Rafe had him by the throat, claws extended, digging into the man who tried to kill his woman, his Queen.

"You have anything to say before I rip your throat out?" His fangs were itching to shred flesh. The albino just stared at him, eyes dead.

"Rafael, it would be best if we take him to the Basement for questioning. He might know where Flanagan is." Frey was trying to talk him down.

"He's right Rafe, we need him alive." Gregor was in his ear now.

"He doesn't deserve to live. He tried to kill Kaya." Rafe could barely hear his brothers. The blood raged through his body, pulsing in his ears.

"My King, you are right, he deserves nothing less than having his intestines ripped out and twisted around his neck. However, the brothers are correct. If you want to find out why he was after Kaya, we require him to remain alive. For now." Dante added his plea to the others.

Rafael began squeezing, the blood pouring down Vincent's neck.

"Please no, Rafael." His grip tightened. "My King, please!" Rafael's head snapped around to his woman. "What did you say?"

"I said please don't." Tears were rolling down her cheeks.

"You called me your King."

"I did. I love you. I want to be with you, be mated to you. I want to be your Queen, if you'll have me." Rafael retracted his claws and dropped Vincent to the floor. Frey and Gregor moved in and secured the shifter, ready to haul him off to the Basement.

Rafael knelt down in front of his beautiful mate, cupping her face in his bloody hands. "Are you sure?"

She didn't flinch, didn't hesitate. "Yes, Rafael, I'm sure."

Chapter 48

Dante gave Kaya an antidote that counteracted the serum in her system. There were no side effects, and Rafe was able to take her home immediately. They stopped briefly at her house to grab some clothes and necessities before heading to the manor. The Clan had managed to take down all of the Unholy with no human casualties and, as far as they knew, no human awareness.

Vincent Alexander's apartments had been combed for any indication of who hired him to take out Kaya. Notes were found around his place detailing Rafael and the Clan. He had been watching them a long time. Schematics of the hotel, as well as lists of the abandoned warehouses, were lying on the table. They did not find out why he was after Kaya, but they had to assume he was behind the murders.

With all of the Unholy that showed up for what they assumed had been a diversion, they now believed that Vincent was working for Flanagan. Gregor decided to put him in solitary for a few weeks to see if he would break down and talk, or write. Vincent being a shifter helped to explain how he was able to slip past Mason, but that opened up more questions like who exactly was he and where had he come from.

Mason apologized to both Kaya and Rafe and said he understood if they wanted to transfer him to the west coast. Kaya told him there was nothing to forgive and she wanted him to stay, if that was okay with Rafael. He agreed as long as Kaya agreed to take time off from the precinct. She gave him one week.

Kaya called Dane to let him know she was taking the next few days off and that he should be expecting a new detective who was transferring in from the west coast. She gave him instructions on showing Jasper around and getting him settled. She also briefed him on the events of the night so he could hold the staff meeting the following morning. Dante let both her and Rafael know that the DNA from the hotel room matched that of the body found at the warehouse. The victim had been part shifter, if that was possible. He and Julian were going to team up to study the blood further. Until they obtained a DNA sample from Magnus Flanagan, there was no way to be sure he was the deceased.

Rafael had quite a bit of Clan business to attend to, but he spent as much time with Kaya as possible. While he was at the office, she familiarized herself with the manor and the grounds. Kaya was taking the week to reflect on her job and her future with Rafael. Ultimately, she knew she would continue on as chief.

She and Priscilla spent much time talking and getting to know one another. The older lady was a wealth of knowledge when it came to the shifters and their ways. The crisp, autumn air combined with the solitude of the garden allowed Kaya the perfect place when she needed time alone.

Many of the brothers came and went, treating Kaya like she was already one of the family. When she would get overwhelmed, Priscilla would talk her down and preoccupy her mind with cooking or tales about various brothers. Her favorite stories were about Nikolas and Julian. Even well over five hundred years old, they still acted like competitive siblings.

With Mason once again acting as her bodyguard, Kaya went back to her house to get ready for the ball. When Priscilla found out Kaya didn't have a mask, she had taken the liberty of ordering one for her. Since Rafael asked her to wear her hair down, it wasn't necessary to go to a salon to have it styled. She threw the hot rollers in while applying a little make-up and listening to the radio.

She didn't care that Mason was in the living room and could hear her singing and dancing. The high she was on was a Rafael Stone induced feeling. If she could bottle it, she'd be a rich woman. She heard Mason talking to someone and figured she better finish getting dressed. He called out, "Miss Kane, your King awaits."

She sighed. Her King. She would never get used to that.

The limousine pulled up in front of the Stone Civic Center. Rafael stepped out, mask in place. He watched a long leg stretch out, foot touching the ground. Kaya held her hand out to him, and he took it, helping her out of the car. The brothers were scattered inside and out, those on the inside having procured invitations.

Rafe held his arm out for his beautiful date. She hooked her arm around his, and they made their way inside. Cameras flashed as soon as they stepped through the door. Rafe felt Kaya stiffen under the scrutiny. "Relax, Love," he whispered in her ear. He was the one who should be tensing, but he felt great. For the first time in his life he felt like he was where he should be, escorting his woman to an event that meant something to her.

Even though Kaya was wearing a mask, hiding her blonde hair and long legs was difficult. She was immediately recognized and the Governor, Mayor, Commissioner, and various others who held office made their way to her saying hello and asking how she was faring since her abduction. Unless pushed, she didn't introduce Rafael. When she was left no choice, she said his name was Roberto Gianni. Roberto was his middle name and Gianni was a shortened version of his mother's maiden name. He allowed his Italian accent to flow from his tongue when required to speak.

Rafael grabbed two glasses of champagne when the waiter passed by and handed one to Kaya. "To the beginning of a beautiful future, I toast you, Amore Mia." He tapped his glass to hers and took a sip. When she didn't follow suite, he frowned at her. "Kaya, what's wrong? Do you not like champagne?"

"Yes, I do but you called me *your love*. I...It's just..." She didn't finish.

"Let us dance, yes?" He swallowed the rest of his drink and took her glass, setting them both down on a nearby table. He led her to the dance floor and pulled her close. "Now tell me, what is wrong? Are you having second thoughts?" He whispered in her ear so that only she could hear.

She pulled back and looked up into his eyes. "I've always thought with the job I have that I would end up alone. Now, here I am, in love with you and it scares me. I just met you Raf...Roberto. I haven't known you long, and this thing between us makes me wonder if it really is love or something else."

"If it is something else, is that so bad? Tell me, Kaya, do you think of me upon waking, before you go to sleep, while you are in the shower, when you are drinking your coffee, when you are staring in awe at the glorious stars in the sky? Do you think of me as I think of you? If that isn't love then I don't know what is. And regardless of why I feel the way I do, all I know is I can't imagine *not* wanting to feel this way."

Kaya pulled him closer allowing him to lead her around the dance floor to song after song. When the Governor asked everyone to take their seats, Rafe was hard pressed to let her go. The dress she wore was showing enough skin that he was certain every man in the room was feeling as he did. If the night didn't end soon, he was going to find a dark corner and discover if she was wearing panties.

The Governor kept his speech short, awards were given, and dinner was served. Kaya excused herself to the restroom and Rafe followed her as far as was appropriate. He waited for a few minutes then reached out with his hearing. Hers was the only heartbeat in the ladies' room, and he could hear her talking to herself. Before she could think too much, he joined her. She gasped when she saw him enter the door. "Rafael! This is the women's restro..." He pulled his mask off his face and tossed it on the vanity next to hers. His mouth crashed down onto hers as he pushed her back into the wall. He slid his hand up the split of her dress, feeling higher until he got to her ass. Her bare ass. A growl came from deep in his chest as he pressed his hardening cock against her.

Kaya wrapped her leg around his thigh pulling him closer. His hand found purchase between her legs and he began rubbing her clit. "Kaya, if I don't get you out of here, we are going to be arrested for indecent exposure, because I am about five seconds away from ripping that beautiful dress off and fucking you right here against the wall. Please tell me we can go."

"We can go." She didn't release him immediately. She pulled him into another heated kiss full of tongue and teeth. Really sharp teeth.

Rafe stepped back and pulled his phone from the inside pocket of his tuxedo jacket. "Jonathan, please pull around to the back door." He made sure Kaya's dress was back in place then he pulled on her hand, leading her out of the restroom. Just before they hit the back door, they met Dante. "We are leaving. If anyone is looking for Kaya, she isn't feeling well and asked that I take her home."

"Yes, my Brother." Dante turned toward the banquet room and stood sentry, giving Rafael and Kaya time to make their exit with no interference.

The limousine was idling at the curb outside the back entrance. Jonathan was holding the backdoor open, allowing Rafe and Kaya to slide in. He returned to the driver's seat. "Home, Sir?" He asked Rafe, looking in the rearview mirror.

"Yes, please." Rafael raised the privacy screen and pulled Kaya into his lap. "You have no idea what you do to me," he groaned against her neck as he pulled her dress up around her waist. He situated her so that she was straddling his lap. He pushed his hand between them and found her wet folds, stroking softly with his fingers as he continued kissing her throat. He

291

let his fangs break free of their skin enclosure and gently scraped her shoulder. The gasp that escaped her was caught in his mouth as he once again pressed their lips together.

"I want to feel your pussy around my fingers, Kaya. I want you to come for me, like this. Can you do that?"

"Yes," she answered breathlessly. Kaya held onto his shoulders and leaned back, giving him room to maneuver his fingers in and out of her body, circling her clit with his thumb. With his free hand, he pushed her dress off her shoulder, releasing a breast. He noticed a scar that appeared to be a gunshot wound. Gently, he brushed his mouth across the puckered skin then turned his attention to a different kind of pucker. Rafe sucked her already taut nipple into his mouth, swirling his tongue over the tip. He nipped the skin around her areola, careful not to bring blood with his fangs. The sensation pushed her over the edge. As soon as the sharp tips scraped her skin, she rocked back and forth on his fingers, calling his name with her release.

Rafe felt the car slow as Jonathan pulled into the driveway. He righted Kaya's dress and pulled her mouth to his for a soft, sensual kiss. "We're home, Love."

Chapter 49

Isabelle was a little nervous as Gregor Stone, her new boss, showed her around the prison. From the outside, it looked big. On the inside, the place was enormous. Staircases led underground to where the worst kinds of criminals were housed. They passed by solitary confinement when Gregor stopped to look in on one of the inmates. Isabelle stood on her tiptoes and took a peek. The man in the cell was sitting on the edge of his bed, head in his hands. His coloring was pale. Not just his skin but his hair as well. She would have to see his eyes to classify him as truly Albino.

"What's his story?" When she spoke, the man looked up, meeting her eyes. She was frozen. There was something about him that called to her. He stood and walked to the door, peering at her through the small window. "He tried to kill the chief of police three times. He doesn't talk, or at least we haven't been able to get him to. Don't worry Isabelle; you won't have to deal with him."

"What if he needs medical attention?" She couldn't take her eyes off those staring back at her.

"He won't. Now, let's continue your tour." Gregor walked away from the cell, expecting Isabelle to follow. The man behind the glass put his hand on the small window. Isabelle wanted to put her hand up to his, but she had just been told he was a murderer. Not the type of inmate she wanted to get to know. She didn't see the man behind the door watch her as far as he could and then whisper, "Izzy."

They continued back up to ground level when Isabelle noticed a door. "Where does this go?"

He kept walking past as he responded, "The Basement."

"What's down there?" She glanced back at the solid door that had an electronic scanner on the wall beside it.

"Storage." Gregor didn't offer any more information.

"Do I get access?" She wanted to know what was down there.

He stopped and sternly said, "No. You have access to all levels with the exception of the Basement. The first floor is maximum security, and you are not to go there alone. You will be escorted to the first floor only when necessary and always with a guard. The people in this prison are the worst garbage imaginable, Isabelle. I will do everything in my power to keep you safe, but you have to abide by the rules. There is no room for error here. If you break a rule, you're out. That's for your protection, got it?"

"Yes, Sir." She was beginning to feel this was a mistake. Why had she taken this job anyway? Oh, to keep from working for her family who had lied to her her entire life.

"Not Sir, just Gregor. I want us to be friends, Isabelle. This might seem like a less than perfect place to work, but it really won't be that bad. Now, do you have any questions?" He stopped outside the door to her new home away from home.

"What happened to the doctor who was here before me?"

"He didn't follow the rules. Anything else?"

"No, I just need to look at the clinic and take inventory." She didn't want to bring her own supplies.

She had agreed to work part-time while they looked for a permanent replacement. She planned on keeping her clinic operating on weekends for now.

"Just make a list of anything you need, and we'll get it for you. If that's all, I will leave you to it. My number is programmed into all the phones. Just pick up the receiver, dial one, and you'll get me. Now, if you'll excuse me, there is something I must tend to."

Gregor strode down the hall toward his own office. She admired his form until he disappeared around the corner. Stepping into her new clinic, she took in the mess. The previous doctor had been a slob. This wouldn't do at all. She would have to clean the place up before taking inventory. She might as well get busy.

Vincent knew that voice, knew her face. The beautiful girl in the window reminded him of someone, but who? He paced his cell, still chastising himself for failing. Now he would never get close to Gordon Flanagan. The boss didn't like weak, didn't like less than perfect results. His plan to use Kaya Kane as bait had almost cost him his life. If it wasn't for her insistence that he live, he would be dead now. Why would she do that? He tried to kill her, and she wanted his life spared. That didn't make sense.

Right now, nothing made sense. His mind was confused. That girl in the window did that to him. Why would she scramble his brain? Fuck, he needed a cigarette. He paused his pacing and looked at his cell.

He had a bed, a toilet, a desk, a chair, some paper, and a crayon. A fucking crayon. If he had anything sharper it could be used as a weapon. Did they not realize he *was* a weapon? Just like them.

When they shoved him in his new home, they told him to write down why he was trying to kill the chief. Instead, he had written one word: cigarette. He didn't know how long he had been in there since he tended to lose track of time, but he did know he hadn't been given a cigarette. Some stupid patch was on the dinner tray after he made his request. He picked the patch up and sniffed it. It smelled of nicotine, so he put it on his arm. It eased his craving for about five minutes.

Maybe the pretty doctor, what was her name, Izzy? Maybe she would get him a cigarette. She was nice. *No!* She had him locked in here too. But her eyes had been kind, hadn't they? Vincent shook his head. No, she wasn't nice either. She was just another useless woman that needed to die.

In the next cell over, Tamian was taking notes. The newest inmate rambled on and on about Gordon Flanagan. Some of his words made sense then he would stop and stutter, like he couldn't remember what he was talking about. Whenever the guards were near, he would clam up. He refused to talk if anyone was around. When Tamian heard the man say the new doctor's name, a chill ran down his spine. He had to get word to Gregor and warn him. When he did this, he was going to have to give up his own secret.

Chapter 50

Kaya was standing in the suite she now shared with Rafael. They were welcomed home by Priscilla who had obviously prepared the room for their arrival. White candles were scattered around, emitting a warm glow. She felt strong arms wrap around her waist as his body melted into hers. "What are you thinking?" he asked against her neck.

"I was just thinking it's going to take a while to get used to all this. I've only ever lived in my two bedroom house."

"You also have a villa on the southern coast of Italy," he whispered in her ear.

"Really? I've never been to Italy." Maybe they could go there on vacation someday.

"I think you should keep your house. We could always use somewhere closer to the city to make a pit stop when we get too caught up in each other to wait. But I am definitely having blinds installed."

"I'd like that." She leaned her head back onto his shoulder, relishing the feeling of being safe and secure.

"What I'd like is to make love to my beautiful woman." Rafe lowered the zipper at the side of the dress then gripped the hem and raised it over her head. She stood completely naked before him save her shoes. He dropped the dress then reached out and squeezed her breasts, twisting and teasing her nipples. The slight pain sent tremors from her chest to her core. "You have the most beautiful breasts I've ever seen."

Kaya didn't want to think of all the breasts he'd seen in his five hundred and some odd years, but if hers were the most beautiful, she would accept that.

She pulled his shirt out of his pants and began freeing each button. She would never get used to a naked Rafael. His bare chest was a work of art. She was surprised he had no ink adorning his body, but he really didn't need it. She pushed the shirt down his arms, and he allowed it to drop to the floor next to her dress. She unbuttoned his pants and slid the zipper down slowly, carefully in case he was commando. She pushed the slacks down his muscular legs and was eye level with his gorgeous erection. The tip was glistening, inviting her to steal a taste. When she licked the droplet, she heard a low growl as he reached down and pulled her up to her feet. Holy shit, his fangs were out.

He kicked his pants off as he growled, "Are you ready for me?" She didn't know how he talked around his fangs without cutting his lip, but she guessed after five hundred years he had plenty of practice.

"Yes, I am. I want to feel you on me, in me. I want to kiss every inch of that powerful body of yours, and I want to suck you down my throat. I want to taste my juices on your lips. I want to feel you come inside of me. I want it all."

She felt Rafael pull away. He ran a hand through his long hair that was now hanging in his face. "What's wrong?"

"Kaya, I can't. I just can't fill you with my seed, not yet. Not until I'm sure…"

Kaya felt ridiculous and embarrassed. Her heart was lost to a man who wasn't sure he wanted her enough to have a child with her.

"I thought you wanted children. I thought…maybe I should go back to my house." She

299

bent to grab her dress when strong hands gripped her arms.

"No, Kaya, you misunderstood. I do want that, more than you know. I want to see the smooth skin of your belly stretched over and protecting my babe. Nothing would please me more than to know that my child is growing inside of you, but we don't know what mating with a human will do. I'm not ready to take that chance. Kaya, if something were to happen to you I would want to perish."

"But *I'm* ready, Rafael. For whatever reason, the fates, or God, or gods, or goddesses have chosen us to be together. If we are supposed to be mates, then I'm supposed to be the mother of your children. If you aren't ready because you want us to spend more time together getting to know each other better, then I will agree to that. If I have to get on the pill then so be it. But I want to feel you. All of you. Rafael, I don't want there to be anything between us when we make love."

Rafael told her he wanted to make love to her. After her admission of wanting everything he had to give her, what he really wanted to do was throw her down and fuck her senseless. She was expecting slow and gentle so that is what he would give her. First. *Then* he would fuck her senseless. All night long.

He pulled a naked Kaya into his arms. He had to feel her. Her breasts were pressed against his chest and her hands were stroking his back down to his ass. He mimicked the movement only he cupped her ass and lifted her until she wrapped her legs around his waist. His hard cock was caught between their bodies and he needed to be inside his woman.

He pulled her shoes off then laid her on the bed. Her legs automatically opened for him. Her pussy was unabashedly on display: an offering for her King. He situated his knees between her thighs, fisting himself. She licked her lips while she watched his hand. Kaya slid her own hands down past her stomach to her lips. Using her fingers, she opened herself up for him.

"Rafael," she begged.

"Yes, Love, what do you want?" He couldn't take his eyes off the show between her legs. Her fingers were teasing not only him but the inside of her labia.

"I want your cock buried to the root." She continued rubbing herself, enticing him to hurry.

"Oh my beautiful girl, you'll get my cock and so much more." He lowered his body so that he was hovering just above her chest, holding himself up on one forearm. He kissed her lips, her chin, and her neck while he rocked his erection back and forth over her clit, teasing, taunting. "Is this what you want?" The thick head stopped just at the entrance to her wet pussy; pulsing, aching, with the need to feel her surrounding him. She removed her hands to make room for his cock and placed them on her breasts, pulling on her nipples.

"Yes."

"Yes what?" He tapped his dick on her mound and her eyes widened.

"Yes, my King."

He impaled her with one long thrust. Instead of moving, he kept his dick buried against her walls, reveling in the feel of his woman. "Gods, you feel so fucking good."

When Kaya ground against him, he set a slow rhythm that had his beast howling inside. He was now on his hands, slowly sliding in and out. Kaya rose up on her elbows so she could watch his cock enter and exit her core. "That's hot." After enjoying the view for a moment, she lay back, her blonde hair spread out on the pillow and began playing with her breasts while watching his face.

"*You're* hot. I want you to enjoy this." He pulled out until only the head of his cock was inside her. "Making love to you is a wondrous thing, but me being what I am, and you being what you are, it's hard for me to go slow, easy." He plunged into her, hard. Closing his eyes, he confessed, "The restraint alone is driving me insane."

"Then don't hold back. Let go. Let me see you. *All* of you."

"Are you certain?" Rafael had never let go in all the times he'd ever had sex, but this wasn't just sex. This was becoming one with the woman he loved even if it wasn't slow and easy.

"I'm sure. And Rafael? I want you to bite me."

"Kaya, that completes the bond. Once it's done it cannot be undone."

"I know. I love you Rafael Di Pietro, and I want to be bonded to you for life."

Rafael lowered his upper body so that their faces were close. He began sliding in and out, slowly at first but when his beast demanded to be let out, this time he obliged. His fangs come out and when he looked into Kaya's eyes she nodded. She wrapped her long legs around his hips and raked her nails down his back. When the blood released from his skin where she dug in, he lost it. He let out a roar. As he pistoned his dick into her pussy, he unfurled his wings then sank his teeth into her shoulder. Their climaxes exploded at the same time and she cried out when they came.

Rafael retracted his fangs and licked her shoulder where the puncture wounds were. At first he was afraid her scream had been from the pain of the bite, but the look in his woman's eyes was a combination of lust and love. The bond was coursing through their veins, entwining their souls together. The smile on her beautiful face set him at ease.

Kaya reached up and touched a leathery wing. She ran her fingers along the thick outer ridge. "Rafael," she rasped. The wings disappeared.

Kaya grabbed his ass and dug her feet into the mattress, grinding her body against his, wanting more. "*Rafael*," she begged with more intensity. He had never gotten hard again so quickly, but it seemed whatever his Queen wanted she was going to get. Without pulling out, he continued stroking the inside of her walls, getting longer and harder with each movement.

"Harder baby, fuck me harder." Kaya was insatiable. He would stay inside her until she made him leave. She was grabbing at his hair, his back, his biceps. His woman was clamping on to any part of him she could, anything to urge him on. He pounded into her as hard and as fast as he could without hurting her. His shifter strength would leave her bruised if he wasn't careful.

Kaya's pussy began tightening around his cock, so he knew she was about to come again. He reached between them, rubbing her clit with his thumb. That was the spark that ignited her flame. His woman screamed out his name as she let go.

When she finally came down he kissed her gently. "I love you too, Kaya Kane."

Rafael called an impromptu family dinner. Kaya was nibbling at her food, taking it all in. There were so many men in attendance, but Priscilla made it seem like an everyday occurrence to cook for that big of a group.

Once they were finished eating, they all made their way to the patio for an after dinner cocktail. Rafael and Kaya were the last ones out the door and what she saw confused her. All the brothers were down on one knee with one fist over their heart. Rafael stopped Kaya and said, "Stay here."

She watched her lover join his men, and he too mimicked their position. As one, he and his men bowed their heads and said, "My Queen." Rafael was the first one to stand then the others followed suit. Kaya was stunned. She couldn't move nor could she find the words to express the emotions running through her heart. She let the tears falling down her cheeks speak for her.

Rafael held out his hand, and she placed hers in it. The men stood still while they watched their King. He dropped to one knee and held out a black box. "When Gargouille find a mate, it is for life. Since you are human, I want to honor your ways of bonding and ask that you not only be my Queen, but also my wife."

Kaya stared at the box then at her lover down on one knee. She knew little about his kind but in her heart she felt that he would never bend a knee for anyone unless they were important to him. *She* was important to him. His Queen. "I would be honored to be your wife, Mr. Stone." He stood and removed the ring from its case and placed it on her finger. She held her left hand out and admired the antique setting that was filled with smaller stones surrounding one larger one. She placed her hands on either side of his face and pulled him in for a kiss.

When the wolf whistles cut through their moment, he pulled her to his side and turned to the men. Frey held out a glass for both of them then picked up his own. "A toast if you will. Now that the bonding has been made official, I speak for the Clan when I say we are honored for you to be Rafael's mate, as well as our Queen. May your days be filled with love and your nights filled with the tranquility of the stars above. And soon, may your home be filled with the sound of little feet running amok." The men chuckled and raised their glasses. "Here, here!"

Kaya looked up at Rafael and smiled. He bent his head and kissed her softy before touching his glass to hers. "Honored indeed, Miss Kane."

Epilogue

Kaya stood at the kitchen table scooping seeds out of the pumpkin she was going to carve. A dark haired little boy with eyes the color of pitch stood in the chair watching intently. The back door opened and the little boy jumped down and ran, strewing pumpkin seeds all over the kitchen floor. "Bas, come back here. Sebastian!"

"Papa, look! Momma's making us a punkin." Rafael laughed, picking his son up, throwing him in the air, causing the child to laugh and seeds to go flying. With his child once again safe in his arms, he leaned over and kissed Kaya on the cheek. She smiled at her son then looked up at the man holding him. "Hello, Papa."

"Hello, my love. How are my two favorite people in the world?"

"Better now that you're here. Always better." Kaya couldn't have imagined the love she felt for Rafael in the beginning of their relationship would get any stronger. She was wrong. When they found out she was pregnant, she was scared. They both were. Not knowing how her body would react or if she would be able to carry their baby to term was terrifying. Soon after she found out, the last journal was located. It was with great relief they read that Caroline Montagnon had carried and delivered seventeen healthy babies to term.

The Di Pietro line would continue and one day their son, Sebastian, would become King. But for now, he was enjoying being a happy, mischievous little boy who had plenty of uncles to spoil him.

The ever rambunctious child began wiggling, and his Papa sat him down. Bas walked over to his mother and wrapped his little arms around her legs and began whispering. "What was that, Bas?" she asked the littlest love of her life.

His sweet face turned up to hers and he said, "I was telling Seven that Papa is home."

Kaya looked at Rafael who was frowning at their son. When Bas was born they finally told each other about their dreams of him and his coming to Rafe during his meditation. "Sebastian, who is Seven?" Rafael asked his son.

"My baby sister in Momma's tummy," he said as he flung more pumpkin seeds off his sticky hands.

Stefania Seven Di Pietro was born nine months later on July 7th.

About the Author

Faith Gibson is a multi-genre author who lives outside Nashville, Tennessee with the love of her life, and her four-legged best friends. She strongly believes that love is love, and there's not enough love in the world.

She began writing in high school and over the years, penned many stories and poems. When her dreams continued to get crazier than the one before, she decided to keep a dream journal. Many of these night-time escapades have led to a line, a chapter, and even a complete story. You won't find her books in only one genre, but they will all have one thing in common: a happy ending.

When asked what her purpose in life is, she will say to entertain the masses. Even if it's one person at a time. When Faith isn't hard at work on her next story, she can be found playing trivia while enjoying craft beer, reading, or riding her Harley.

Connect with Faith via the following social media sites:

https://www.facebook.com/faithgibsonauthor

https://www.twitter.com/authorfgibson

You can send her an email to:

faithgibsonauthor@gmail.com

Other Books by Faith Gibson

The Stone Society Series

Rafael

Gregor

Dante

Frey

Nikolas

Jasper

The Music Within Series

Deliver Me

Release Me

The Sweet Things Series

Candy Hearts – A Short Story

Troubled Hearts

Spirits Anthology

Voodoo Lovin' – A Short Story

48584598R00177

Made in the USA
San Bernardino, CA
29 April 2017